THE CHIMERA CLAN

THE CHIMERA SERIES

P.A. POWER

This book goes out to my husband and all my friends who helped push me to continue this journey. Allow no one to tell you that you can't do something. A special thank you to everyone who has accompanied me on this journey. I wouldn't be here without you.

PROLOGUE

Today was to be the most fantastic day of Austin and Danny's lives. It was their wedding day.

Austin wondered if he'd ever had such a great day in his life. He thought of the time he had gone back to the Genesis Moon Pack to pick up his brother, Brian. Six years ago Brian had taken a silver dagger for him that night in battle and lost his wolf, and he hadn't been the same since. Not that anyone wanted the Brian they had grown up knowing, but they all surely missed the man he had become before the tragic accident.

Austin walked into the pack automotive repair shop. It was time to forget the past and live the day he had been waiting for so long.

"Brian, come on, we've got to get going here," Austin yells out. They hadn't been close growing up, but that was Brian's father, Alpha Joe King's fault. Even though Austin hadn't officially been adopted into the family they still considered each other as brothers; a feeling that continues to grow over the years.

"Keep your shorts on, short stuff," Brian shouted from under the jeep.

"Kind of pressed for time, brother," Austin said, tapping his watch. He reached down and dragged Brian out from under the jeep then headed for the pack house with him in tow.

"Where are you dragging me to?" Brian asked, as if he didn't know what today was despite having been reminded nearly every day for the past month.

"The pack house. God, Brian, you are such a knucklehead," Austin growled out in frustration.

"Ouch... I'm so hurt dear brother. I'm only *human* after all," Brian said, putting extra emphasis on the word with deep sarcasm as a smile played across his lips.

"Well, then get up to the house. We've still got a little time. Phoebe brought you some fresh clothes, so please go shower. You smell like diesel fuel," said Austin nearly gagging on the smell of gas, oil, and grease.

"I'm a mechanic," said Brian, shrugging his shoulders and walking up to the pack house. "This better not be another false alarm like last time. You had me rushing off to your family's clan land only to hoodwink me into staying and not moving into the human town. I still find that unfair. I'm human now that I lost Ted."

"Just shower. You stink," replied Austin, placing his hand over his mouth and nose for emphasis.

Soon after, with Brian showered and changed, they took off running toward the portal leading to Austin's family hatchery.

"What is this place?" Brian teased Austin every time he visited.

"It's a colossal incubator for all of our clan eggs. So many families are still getting over the war, that they aren't ready to hatch their eggs. But if I had made Danny wait one more minute, I think he would have beaten me to within an inch of my life," Austin said joked as Brian tagged along behind him.

They were just inside the door, when they heard Katie squeal.

"Brian, you made it. Thank goodness. I was sure you would try to bail and run," she chastised, while cupping her enormous belly in her hands. She was due to pop with Sam any minute now. It was sad that she had lost Samantha but gifted with reincarnation by Selene, and yet she still chose the name Sam or Sammie.

"I tried one time, Mom, and you sent Austin after me. Like that would be a fair fight." Brian rolled his eyes and crossed his arms, shooting Austin a dirty look.

"Austin, thank you for going to get Brian. I know today is your special day. Welcome to fatherhood! You will make such an amazing father," said Katie, placing a hand on Austin's back to let him know she was entirely behind his decision to become a father.

"Or should we say he would make a wonderful Mr. mom? He is by far the more motherly of the two after all. He has always had a sweeter disposition, wouldn't you say?" Brian attempted to joke, although nobody laughed at the inappropriate timing of it.

The group gathered around in wonder as the three eggs shifted and bobbed before them. Austin couldn't believe that for the past three and a half months he and his family had been coming here to sing to and hold each of these eggs.

"I'm glad I don't have to work unless I want to," he declared. "Since Daniel came home and took over his company again, market shares have done nothing but climb. I have an amazingly straightforward job as second in command. I know my kids will have a topnotch education, because not only my father, but my father-in-law have already set up accounts for them. Could life get any better than it is right now? Danny is even trying to go for maybe four to six more eggs."

Just as he finished speaking, Austin suddenly heard a familiar voice from behind him. "Hey, stud muffin," said Danny, as he wrapped his arms around Austin and kissed his neck on the mate's mark, sending shivers down his back and electricity right down to his root.

"Danny, you're a real horn dog. Our kids are about to hatch, and I can feel what's on your mind," said Austin.

"Don't blame me, Mr. George-Blazek. It's not all my fault. You are the love of my life. I just can't help it sometimes. I want to fill this world with our babies," Danny said sweetly in his ear.

"Well, try to have better etiquette. Our kids are coming into this world. Last I checked, I'm far from going into man heat. Besides, our last fun attempt didn't get an egg from you," Austin said with a wicked smile playing on his lips.

"Excuse me? As you call it, that last fun time was not all fun and games. You had me cuffed up in a hotel room," Danny said, straining to keep his voice down.

"The problem with that was?" Austin gave him a wink that he knew would drive him up the wall, filling his already dirty mind with ideas he had no chance to act out.

"You had me cuffed without my powers and against my will." Danny gritted his teeth. Pulling Austin tight to his body allowing Austin to feel what awaited him later that night.

"Umm, you enjoyed yourself, so don't give me that against your will stuff. Oh, Shh, it's starting... look, Danny!" Austin said, pointing to the movement of the first egg. Breaking free from Danny's firm grasp.

"Danny, it's our son, Logan. He's the first one to hatch out of his eggshell. He's the one that has the blueish-green shell with flecks of gold throughout." Austin was worried at first, knowing a regular wolf's gestation was usually longer, but he realized that the time they were in limbo before they hatched must influence the hatching process.

Logan was one cute baby, even before he opened his eyes, and once he had, everyone could tell he had inherited the best features from each of the two lovers. One eye was blue like his daddy Danny's, and one was green just like Austin's. He had Danny's blond hair and Austin's cute dimples.

"I know it's too early to tell, but whoever gets to be this boy's mate will have their hands full," the doctor stated while weighing and measuring him. "He is 68 cm, and an astonishing 10 pounds 8 oz. Oh, look, I think Logan's siblings don't want to wait any longer either," continued the pack doctor, pointing to the other eggs.

"Oh, Austin look! It's Ethan, right? Wasn't his shell the color of spring sunrise over calm waters?" exclaimed Danny, looking down at Austin with a questioning gaze.

"Well, he is his daddy's son. He has Austin's brown curly mop on his head and the darkest green eyes you've ever seen. Ethan is only 65 cm long and weighs 10 pounds 4 oz," Nurse Bean announced.

Ethan already showed a sweet and calm personality while the nurse cleaned him up and measured him.

"Austin, am I to assume your mother would describe you the same way as your own hatchling?" said Danny as he gently tickled Austin along his ribs. Just as the doctor was wrapping Ethan up, the next egg moved. Clearly, the guys were about to have their hands full.

"Well, it looks like my little Aurora doesn't care if we're ready or not, either. She is going to shine," Amy said, clapping her hands and walking up to the nurse. Both the name "Little Aurora" and that personality stuck with her long after she had hatched.

"Austin, I love her eggshell. It is a mother-of-pearl on top of pale blue," said Amy, almost unable to keep her hands off the hatchling, while impeding the nurse who was trying to measure her.

"This child is a handful," said Nurse Bean. "She comes in at 64 cm and 9 pounds 8 oz, and she has hair as black as ravens and eyes the color of the Caspian Sea." Nurse Bean held the child up for the clan to see.

The kids were huge, and both Danny and Austin were quite happy that it would take a few years before they would come into their powers.

"Boys, your hands are full. Let me help," Amy said, reaching for Aurora, who instantly became calm in her arms.

"Well, I see she's going to be a grammy's girl," said Austin with a proud smile on his face. Little did they know then, he could not have been more on point, as from that day on, Austin's mother doted on her whenever she even quivered her lip to let out a cry.

"Austin, Danny, I need you to stand here with the boys. Amy, you get between them with Aurora. All right everyone, big smiles," said Daniel as he pulled out his camera and took a few pictures.

"Here, Mr. Blazek, go stand with your wife. I'll take pictures for you guys," Candy said with a soft smile as she took a few pictures herself.

"Okay, Grandpa Zack, you and Laura join in with the family, Hank get in here as well." she called out as she took a few more.

"Doug, Julie, you guys join. That's right. Liz, you can join the group pics in just a few seconds." Candy could be a natural people's person when she wanted to, but everyone knew to watch out for the fire and brimstone if she ever got mad.

Once she had all the group pictures done, she broke them down into separate groups within the family. The parents only, then just the grandparents, then came the siblings.

"Candy has always been there for Austin. She helped him when he was getting bullied at school. She was always by his side when he called to complain about me. I don't know what he had to complain about, though. I mean seriously, I am like perfect. Have you seen my abs?" Danny couldn't help teasing the group.

"Austin always complained that Danny had been too perfect. Candy never let him forget he was perfect, because she knew he was Austin's ideal mate. A day will never go by when Austin doesn't desire waking up next to him," said Brian, reaching over to tussel Austin's hair, while Austin looked over and smiled at the love of his life.

"Liz, I need you to stand here. Brian, hold Aurora and Bou, would you? Where is Bou?" Candy called out.

"Here!" Bou shouted from the back of the room.

"Get up here. You're due in the shot," said Candy.

"Really? But I'm—" Bou started, but Austin quickly cut him off.

"Bou, I told you before, blood is not the only way to be family to someone. You are a part of this family, and you need to come up here and be a good uncle." Little Ethan giggled and cooed in Austin's arms as he spoke.

"Let's not forget GG folks. Betty, we need you," Danny called out.

"I was going to say my boys better not forget me, or I might have to pull up some litigation between them for failing to recognize my importance," Betty said as she picked up the little princess.

Once all the family and friends had finished taking photos with the kids, the brood house nurses came in to take the children for their feed and put them down for a nap. Austin was ready for one himself. The family all sat and talked, but his mind drifted.

"*Austin, what's wrong? You look worried.*" Danny linked with Austin's mind.

"*I know that full-blood dragons grow at a different rate and can reach what the outside world calls adult in five to seven years,*" Austin's mind conveyed to Danny.

As they did not know how long they would have with their children, he prayed and hoped they would age as he had.

The Clan gathered round. They had dragons, sirens, and werewolves, and even his friend, Candy had made it to their hatching. It was a joyous time as they made memories they would hold dear.

🌙

It is hard for one to believe, but this is just a glimpse of life in the Chimera clan, and if we fast-forward a few years, both Danny and Austin have been through all the endless dirty diapers, the tantrums, the teething, and everything else that comes in threes. Oh, sweet Moon Goddess, everything always comes in threes.

"*To think Danny wanted three more the very day they hatched. "I swear this man wants me to be a nonstop egg factory,*" Austin spoke in his mind to Trey.

"*Hey you had to shift into your dragon form and lay a magical egg the first time. Thankfully, the Fae queen, Tatian helped bring out our eggs. Once we freed the gods, Eilei-thyia, the goddess of childbirth, gave us a gift so that having more children would be easier on the hosting parent. If we hosted the children like a traditional pregnancy, we could manage it but our bodies would snap right back to when the child was born. Austin, you or Danny* now could choose to give birth or hatch more kids from an egg," Trey responded with bounded glee in his voice.

"Yeah, and once Danny figured out neither of us would lose our figures, he was all for it. He even offered to carry the following three children. Why not? He had nothing to lose. Only a week's worth of pain and discomfort for an egg, or nine months of pampering to snap right back into his perfect body. I warned him that if he went that route, the ladies in our lives would make sure he paid." Austin's mind was in a faraway place while talking with Trey, when suddenly he heard his name being called out. Danny was drawing him back to the present and out of the shadows of the past.

CHAPTER I
WEDDING DAY

As Austin stood there at the end of the aisle, looking out over the crowd that would witness this joyous day, he was lost in his own thoughts, as he relived all of the fond events that had led them to this moment. The hands of time seemed to have come to a stop, and so had his heart.

Across from Austin stood the man he had claimed as his mate all those years ago. He was his mate, the love of his life, and above all, his equal. With them stood their two boys, who would be the best men at their wedding, while their loving daughter Aurora was the flower girl. The best men's suits had been gifted by Charles and Brad, who had places of honor at the wedding, and whose generosity Austin would not forget. Their sweet little Aurora had picked out her own dress, and it had also been created by Brad. The pale pink reminded Austin of new soft coral on the seabed.

Austin was glad his children had gotten the chance to live as humans, even though they were Chimeras. It was only a matter of time though, before their gifts and powers began to show.

A voice drew his attention back to the wedding ceremony that he already knew he would cherish for eternity.

"Earth to Austin. Come in Austin," Danny whispered to him across the aisle, concerned that his mate was staring into space on their wedding day.

"Hum, sorry, I was just remembering the day we became a family," Austin said, coming back to his senses and looking down at the boys dressed in their little suits, while their little princess scattered rose petals down the aisle around them.

"We have come a long way, Austin. We have been a family for five years now, and you have been my mate since long before that," Danny said, looking up at him with those amazing eyes he could never get tired of seeing.

Just then, Little Aurora walked up to Austin and sprinkled rose petals at his feet while letting out an angelic giggle, bringing a huge smile to Austin's lips just as Danny stretched out his hand.

"Aww, baby, you look so pretty in your gown; just like a little princess," said Danny, smiling down at his daughter.

"Thank you, daddy," replied Aurora blushing and twisting her hair in her tiny hand.

"Do you want to do a little twirl and show daddies your pretty dress?" Danny asked, taking Aurora by the hand.

"Yeah, spin me daddy," Aurora giggled.

As he watched them dance, Austin knew he had to soak up every moment, because it would only be a matter of time before it was their turn to walk her down the aisle. Hopefully though, it wouldn't be for a long time, even if the thought of it brought tears to his eyes.

"Baby, why are you crying? Are you okay? What's wrong?" Danny was quick to ask as he saw the waterworks running down Austin's face.

"Life with you has been so amazing. We have our family, and now the law of the land, the supreme court, will allow us to marry. The outside world doesn't follow supernatural laws. So, to protect our family, we must follow their law. Now I get to have you as my husband. On this day I have so many wonderful fresh memories. I'm trying to hold on to them tightly so I can cherish them forever. This moment is fleeting, but what it stands for is eternal," said Austin as he gazed lovingly at the family gathered before them.

Just then, someone cleared their throat. "Can we get started, boys, or would you like teatime first?" Stephanie said with a smile. Paul had made his life with this girl, and she had made him a better man, but Austin could see where Candy got her sassy attitude from. She had come a long way since that night at the zoo.

Austin looked up and blushed as he and Danny both nodded their heads.

"Ladies, sorry to break your hearts, but these two amazing men standing before you are here today to join their souls together forever." Stephanie continued addressing the crowd as she went through all the highlights of their crazy life together, and told them about all the battles they had experienced to get to where they were now.

"The grooms have made their vows, and knowing Austin it will be a rendition of a song that he has twisted and tweaked to suit his needs. He can't help it. It is the siren call within him," Stephanie said, letting out a small giggle.

Austin stood there with Ethan at his side holding onto his leg. Then he looked over at Danny with Logan doing the same thing, and he smiled and started his vows.

"It's a beautiful time
To make this man mine.

I found forever in you.
Hey, yeah, I am going to marry this dude.
It's the light in your eye,
Or is it our kids by our side?
Without a rhyme,
It is right on time
We're here at the lakeside chapel
Where everyone can see
We can't be crass.
They parked your folks on the grass
Please tell me I do.
My love is only for you
So come on,
Let's be one
Join our lives together
Now till forever
With our kids outside, are you ready?
We are home,
Home
Home
Because of our love
With peace from above
It's a beautiful time.
We finally can be one
So come on, baby, say I do
I want to marry you
Now and forever."

When Austin had finished, he took Danny's hands and kissed them with a sparkle in his eyes.

"Danny, do you take this singing man, who has no shame in calling out his in-laws for parking on the new grass?" Stephanie asked.

"I Do," Danny said with a beaming smile.

"Danny." Stephanie gestured.

"Austin, I might not have a song, or a fancy way to express all that you are to me. But you drew me to you from the day I first saw you when we were just pups. I have known you were my better half since grade school. Throughout my journey in life, nothing has come close to the feeling I had when I took you as my mate. We have grown together more than anyone could expect. We have had epic battles and an amazingly fun journey with our family. So, join me and say I do as my husband and father to our kids and pray to the gods we have more." Danny added the last part with his eyebrow raised. "Sorry about the grass. I'm sure it will be fine. So will you take me as your husband?"

"I do," Austin responded before Stephanie could even ask.

"Well, with the power given to me by the local human government, you two are now entered into a marriage contract for all time," Stephanie said smiling while taking their two hands and bringing them together. "You may kiss your groom."

With that, Austin lent over and respectfully kissed his man. But Danny had other plans, as he pulled Austin into a fervent kiss and tipped him over in front of the crowd. Of course, they all started cheering and encouraging him further.

"I now present the official Mr. and Mr. George-Blazek. May their love be eternal," Stephanie said winking at them, and the crowd erupted in applause. Austin looked over to the Salt Lake he had created, and they filled it with merfolk, as he looked out at them, he saw werewolves and dragons standing side by side in human form, while two lone humans stood amongst all the supernatural.

Austin looked down at his boys, and they both gave him the universal sign for please pick me up. They looked so cute in their little black and white tuxes that Austin couldn't help bending over and taking Ethan in his arms, as Ethan hugged his daddy tightly. Then Ethan pointed to Austin's lip and said, "Daddy, Ouchy?"

"It's okay, Daddy didn't hurt me. Daddy kissed me. I don't have any boo-boos," said Austin as he watched Danny pick up Logan and give him a fist bump. Ethan was ever so the mini-me of Austin, while Logan was the spitting image of Danny.

Ethan was the gentler one of the two boys; he had his father's soul, while Logan knew how to be strong, and it showed. He had an Alpha bloodline from both of his fathers. His destiny was yet to be written, but it was clear there would be great things on his horizon.

"Danny, I can't believe our kids will be six in just a few short months," Austin said, looking at their fantastic family.

"Yes, and what a wonderful venue for our special day. I can't believe that Candy and my sister planned all of this." Danny gestured to everything spread across Grandpa Zack's land. They had chosen the spot by the lake because it had always brought them so much peace before when the boys were being fussy. Aurora had always been the angelic one, even though both Danny and Austin knew the halo would fall one day, and she would break their hearts.

"It wasn't easy to set up all of this. I'm grateful for the effort our mothers put in looking after the kids and helping set up the labor workers. We are fortunate to have so many people who love us and who wanted this for us. Tatian had her Fae friends grow all the flowers for our ceremony. The Siren pods provided the music for our walk down the aisle. Everyone has blessed us with help," Austin said, pointing out how grateful they should be to be so blessed.

It had been a few years since any gods or goddesses had tried to show themselves. They kept telling themselves that it was for the best. As he looked around the clan lands, Austin realized he had missed them almost as much as he missed home. Since the children had hatched, he had genuinely tried to enjoy life with his family and still travel until the kids reached school age. Then, Doug and Grandma Betty needed Danny back in Nebraska.

"Baby?" Danny pulled Austin back from his revelry with only one word.

"It's okay. I was taking in the sights. It's hard to believe that tomorrow we will head back to where it all began for us," Austin said, shifting Ethan from one hip to the other.

"Luna Katie has done a wonderful job over the years. They have repaired most of the ground. You would never have guessed a supernatural war hit the place," Danny said smiling.

"I know, but why do we need to go back?" replied Austin, not bothering to conceal his displeasure.

"You know as well as I do these humans struggle to keep their frail everyday lives in order. Malcolm and his vamps are under control. It was not always so risky to be supernatural in Nebraska. It has gotten so bad Malcolm's father has threatened to take over the territory. If he did that though, we all know it would be another war. So, we don't bother that man as long as he stays on his side of the river. Malcolm is lucky Elena could negotiate a treaty to keep them on the dairy farm grounds. Everything that the hybrid daughter has done kept her father at bay. As a lawyer, I can easily make land grabs; I can void sales on the property and get the county to evoke eminent domain. Anyway, we will wait and know more about what new battle awaits us once we return to Genesis Moon," Danny said as he took Ethan and gave Austin his little princess to dance with.

"Daddy, I hear we are going where you met daddy," Aurora said as she hugged his neck and continued to dance.

"That's right sweet pea. We're going to go stay awhile at Luna Katie's pack," said Austin, spinning around and making her giggle.

"You know Luna Katie is also another mom to me, don't you princess?" Austin asked, knowing full well already that she understood everything, even at five, going on six. His kids were brilliant.

"Yep, and Uncle Brian and his girlfriend Phoebe come from Genesis Moon. Is Uncle Brian ever going to get his wolf back, or perhaps another wolf? It's not nice seeing Aunt Phoebe feeling so sad." Aurora laid her head down on Austin's shoulder.

"Hey, squirt, got a dance in you for old Uncle Brian?" said Brian as he approached them with his arms open wide.

"Uncle Brian!" Aurora practically leaped out of Austin's arms and into Brian's, as a beaming smile covered his face at having his dear niece so close to his heart. Both Austin and Danny had witnessed the positive changes in Brian's life since the kids were born, and Austin truly hoped that moving back home to settle the vampire issues would give them more time to be brothers.

Austin walked over to Danny and took Logan off his back as they all made their way over to the dinner table.

"Why does Uncle Brian always take Aurora?" Logan pouted.

Before Danny could answer though, Grandma Amy interjected, "Well, because she won't trip on herself as you would. You have that lip of yours so far out with all that pouting. You better pull yourself together, Logan. Grammy won't hold back, you know this by now. Your sister goes, so she gets girl time with Aunt Phoebe. Logan, unless you want to wear dresses and do makeup and nails, let your sister have this."

Only a grand-mother could ever pull off that kind of voice.

"Yuck, no. Nope, I 'd rather not," Logan said, waving his hands franticly.

Austin did everything he could to stifle the laugh that was building up inside him. Logan really was his father's child. He had a few of Austin's attributes that showed up from time to time, but it was clear he took after Danny the most.

CHAPTER 2
MOVING BACK TO GENESIS MOON

T
he days following the wedding seemed to fly by, and soon they were all packing the car up ready for the big trip. The same car they had taken the kids to the Grand Canyon in just the previous week. "Baby, I know you like road trips and we're leaving with enough time, so let's take the kids back down to white sands. How does that sound?" Danny asked Austin as they drove away from the family land.

The suggestion of an epic road trip weighed heavily on Austin's mind. Finally, after a simple internal debate, he agreed with Danny.

"Let's do it. Once we get back to Genesis Moon, we will have to enroll the kids in school, and I hated that school. It could be just as bad for our kids as it was for me," Austin said as he recalled the horrible days in that tiny prison for children. "I agree to this road trip, Danny, but it better be epic and educational for the children. There are no more portals, and no shortcuts, just endless miles of family time."

The kids had fallen asleep and they weren't even five minutes into the drive.

"Sounds good to me. So where does this journey start, my love?" Danny said, doting on Austin. This man and his silver tongue always knew how to get Austin distracted enough that he could get almost anything he wanted.

"We should go in the opposite direction to our final destination. Let's head west to the sea. I want our kids to see the ocean one last time. I don't know how long it'll be before we can return to it again."

"So, we visit the sea and say our goodbyes?" Danny raised his eyebrow suspiciously.

"Sort of. We will go to San Diego. It's safe now, and once we're there, there's no end to the sightseeing opportunities. Plus, I want our children to know where Grandma Amy comes from and allow them some time with the sea. I don't want to hold things back from them. The sea is a vast space, and if we hold them back from it, they will want it enough that it will be hard to pull them back to the land again. The freedoms that can come from the sea are nothing like the restraints of being on land." Austin sucked in a deep breath and let it out slowly as he watched the mountains drift off behind them.

"Austin, it's going to be okay. I know this is all a bit much. Dad needs me, and GG Betty is getting to the age where she wants to retire. Once we get home, I will have two jobs to balance. Working in my father's law firm again besides the security company, WIZ." Danny drummed his fingers on the steering wheel.

"You know, sweet love, I knew you were the owner and CEO of WIZ, but what is it exactly? I know you're a security company, but you never said what WIZ stood for," Austin said, dumbfounded. He had never asked before.

"The actual name is TEC WIZ. The TEC part is easy enough to figure out though, it's Technologies. The WIZ? Well, that's the watchful intelligence of Zelus," Danny said, all too smugly for Austin not to break out into a smile.

"You know as well as I do, he was the minor god of rivalry. So, I take it your security company is the rivalry of all other security companies," Austin said as he pulled out his magical journal.

"I see you've picked up a habit or two from your mother. Are you enchanting them with magical keys as well?" Danny looked at the key around Austin's neck that once belonged to his mother.

"She gave them to me and the key to open them. She has inspired me to enchant this book and to transcribe three others. So, I have my master that god forbid will magic its way to you or my folks if something happens, but our kids will have one of their own," Austin said while tapping the pen on the blank page.

"That is why I love you, my sweet cheeks, always and forever. You are always the one to share yourself with others, so they can come to know love and kindness. Selene truly blessed me when she fated you as my mate," Danny said, taking Austin's hand in his and kissing it as he glided along the open road.

"First stop along the way is the Garden of the Gods, as the humans call it here in Colorado. Then, we hit up arches in Utah. Then we're off to the sea. Once we've spent a week at the seaside, I want us to head inland again. We will visit your family's traditional pack in Arizona: The Blue Sapphire Ridge Pack. I'm sure your uncle would love to see our kids. Then we will travel on to the White Sands National Park. We can even buy sleds and have a time of it, but promise me this time not to let little Logan go running off." Austin poked Danny in his ribs as he spoke, reminding him of the last time they had lost Logan for half an hour because he wanted to play hide and seek.

It had taken Austin using his hearing to listen for the rapid heartbeat of an over-excited child before they could find Logan hiding in a sand cave.

"Okay, Mr. I got plans. I say we keep to the south. We will go east on into Texas to the gulf. We will travel to New Orleans, then we can go north, and we can have a go at farming for diamonds up in Arkansas. Our little Aurora loves shiny things; she picked that up from her daddy." Danny shot Austin a smug glance. He could do nothing more than put his hands in the air and surrender to the truth.

"What I like is shiny things: cars, stones, and one guy when he is all shiny from a hot day's work." Austin grinned and teased Danny, knowing he was helpless because he was driving. Cat and mouse games were always delicate with him. If he teased too much, he would find himself in a world of hurt, but of the good kind.

"Clever, you tease while I drive, but we will have to stop sometime; how foolish of you." Danny gave Austin a mischievous stare.

"Clever still. We are with our children. We have no sitters, so it's all G or PG from here on out." Austin stuck out his tongue and teased him further.

"Okay, once we've dug for our precious stones. What will it be, a day, maybe two?" Austin asked, wondering about his husband's plans, while changing the subject before it got too heated and Danny called for backup.

"Look, my love, I'm in no rush to get back, but we will need to get to Genesis Moon; Luna Katie is looking forward to time with her grandchildren. Though they cannot take over the pack, we all know that right still falls to Brian. He has an obligation to the pack," Danny said biting his lip, knowing Brian being without his wolf was all Austin ever blamed himself for. He had sacrificed to save Austin afterall.

Thankfully, he didn't die, although he hadn't been the same since that night.

"I know, so we will take the kids to Fun Worlds and Funnier Oceans after hunting for treasure. Then we can head home. Home to, as they say, welcome the good life," Austin said in a mocking tone.

"Since your dad would not let you take his clock, he at least gave you the blueprints. Austin, once we settle in, we can make our version of your father's clock. You know you still owe me an explanation on how you knew it was your father's clock, and how you knew of its secret compartment," Danny said, raising that one eyebrow that let Austin know it was not up for discussion.

"Even as children things happen that forever stick in our minds. It's part of growing up. I forgot everything I knew before Genesis Moon to protect myself. But as fate and events would have it, things clicked into place as one puzzle piece fell into another. It also helps that I noticed my father's initials on the clock face. My father and I used to hide things from Mom at that clock. From Mother's Day gifts to birthday surprises or whatever we chose to hide. So, when I saw the clock, it all clicked and came back to me. Sorry if it was no open sesame and a mystical door opens into a new world," Austin openly teased.

The trip went ever so according to their plans. When they were out in sunny California, the family ran into a few of their old friends. Oscar put them up in his hotel and would not allow them to pay for anything. He spoiled the kids beyond anything a godparent should. Naming him the children's godparent was more like mocking the system that tried stopping their family every step of the way. Danny had to play into the broken system to beat it; Oscar took his duties seriously. He knew that if anything happened so they could not care for the kids, they wanted him to help guide them.

Supposing the grandparents were out of the picture and unable to look after them, then it would be up to him to look after the little clan. Nelly and her sister Cassy had moved back to the town, and Cassy was better behaved. She no longer chased after Austin's husband around town. She found herself a charming woodland nymph by the name of Jupiter. His folks were the kind to name all of their children after celestial bodies. Jupiter even joked about his one brother, "Don't dare say his name three times, or he very well might appear." The good news was though, that they spelled differently it.

The kids enjoyed their time at sea and all the other adventures. Danny had home schooled the children along the way. Once they made it to Arkansas, they spent three days digging and hunting for diamonds, and they walked out with eight rather enormous diamonds ranging from one to two and a half carats. On the last day, Austin found a yellow 7.8 carat diamond. The boys seemed to have fun digging and playing around, finding many unique stones and goodies. The one that surprised Danny the most was the little princess. She staked out and roped off a small area and worked it. She kindly asked the others to please allow her this small space to work. Ever the young minor diplomat. Some of the other diamond hunters even asked the couple how old she was because her behavior was far from her age group. With the respect she earned from them, one of the older, more seasoned hunters showed her a few tricks to finding stones. Danny and Austin thanked the older man, but he was too eager to sit with Aurora and show her anything she desired to learn. When it was time to go, Aurora asked if she could keep in touch with her new friend. Danny and Austin gave the older man Danny's business card to the office in Nebraska. The kids all had fun, and they made their way to the amusement park for the last bit of fun before settling down back in Nebraska.

"Danny, this road trip has been epic, but oh so short-lived, I cannot believe we have spent the entire summer already. There are only three weeks before we have to have the kids enrolled for class," A tired Austin said, shaking his head.

"Well, Venessa has been the point of contact for our kids for remote learning at pre-K. Venessa is moving on with them to kindergarten. It will be fine. The kids are well beyond the point. So, you don't have to worry." Danny tried to soothe his mate's nerves, but it was no use. Austin was not too fond of that town, that school, and above all else, he had already lost far too much to that place. He had lost Grandpa J and he never got to tell him how much he loved him one last time. Austin only hoped he would look over his great-grandbabies.

"My only hope is he is as proud of me in death as he was in life," Austin spoke quietly to Trey, his wolf. As they approached the town, Austin looked up from his journal, looking back at his sleeping little ones. *"I will not allow what happened to me to happen to them,"* Austin vowed to himself and to Trey.

CHAPTER 3
BRIAN STEPS DOWN

"This life with Austin has been such a blessing for us. We have had our ups and our downs, and some playful merry go-rounds. I would not trade even one second with this man for anything in this world or the next. Coming back to Genesis Moon was my idea, but it was not just for the sake of my family. I knew that Luna Katie was without an Alpha, and Beta Jeff was trying to help. If only the pack were more forgiving and open to the idea that Brian would be a good Alpha, even without Ted. That poor fool Brian, dealt a wicked hand, but he risked his life for our beloved. All his past transgressions became nothing but a fading memory, as vile and evil as they were. Austin and I both forgave him and welcomed him into our family. So, we now come home to help him with his family," Danny spoke with Adonis.

"Brian, do you by chance know where this little one got off to? She is oh about yay high, has an infectious laugh, and is my little princess," Danny said, winking at Brian as he could hear her trying to hide in the broom closet.

"Nope, haven't the fuzziest of ideas. She won't sit still. I told her to wait here, and when I came back from getting us cake and

27

ice cream, she was gone. So, I guess you will have to have her share." Brian stretched out his arm with the dish of sweet delights. Then suddenly the little princess jumped out of the closet.

"Boo, got you! Hey, you can't give daddy my snack. That's mine." Aurora snatched it and ran off to the table.

"Hard to believe that she and her brothers start school together tomorrow," Brian said, shaking his head.

"When are you and Phoebe going to accept each other and start your own family, dear brother?" Danny questioned him. Everyone had gotten used to that wounded look. It no longer had the same effect the family was accustomed to seeing.

"Ouch, my brother sends my brother-in-law now to play matchmaker. He truly has rubbed off on you." Brian overdramatically grabbed at his chest as if reaching for a dagger.

"Your brother was right, you are one to be perceived as, what did he call it? Oh yes, the melodramatic drama queen," Danny said with a smile curling up on the edge of his lips.

"Drama queen? Oh no, that title belongs to oh... what is his alter ego? TreyVana? I say my brother makes a shockingly attractive girl. I see where little Aurora will get those feminine looks. Also, if I catch any wolf, merfolk, or dragon; hell even human that tries to flirt with her, I will break some legs. We even need to worry about the vamps. That's the last thing she needs, a bloodsucker for a mate," Brian said over the top of his coffee.

"You will make an excellent father. Your brother and I want you to know that you are still our family, with or without Ted. When you decide to lead this pack, we will stand by your side," Danny said, as he took a bite of sweet Aurora's cake while she wasn't looking.

"Why won't you all just let it go? How can I be an Alpha without my wolf? I can't shift or fight. I can't heal like a normal wolf anymore. For everything I have done to Austin, and most of the pack, I don't deserve to be a leader." Brian let out a deep sigh.

"You would still make an amazing leader," Danny tried once again to inspire him.

"Phoebe is amazing. She is sweet. I knew she was my mate before the battle. I saved her! Now, look at all of this." Brian gestured to his condo.

"It looks amazing. Very well put together," Danny said, looking around.

"That's because Aunt Phoebe and I decorated it," Aurora piped in.

"See, even my little peanut gets it. This woman is the best thing for me, but am I what is best for her?" Danny could hear the depression in Brian's voice as he spoke. His shoulders sank lower and lower.

"Aurora, sweetie pie, why don't you take your cake and ice cream on the deck? Uncle Brian and Daddy need to have a big boy talk," Danny said as he kissed her forehead.

"Okay, Daddy, but if anyone asks why I am outside all by myself, I'll just have to tell them Daddy and Uncle Brian are talking about girls and didn't want me to hear."

"That's okay, pumpkin. We are on pack land, and the patrols are not far off. You will be safe," Danny told her as he assisted her to the door.

"Wait. That's not how it works with GG. I pull that one, and she gives me a quarter." Aurora insisted on getting paid.

"GG does that, not your daddy." He looked over at her with that look she knows.

"Don't Tell her I told you, or she said the gravy train will stop." She does her best to look so severe, like she was the one to correct his actions.

"GG needs to stop. No little girl of mine will extort money

from people to do what I asked of her." Danny gave her one last look of don't press the issue.

"Okay, I am sorry, papa." Aurora gave Danny a big hug and grabbed her cake and ice cream.

Brian looked up at him and mouthed, "papa?"

Danny gestured for him to wait a minute until she was gone. Once the room was vacant, he said, "She calls me papa when I have laid the law down. That's her way of branding me the bad guy."

"Oh, when did this all start? Because that doesn't sound like my little peanut," Brian said, stuffing a piece of cake in his mouth.

"On our road trip. Well, more like on our way here from my family's old pack. She picked up this lovely behavior from one of her cousins." Danny watched his little girl dancing on the deck with her doll in one hand and cake in the other.

"You came from Blue Sapphire ridge, right?" Brian asked in a very carefree manner.

"Yes, sir, I sure did. Is it that obvious?" Danny questioned him with just a brow raised.

"Explains why she has blue sapphire earrings," Brian said as he drank another swig of coffee.

"Don't even get me started on those things. Austin is still mad my aunt took her shopping one day and brought her home full of holes." Danny shook his head, remembering how Austin hit the roof when he allowed his aunt to pierce her ears.

When he was just ready to start in on his brother-in-law, Phoebe walked in with Luna Katie in tow.

"Well, this is a sight for sore eyes. How are you, Danny? How is Austin? You boys let her have her cake and eat it too." Katie pointed out that Aurora was on a sugar high on the deck.

"Oh boy, that's my cue, poor Uncle Brian. Shame on you for

giving my sweet little girl so much sugar before the party," Danny said smirking.

"What party?" Brian asked, completely surprised.

"Oh, it's just a little get-together tonight at the pack house. Here is your suit, Brian." Luna Katie handed him a suit.

"Mom, what do you have planned?" Brian looked to Danny for answers, and he put his hands up.

"Aurora princess, it's time to go. Daddy is expecting us at home. We have to get ready for Grandma Katie's party," he said out the door, and they ran off to the condo before Brian could stop them and ask any more questions.

Danny took his daughter home and found all the men in the house already dressed for the night.

"Danny George-Blazek, you have thirty minutes to get ready. Give me our princess, and I will get her changed. Why is she covered in I-C-E-C-R-E-A-M." Austin spelled the last part out, so that the boys wouldn't figure it out.

"Sorry, can't talk. I have to get ready. Love you," Danny said, running up the stairs.

"Love you more! Aurora, come here. Let's get cleaned up." Austin took Aurora to get ready for the party at the pack house.

☽

It didn't take the family that long to get ready and head to the pack house. They walked in and the welcome was warmer than ever. The couple read the room, and everyone was waiting for the chief person to join the crowd. Danny sent the kids with the Omegas to take them to the daycare, so all the adults could mingle and have a good night of merriment. The two were all having a swell time sharing stories of the kids with the pack that Austin once hated. It makes a difference when leadership is filled with love and not hate. The pack back then was nothing to how they were now.

Austin felt free to be out and open about his love for Danny and their wonderful kids. So much so, that with any luck they would have an egg to put in the hatchery Danny had built here on the pack land. It was getting close to the time for dinner to be served, when the pack all heard the bells ring and the older gentlemen of the pack guard clear his throat.

"Announcing Luna Katie," the guard announced, as Katie walked down the stairs.

"Thank you, Genesis Moon Pack. Welcome to my retirement party. It has been my pleasure to continue as your Luna, but my time is over. I am stepping down now. My son Brian King is in charge of the pack. We have struggled as a pack, with my mate turning his back on us and making the horrible deal. He paid for it with his life. My son lost his wolf by being a good leader and protecting his pack and his brother. Brian has grown up a lot and I feel like his grandfather, Elder J, would be proud of him as your new Alpha." Luna Katie turned to face her son.

"Mother, why? We have talked about this. I am not ready. I don't have a wolf now. You leave me with no other choice." Brian turned to the crowd below.

"I, Brian King, newly appointed Alpha of the Genesis Moon Pack, turn my rights to rule to my chosen Beta, Kevin. He will be a powerful leader. I am sorry." With that, Brian took off from the pack house without looking back, but everyone could hear him crying. He gave up the one thing he was born to do: lead.

Kevin stepped forward and bowed and took a knee. When he stood up, he nodded to Luna Katie. Turning to the crowd, he spoke with vigor and embodied strength. "I, Kevin Quinn, accept the offer and title of Alpha. I will rule this pack in

Brian's absence to the day I hand it back over to him or to my son."

"Well, this is not the night I had planned for my pack, but I accept this change of power. Kevin, face me please and we will officially exchange power from me to you. Sara, you will become the Luna, I hope you are ready. I know you will do wonderful things. I am always here to help both of you out." With that, Luna and Katie set out to complete the Alpha ceremony, and Danny took Austin to collect the kids.

"We will congratulate Kevin and Sara, and give our good wishes to Katie, but we need to go spend time with your brother. He is hurting right now," Danny whispered in Austin's ear.

"We are a pair matched for the best. That is exactly what I was going to tell you, love," Austin replied, as they entered the daycare to see Brian walking the boys out.

"I kind of figured you two would look for the kids, then me, so why not kill two birds with one stone?" Brian led them out to the crowd.

"We will give our blessings and congratulations, then I am taking all of you out to have pizza," Brian said as he was walking up to Katie. Austin watched as Aurora pulled her magic over on him.

"Yes, p eanut. we will invite Phoebe to come with us for pizza. She might not come though, I know how much she loves steak and lobster," Brian whispered.

"I might love steak and lobster, but I will go anywhere with you and your family. Especially little peanut here," Phoebe said, reaching out so that Aurora could jump into her arms.

CHAPTER 4
PHOEBE'S WISH

As Phoebe held little Aurora, Brian looked deep into her eyes. "Why me? Why did Selene bless me with you as a mate but curse you with me as your mate?"

"Brian, stop right now. You know what I wish with all of my heart?" Phoebe let out a deep sigh.

Brian took a deep breath and swallowed hard, shaking his head and letting out a meek, "No."

"I wish you could see you the way I do." Phoebe brushed her hand across Brian's cheek.

"We were fine until I lost Ted. I—" Brian started off.

"You are not the only one to have lost Ted. I lost him, and my wolf lost him as well. But regardless of that, we both still love you," Phoebe said with tears in her eyes.

"I know. That's the reason I don't feel like I deserve you." Brian kissed Phoebe's hand.

"Brian, even without a wolf, you are my mate. So, it's time to find the courage and accept what we have. I have fallen for you, and I know you feel the same way." Phoebe's shoulders slumped as she tried to get it across to her mate.

"Why don't we talk about this over a simple dinner and a nice long chat?" Austin suggested to the pair walking behind him.

"Should we leave the kids?" Danny questioned.

"Um, no, they will help to keep everyone calm. Besides, this is a real-life lesson on family bonds—the mate bonds we all share. I want our boys to do what is right when the day comes to find and claim their mates. I want our daughter to know what true love is, and to know to fight for that love," Austin said while looking over his shoulder at his fantastic family.

The group approached the oversized SUV that Austin called his soccer dad's car, they got in, and Brian buckled up his little peanut, as Danny and Austin buckled up a boy each. Then, Danny slid into the driver's seat, while Austin took the passenger seat, leaving the open seats to the struggling couple; forcing the distant love birds together even briefly, so they could open their hearts.

As they drove into the town, Brian looked out the window at the passing pack lands, and Phoebe reached over and placed her hand on his. Everyone could see the love they had, or could have, if only Brian could open his heart a little more.

"All right group, we have a few places we can go for pizza, but I figured we could go where they have games the kids can play while the adults have a little chat," Austin spoke up while mapping out where they were going.

"Aunt Phoebe, Uncle Brian, can we be in your wedding like we were for Daddy and Dad?" Aurora asked.

"We have to wait and see how things go, sweetheart. We're not ready for a wedding," Phoebe responded honestly, and it set the mood for the rest of the ten-minute drive.

They pulled up to the Pizza House, as they called it, because it kept changing owners and names. It was the one place where the adults could chat, drink, and eat while the little ones spent money and played safely. This place was safe mainly because something enchanted it with good magic to protect the children.

As they unloaded, all the children were getting ready for a fun night, especially once the boys saw where they were. They immediately ran for the door and were inside in a flash. Danny ran to catch up to the boys, while his princess waited for him at the door.

"Well, thank you dear, for waiting for me. At least one of my children listens to me when I tell them to wait for dad." Danny looked down at his little princess and could only smile lovingly.

Just then, a stranger came over with his group of goons and encircled them. The stranger said, "Well, what do we have here folks? Looks like we got one of them yellow bellies. You know, the kind that typically has his tail between his legs? Oh, wait, that can't be right. This here fellow is nothing special anymore, just a worthless human. I'm surprised another pack has not taken over this pack already. Maybe I will challenge the new Alpha since he is not a real Alpha. I could take his title, but I think I will mostly take this she-wolf. You humans have no claim to our females. No need to muddle bloodlines. No one likes a mutt anyhow."

"Jed, grab that twinkle toe and show him what we do with his kind. I want to introduce myself to this little desirable piece of—" The stranger didn't get to finish his words.

"Lay one finger on my mate and so help me I will end you, sir!" Brian growled out with such power, if you didn't know any better it would be impossible to tell that Ted was gone.

"Sir? Nice to hear some respect from a human. Call me Charles. I'm the pack Alpha from North Dakota. I came to show respect to the Genesis Moon Pack after a very odd turn of events last year. The only son born from Alpha Joe lost his wolf and the pack has no respect for him. So, he ran away with his head down refusing his mate, oh, and hangs out with twinkle toe mutt trash. Jed, how's it coming over there?" Charles asked. When he got no answer, he looked over at his Beta.

Beta Jed was playing hopscotch, or what appeared to be some type of game, but with no markings on the parking lot it was hard to tell precisely. All the while, Austin's eyes were glowing.

"I don't have time for this she-wolf. I, Alpha Charles Saints claim you as my concubine," said Charles as he reached out and pulled Phoebe from Brian's hands.

Brian snapped at this, his eyes turning jet black. "I, Brian King, son of Alpha Joe King, swear to the Moon Goddess you will not touch nor claim my mate!"

"Whatever, you puny human. You can't do anything to me!" Charles screamed the last words as Brian yanked him up and away from Phoebe before throwing him across the parking lot where he landed with a loud thud.

Then, Brian turned to Phoebe and said, "I am sorry, my love that it took this fool this long to stand up and declare his love. But fear not Phoebe, my mate, my love, and who will one day give us a house full of pups, I have a disrespectful Alpha to mop this parking lot with if you'll excuse me. Brother, busy his goons, then take my bride-to-be inside. No need to have her around such violence," Brian said as an evil grin stretched across his face.

"As you wish, brother." Austin turned his attention to the five other men in the group and sang a song. They all tried blocking it out, but they couldn't stop themselves from pairing up and dancing a Tennessee waltz.

"Come, sister, my brother is waking up from a long nap. Let's allow him his fun." Austin took Phoebe by the hand as she had already sensed what Austin had picked up on.

"What is going on out here? I have the kids in there and I've already placed the pizza order. Austin, what is going on?" demanded Danny as he poked his head out the door.

"Calm down, don't get your panties all in a bunch. Take our soon-to-be sister-in-law in to the kids. I need to help my brother. As you know, we're a family, and no one messes with family," Austin said as he turned to join Brian.

He could see that the Alpha was trying to shift, but try as he might, he could not shift into his wolf.

"What black magic is this? You know we have laws against the use of magic on unwilling wolves," Charles growled out.

"Well, listen to me then; I will make it quick. We may be in the town where the humans run things, but this is still Genesis Moon Pack territory. You fall under the rule of law set by us, not you." Austin's eyes were now a pair of lightning storms.

"Oh boy, now you have done it. You made the wrong man mad," Brian chuckled.

"You call that filthy thing a man?" said Charles, pointing over his shoulder.

"Watch your mouth. He is my brother. I am the only one who can tease him. I suggest you apologize to him or I will tell him to use his powers to have your men do more stupid crap," Brian barked out.

Charles spat toward Austin, "I don't care about fairy boy here, or you. Both of you are a disgrace. I WILL TEAR YOU TO SHREDS once I am free from whatever this is." Charles fought against the invisible force holding him down.

"Well, you're an Alpha, but you must be new," Austin said as he walked up to Charles, who was bound to the ground by invisible chains.

"So, what does that have to do with my power grab? I will take this territory and make it my own," growled Charles.

"I have to say thank you, Charles was it?" Austin gloated.

"Why are you thanking me, fancy boy? I have done you no favors," said Charles.

"Oh, it's not for me. It was for my brother here." Austin turned to his brother. "Sorry Brian, but you will have a massive headache. I will see if Candy can come and relieve the pain you will be experiencing." Austin slapped Brian on the back.

"What on earth are you—" Just then, a searing hot pain cut Brian off, as a skull-splitting headache that felt like someone was digging into his head with a red-hot poker hit him.

Austin squatted down and squared off with Charles. "You see here, Charles. My brother took a silver dagger to save me. Unfortunately, in doing so he lost his wolf. Brian has struggled to get better and heal as a human. It was not until he accepted who he was with or without his wolf. You don't have to have your wolf to do what is right. Because of that, he's getting blessed by Selene, and if you are foolish enough to attack us here on our lands and not know your history well, I am sorry I can't help you."

"What are you talking about?" Charles was now turning red in the face as he tried desperately to get up.

Suddenly, a blue light flooded the parking lot, and a beautiful maiden stood before them. She reached out and caressed Brian's face. "Calm. Take a deep breath. The exchange is almost complete. Brian, you will be okay." Selene turned to the Alpha that was under her thumb of power.

"Charles, this will be a hard pill to swallow, but these boys are under my protection. Your actions here tonight disgust me. Austin is a blessed wolf. Well, the actual term is Chimera. Brian is his brother by choice, not law or blood. Do you see the bond they have? All my children should have that. You seem to have forgotten this, so let me remind you. As of right now, your pack has forgotten who you are. Your wolf will sleep, and you won't shift. You won't heal. You will be a puny human as you call them. Austin, can you be a dear and open a portal to say, the swamps of Florida?'

"Anything for you, Selene." Austin closed his eyes and opened a portal, and he watched as Selene pushed this seven-foot-four, two hundred and eighty-five-pound man into the unknown with a flick of her wrist.

"Your men can go with you under the same fate, cut off from the pack and clueless about their wolf. Austin, please look after Brian as his wolf pup settles in. It might be a little hard on him, but I am so proud of how far he has grown. I will not hold you boys up from your night," said Selene, and with that she faded away in the light of a moonbeam.

"Austin, I'm not sure what is happening, but let's not tell them right away, not until I have gotten my head on straight," Brian said.

The scent of eggnog and cinnamon caught his attention, and he whipped around and whispered "mate."

Phoebe immediately came running and jumped into his arms, peppering him with kisses.

"I love you. Phoebe, will you be my mate? Do you accept me as I was or will be?" Brian asked in a strained voice.

"I, Phoebe Cassel of the Genesis Moon Pack, accept you, Brian King, as my mate. I care not that you lost your wolf. You are my mate. A blessing from Selene." Phoebe hugged her man.

"I, Brian King of the Genesis Moon Pack, declare you Phoebe Cassel as my mate, always and forever." Brian spun her around in happiness. He had never felt so alive.

CHAPTER 5
GROWTH SPURT

"Austin, Danny and the kids have ordered. Let's go enjoy a family dinner," Brian said while smiling and holding his mate close to his side.

"Yes, let's go. I know now that you two have accepted each other. So, the girls will have to gossip while us boys celebrate," Austin said, patting his brother on the back.

Once inside, the ladies sat together, as did the men with the boys. The girls sat close together and started gossiping about boys and clothes. Meanwhile, the boys were talking about upcoming school and sports when the waitress walked up.

"What shall I start for you all?" Danica said with no life in her voice.

"Okay, we already have our food order in, but we have an odd request here. All the adults will do a single shot of three tequilas and one whiskey. For the kids, can we do milk in a shot glass, so they don't feel left out of the celebration?" Brian raised his one brow, trying to charm the waitress.

"We don't serve alcohol to minors sir, it's against the law."

"Here are the adults' driver's licenses. See, we're all of age. I was only asking for milk in the kids' glasses. I would even settle for a small rocks-style glass," Brian pleaded his case.

Suddenly, a voice they all knew so well came from behind Danica. "Danica, it's fine. The munchkins can have the shot glasses. I have little fun ones you can use that have cartoon characters, so you can tell from a distance that it's not a real shot," Candy said with a smile, handing Sue the sleeve of the kids' shot glasses.

"Candy, nice to see you tonight," Austin said as he stood up to greet his old friend.

"Boy please, you texted me to alert me you were bringing in my buddies. Here you go Logan, Ethan, and then I have one for my little princess." She handed each of the children token cards so they could run and play in the arcade room.

"Thank you, Aunt Candy," the children said in unison as they looked at her and then at the cards.

"No problem my little people. So what is the big celebration?" Candy looked the table over, waiting for a response.

"I accepted Phoebe as my mate, and she accepted me. I am going to marry this perfect woman," Brian said, kissing the top of Phoebe's hand.

"Aunt Phoebe is having a wedding. Yes!" cried out Aurora.

"Well, that is a cause to celebrate!" Candy ran her hand over Austin's and Danny's shoulders.

"Okay, here are the shots. I got my shot," Candy said, holding up her Chada.

"Here is to a smart, beautiful woman who saw me at my lowest, and now whenever I see her I am always at my highest. I love you, Phoebe. I know you love kids, and so do I. With that, I hope you are ready, because I want a litter of our own pups, even if it takes a lifetime. No amount of time with you will ever be long enough. I have wasted so much time. No more. I love you Phoebe." Brian raised his shot glass at the end as the crowd tossed back the shots.

"All right, guys, pizza is in the oven. You have about a good fifteen minutes." Candy looked down at her watch.

"Daddies, can we go play?" Logan asked, using his big puppy dog eyes.

"Yes, you can, and be nice to the other kids," Danny said to the boys. Then he turned to address his little girl when she piped up.

"What about me, Daddy?" Aurora asked with a smile. "If any boy comes near you, well, they better not, let's just say that," Danny said, looking down at his little princess who seemed to grow older by the second. In a flash, she was off chasing down her brothers.

"I can't imagine they will be in school in only a few weeks," Brian said, shaking his head.

"That reminds me, they all have to go in for the doctor's visit for their checkups before school. I am not looking forward to that school," Austin grumbled.

"We have the pack doctor ready to fill in all the paperwork. It's going to be a pain this state is not too keen on a two-dad birth certificate," Austin said, letting his shoulder sink a little lower than usual.

"Screw this state. They were born in another state, and it allowed two dads. They cannot deny the parentage," Brian said, shooting Danny a quick look.

"That's right, they should remember the town now has a crappy law firm covering them. My father's office will hit them with litigation faster than the kids are growing," Danny said, kissing Austin on the top of his head.

"Danny, why is Logan wearing high waters?" Austin asked, watching the boys play on the pinball machine.

43

"High what?" Danny looked at Austin, confused.

"High waters. It's where you are wearing pants that look more like man capris," Austin said, rolling his eyes. "Those pants are shorter on him now than when we left our house for the party."

"Capris?" Danny looked over at Logan. "He is not the only one. Looks like Ethan grew two inches already."

"Don't tell me they hit their first growth spurt." Austin looked over at the kids.

"We can buy more clothes if we have time. I am not worried about the money we just spent," Danny said, pulling Austin into him.

"You say that till you see the card statement." Austin bit his lip, waiting for Danny to look at the e-statement.

"AUSTIN!" Danny screeched, a little louder than he planned.

"I know we don't have to worry about money, but that is a lot to spend on kids' clothes. It looks like you spent three thousand dollars. What do you plan on doing with the kids' outfits that already don't fit now?" Danny looked up from his phone rather sternly.

"They still have tags on them. I will take them back and get bigger sizes. I will check what each of the store's rules are, and what I can't exchange, I will donate to Genesis Moon Packs orphanage. The war did a number on the families and many people go there to get help." Austin looked up at Danny.

"Is that the Elder J project?" Danny could see the pain in his mate's eyes.

"Yes," Austin mumbled.

"Donate all of it. We're taking the kids shopping again tomorrow. That project has been your baby to get off the ground. I want it to be successful." Danny put away his phone and looked down at his mate, then at the kids who were growing like weeds.

"All right, munchkins, dinners on. Get to your tables, and don't make me shut the game room down," Candy called out as she carried two pizzas over to the table. "Don't worry, I have two more coming."

"I didn't say a word." Austin put his hands up in self-defense.

"You don't have to. I can see it on your face. Did you forget I am not new to being around you? I can read you like a book without busting the cover open," Candy said with such sass it brought a smile across Austin's lips.

"Boys, here are some sanitary wipes. Wash your hands, because I know you didn't wash them before coming to the table. The table is for food, not dirt, grime, and germs," Austin said, handing the boys the sanitary washcloths.

"Sorry Dad. Wait, why did you not give one to our sister?" Logan pointed to his sister, who was already eating her cheese pizza.

"That's because Aunt Phoebe took me to the girl's room to wash up. You boys are so dirty. I hope my mate is not like the two of you." Aurora stuck out her tongue at her brothers.

"Aurora, you are only going into kindergarten, grade K. You will have no talk of boys until you're an old lady in a retirement home." Danny squinted his eyes at his little girl.

"Oh, Dad! Stop it." Aurora pouted.

"Speaking of that, we will go shopping again. Looks like you boys are growing out of the clothes we just got," Austin told the boys.

"Not shopping! We like what we have already," Logan pouted.

"Fine, I will get a couple of sizes bigger and hope it's not too big," Austin said, rolling his eyes.

"I will go shopping, Daddy," Ethan said with a smile, knowing when you go shopping you get to eat out.

☾

Time flies when you are older, and you don't want things to happen so fast. Sadly, none of us can slow down the hands of time. All the George-Blazek children once again got new clothes. While the kids donated the new garments they just received days prior as they no longer fit and the pack orphanage was in need. The pack doctor did his exam on the children, finding nothing wrong or out of the ordinary. It was all or nothing. The kids had to pass as humans while in school. Once the children and the doctor completed the exams, they sent the paperwork to the school. That's when it all went downhill.

"Hello, this is Scout public school. We're calling to speak to the mother of Ethan, Logan, oh, and little aurora," Pam, the school secretary, said sweetly.

"Mother? Ms. Pam, you all received the paperwork. Our children have two dads, no mother," Austin remarked, thinking about the paperwork Pam should have with her.

"Sir, I assume you know basic biology?" Pam started with a rather snotty tone in her voice.

"Can you tell me this, Pam? Do you see who my husband is? Please don't make me turn into a Kevin or whatever you call a male Karen," Austin said, a bit more irritated than he wanted to be.

"Excuse you, sir," Pam rebutted.

"Did I burp? Did I stutter? Was I unclear in any way? Our children have two fathers. The birth certificates are legal. You cannot discriminate. So, what is the issue now, Pam? Think long and hard before you respond," Austin said coldly.

"It is unorthodox. We are a simple Christian—" They cut Pam off.

"Stop right there. Do you want to bring religion in on this? Step outside and walk about a quarter of a mile east. There you will find Aquinas, an all-Catholic school. They have religion in that school, not the public one. If you want to thump on a bible and have a chat, come on over to our home and we can talk scriptures. With my kids going to kindergarten, your religious opinions have no place," Austin said smoothly but with conviction.

"Mr. Blazek, is it? Can we lose the attitude?" Pam's voice was flat.

"My name is Mr. Austin George-Blazek. I am the father of three wonderful children attending kindergarten in your school."

"No, Danny appears to be the father to Ethan, and Aurora. You are the paternal father only to Logan. So just know only you can get Logan, and Danny can only pick up Ethan and Aurora. Parent-teacher conferences will go the same way. We will not take both of you listed as the father for all instances. We need the name of the female parent," Pam said with more force.

"I want all of this in writing and signed by all parties in that school who agree with this. If you all want to play this game, you picked the wrong ones to play with," Austin said while tapping his pen on a notepad. He was taking notes of the conversation.

"Mr. Blazek, I assure you this is no game. Also, once more I will ask you to lose the attitude before I have Sheriff Tate ban and bar you from school grounds."

"Pam, I am calling Doug." Austin picked up the landline, and Pam could hear him dialing.

"Doug, what does he have to do with anything?" Pam said, flustered.

"Doug is the children's grandfather and our family lawyer," Austin stated as Doug answered.

"Austin, what can I do for you? Are my little grandkids being good?" Doug's voice rang out over the phone.

"What!" Pam screeched.

"Pam, you have our packet before you, correct?" Austin inquired.

"Yes, I called you Mr. Blazek. Unfortunately, it is incomplete, and your son Logan cannot attend unless it's completed," Pam's voice was now ice cold.

"Pam, is it? You will refer to my client and son-in-law with his full legal name. Mr. Austin George-Blazek. I prepared the papers you are questioning. My son and son-in-law have three children, not just Logan. If you take the time to go over all the paperwork, you will find it all in order," Doug informed her in a monotone voice you could tell he had perfected from years in the courtroom.

"Pam, did you look further into the packet?" Austin asked.

"No, not yet."

"Whose packet are you working on now?" Austin inquired while Doug sat quietly, listening to the conversation.

"Just opened the first one. Ethan's." As she read the student's name, "Ethan George-Blazek."

"Look on page four through page eight," Doug chimed in.

They all sat patiently, as you could hear Pam rustling through the papers.

"By the way, Pam, if you are only on Ethan's packet, why did you tell us Logan's paperwork is incomplete? You just told me and my lawyer, LOGAN's paperwork is incomplete." Austin was firm, but Pam poked the bear and now was going to pay the full price.

"What? How? I don't believe it. This doesn't seem right," Pam said, now flustered by the paperwork.

"Pam, Danny and I got married. The legal copy of the certificate is on page four. We had the kids before. The birth certificates show both of us as the father. But because we knew we were coming back to this bible loving state, we legally adopted all the kids, even though biologically they are already ours. The DNA blood paternity test is on page ten. This shows that Danny and I are both the parents of all three children in question. With that said, I am not Mr. Blazek. I am Mr. George-Blazek. Our children will be there on Monday for their first day of school. Once you go through all the kids' paperwork, you will see everything is in order," Austin's voice never wavered.

"This is not right," Pam replied.

"What's not right?" Doug inquired.

"They are pushing their lifestyle on the rest of us." Pam's voice was now licked with anger.

"Do you want to start that up, Pam? Do you understand you are breaking the law, or on a razor-thin line? A pushing lifestyle comes naturally, wouldn't you say? What about pushing people off their land, pushing your God on them, and even forcing our language onto them? Sounds like what early Christian settlers did here in America, remember Pam? I have my father-in-law on the line. You know our family's lawyer. Oh, let's not forget Grandma Betty W. Anderson. One of the three Judges this town has." Austin's voice was straining to hold back Trey.

"That's right, Betty is Danny's grandma," Pam said aloud, more to herself than anything.

A few moments of silence pass between the three.

"Pam, is there anything else you need?" Doug asked.

"No, sir." Pam sounded defeated as she sat down.

"Okay, have a wonderful day. Austin, I expect to see the

kids as payment tonight," Doug said and hung up before Austin could object.

"Mr. George-Blazek, please pick up your children's starter packet Thursday or Friday." Pam quietly let a tear fall from her face.

"Will do." Austin knew he had upset one of the many people who would have it in for his kids.

With that, Pam slammed the phone down, and the principal walked out, having heard the entire conversation that Pam had to deal with.

"Monday will be fun," the principal joked.

Meanwhile, looking in on the George-Blazek home, the children were playing happily... Oh the beauty of innocence.

"What has you upset, Austin?" Danny questioned as he walked into the room.

"One word," Austin looked over at Danny, "PAM."

"Let me guess, she had issues with our paperwork," Danny said, rolling his eyes.

"She had the nerve to demand the mother's name that was to be placed on the birth certificates." Austin sat down on Danny's lap at the kitchen table.

"We even went the extra mile to order the paternity test, and the real kicker is, she didn't even look that far into the paperwork before she called raising Kane." Austin leaned in to smell his mate's scent and calm himself down.

"Well, it is all cleared up, correct?" Danny hated loose ends.

"For now," Austin replied, nestling into his lover's arms.

"Well, let's let sleeping dogs lie. Dad called me. Looks like we're making dinner at his house. He said you would know why. I am assuming you called him while dealing with Pam?" Danny raised one eyebrow.

"Yes, sir, I did, and I have no issue going over for dinner with the kids. We pick up the kids' packets on Thursday, by the way." Austin stood up, kissed Danny, and walked out to get the kids ready.

⸱⸱

The week passed, and Austin and Danny walked into the school to pick up the packets for the kids. As they entered the building, Austin already had a sinking feeling in the pit of his gut.

"Here you go." Pam handed Austin all of Logan's paperwork packet, then turned to Danny and passed Ethan and Aurora's paperwork.

"Here you go, honey," said Danny, handing all the paperwork to Austin, while locking eyes with Pam.

"Pam, this is my husband. All three kids belong to both of us. I let it slide how you spoke to Austin the other day. I will even let this slide, but know that they have already served the school district notice, we won't tolerate discrimination or acts of hatred or harassment to our family." With that, Danny turned and walked away leaving Pam with her mouth agape.

"Austin, let's go show our kids their classroom." Danny took Austin by the hand, but Austin pulled away.

"Danny, they changed classes on us."

"What?"

"Yeah, Ethan and Aurora go to the morning class, and they set Logan for the afternoon class."

"Pam!" Danny said with a clenched jaw.

The principal came out of his office. "Pam, I put logan in with his siblings. Why was this changed? You need to put him back in the morning class. I want all three of the George-Blazek kids together."

"Yes, sir," Pam said, less than enthused.

"I am truly sorry about that Mr. and Mr. George-Blazek. I

will do my best to educate the staff not to act like this again." Principal Dr. Johnson showed his notable concern which was appreciated by the guys.

Next, they went out into the hall with the fixed schedule in hand, where they were greeted by the kids and Grandpa Doug. The children were excited to be starting school so they could grow up and become highly intelligent like their dads.

"I heard they tried to pull one on you, son. I will note it in the file. Let's get my grandkids to class to meet their teacher. I want to know where they will be when you're not watching them. Since they will be in school, are you coming back to the office to work with me?" Doug asked his son, knowing the answer.

"Dad, you know I will be back in the office. My security company is up and self-running. They contact me when we have issues. I need something to occupy my time. Austin is opening the Thermal NRG office here in Nebraska, so he will be busy too." Danny wrapped up their conversation as they walked into Ms. Venessa States' classroom.

"Welcome to my classroom, and who do we have here?" Venessa got down to the childrens' eye level.

"Hello there again. Let's see if I remember your names. Logan, Ethan, and Aurora." Venessa beamed at the kids.

"Ms. States, we get you again! So does that mean we didn't pass?" Ethan asked with sad puppy dog eyes.

"Oh, no, little man, you all passed so well I had to follow you. The grown-up that was the teacher before is retiring, so I got her job." Venessa passed all the kids a juice box and walked them around the room, showing them where to put their things.

"So, it's safe to say the kids will be happy they had her for pre-k, now they have her this year. I think the change from virtual class to in-person will be fine," Danny said, while kissing the back of Austin's hand.

"Austin, don't worry. The principal explained the error to me about registration with Logan. He is on my morning roster again." Venessa smiled up at Danny and Austin, making them at ease.

CHAPTER 6
MAKING A SPLASH

The first weeks in scout public did not let Danny or Austin down. The class filled with the kids whose parents were the bane of Austin's existence. It came as no surprise when Logan came home after a week of class and had a quickly fading bruise on his face.

"Logan, what happened to your face buddy?" Danny asked his little man.

"Some guy in my class called me a fruitcake on the way home. I was like, why did you call me that? He told me his daddy told him my dad was a fruitcake because he likes other guys." Logan let out a huff. "Family is more than blood, and we defend the family in our house, daddy. So, I punched him after school on our way home. Do you think I look bad? You should see him." Logan laughed, thinking about what he did to Chuck's face.

"Son, no, we can't do that. You know we are stronger than humans. We share this world with them, but we need to be careful," Danny said, picking Logan up and placing him on his lap. "Who is Chuck's father?"

"I don't know. It's rude to call adults by first name. Chuck's name is Chuck Travis."

"Wonderful. His dad's name is Andy. Your father and I will reach out and talk to him—"

A hard pounding on the door cut Danny off.

"Open up, queers, or I'm kicking in the door!" Andy yelled.

"Logan, take your brother and sister to the basement," Danny said as he ushered the kids out.

Once the kids were safe, Danny and Austin were at the door when Andy started kicking it. Austin opened the door, and Andy came charging in and went right for Austin.

"Get over here, queer. I am going to beat the hell out of you, and my boy will beat that queer kid of yours, too." Andy went to swing at Austin.

Austin sidestepped, then grabbed Andy and picked him up above his head. "What the hell Austin? When did you get so strong?" Andy was struggling to get free.

"You threatened my children when you taught your son to be as simple-minded as you. He hit our kid, and I won't stand for this for my kids." Austin tossed Andy out on the lawn, where he saw Chuck.

"Come on, dad, kick the fairy's ass," Chuck said, tugging Andy to get up.

"Son, I made my point. If his boy touches you again, tell a teacher he touched you in your no-no square," Andy said, looking at Logan's parents.

"Andy, get off our property. Never come here again, and your son needs to stay away from our kids," Danny said, pointing at the cameras.

"Andy, don't forget I own the best security company around, and I am a lawyer." Danny stood firm at the door.

☽

The kids had a sink or float contest for a science class the next day at school, and as Ethan was getting ready to set up his project, Chuck walked up and tipped over the table, soaking Ethan from head to toe.

"Oh, look, Ethan peed his pants," Chuck yelled, high-fiving with Deven. Ethan immediately ran from the room as the class laughed. Venessa ran after Ethan and stopped him in the hall. "Ethan, stop. You cannot just leave class like that."

"I am wet. I need to get dry. Please call my daddy." Ethan's plea hit Venessa, and she quickly led him to the private boys' room. Pulling out her phone, she dialed and said, "Yes, Austin, this is Venessa. We had a minor accident and water got spilled all over Ethan. He is upset, and I got him to the bathroom where he could try to dry off, but he asked if you could bring some clothes up. Thank you. I will tell Ethan you will be here really quick."

"Ethan, open up, buddy. Your dad is on his way," Venessa said sweetly, tapping on the door.

"Yes, Ethan, listen to your teacher buddy. Daddy is here, and I have some clothes for you," Austin said, scaring Venessa, who didn't know how he got to school so fast.

"Venessa, you should know that Danny and I run fifteen miles a day. So, six blocks are nothing for me to sprint here," Austin said, calming her.

"Well, I will give you some time. I need to get back to class. Ethan, when you are done, please come back to class."

"Okay," Ethan said in a lovely voice.
"Ethan, open the door. It's just me. Tell me what happened buddy."

"Chuck tipped the table over during sink or float on my turn, and I got wet. I felt pins and needles on my legs, so I had to get into the bathroom. I thought we couldn't get our tails. I have the bracelet Aunt Candy gave me to keep my tail away," Ethan cried.

"Ethan, you're fine. Let's get you into this nice dry outfit." Austin got Ethan to open up and change quickly. "Now get back to class, and we will deal with this later." Austin hugged his boy and sent him off.

Once he sent his son back to class, Austin walked down to the office to see what the principal had to say about this sink or float drama. "Mr. George-Blazek, you cannot just walk into the school and disregard policy," Pam started in.

"Pam, one of the other students dumped water on my son, and I dropped off dry clothes for him at Venessa's request," Austin said, rolling his eyes.

"Austin, I don't care if he shits his pants. You will check in, and we will retrieve your spoiled brat son." Pam was seething.

"Oh, that's right, Pam, you're Chuck's grandmother, keep that boy away from my kids, and we won't get Doug involved. Have a good day." Austin walked out.

"Mr. George-Blazek," the principal, Dr. Johnson called out.

"Yes, Dr. Johnson, I was dropping off dry clothes for the boy, you know, kids and water. It's not a day until we have a mess," Austin said politely.

"Very true. I am sorry for Pam's outburst. I will chat with her, Andy, and Chuck."

"Yeah, please have the staff and the crossing guards watch the kids better. I guess Chuck and Logan got into a fight after school. I know you all can't do anything about that, but since he lost his fight with Logan, I feel he is now targeting Ethan." Austin pulled up the feed on the home cameras, where it could be heard loud and clear.

"Chuck, I don't care what you do. Daddy has your back. This family needs to go. If you have to beat the hell out of

Ethan because I can tell Logan beat the hell out of you..." Andy was telling his son it was okay to fight.

"Austin, I understand that this is unsettling. Kids will be kids. I take the welfare of the children seriously. You are more than welcome to pick up your child if you feel the need. As far as checking in at the main office, please check in with us before you go about the halls. It's for the safety of our students and the staff.

Meanwhile, back in class Ethan had his hands full. As he went back into the course, he could feel all eyes on him.

"Ms. States, Ethan just walked in the door!" called out Deven.

"Thank you, Deven. I can see that," Venessa said with a smile.

"Ethan, is everything okay? Did your dad go home?"
"No, he went to Daddy and Grandpa's law office. He has some paperwork to do," Ethan said smiling, knowing the paperwork was for permits for the new privacy fence.

"What, is your gay daddy going to take people to court when you get wet? You are a crybaby, just like your dad. We don't need or want your family here. So go back to whatever hole you crawled out from," Chuck spit out with anger in his voice.

Unfortunately for him, Mr. Johnson was standing in the doorway.

"Chuck, that's enough. It would be best if you came with me to the office. Your grandmother and father are waiting for you. Now to the rest of you, orientation is not to be brought up. We don't need to talk about one mom, one dad, or two moms or two dads. You are here to learn and become educated the proper way. If you are so concerned about what the bible says, your parents can enroll you down the street," Mr. Johnson said with a firm, authoritative voice as they walked down the corridor and arrived at the office.

"Chuck, sit next to GG, honey, we will get this all sorted out. I will call Reverend Louis. This won't go unnoticed. Has that boy touched you or said anything? I swear if I was not a good Christian woman," Pam rambled on.

"Pam, we enjoy having you here at scout, but this is now an official investigation into your grandson and your actions. Also, Andy, I will have to ask you not to press upon your son that violence is okay. If I catch him doing anything of what the video I saw suggests while he is on school grounds he will face the consequences. I do not care if it's spring break. If I catch him fighting on school property, the school will act. Is that clear?" Mr. Johnson asked from across his desk.

"That boy better leave my son alone, because I will get the law and the state involved if he doesn't." Andy glared at the principal.

"Moving on, Pam, you are relieved of your duties—" Pam cut off the principal.

"Are you flipping kidding me right now?" Pam hyperventilated.

"Pam, as I was saying, you will have no contact with the George-Blazek children. You will now become the vice principal's secretary and will have nothing to do with that family."

"It was just water. I thought it would be a funny joke. Why do you have to be so mean, Mr. Johnson?" Chuck cried.

"If it were only that simple. Chuck, is this your backpack?" Dr. Johnson asked, raising an eyebrow.

"Yes, sir." Chuck hung his head because he now knew what this was about.

"Mind if I open it and share what you have here with everyone?" Dr. Johnson tapped the bag.

"Mr. Johnson, what does this have to do with anything?" Andy questioned, more out of the loop than he was aware.

"When I went to collect young Mr. Chuck, I saw his bag on

his hook and thought after our meeting you two might be upset and would want to take an early day. When I picked up the bag, I noticed at first the weight and how it sounded like it contained some liquids. Nothing unusual till when you hold it by the strap, the shape of the contents is obvious." Dr. Johnson showed them.

"I don't see it. What am I looking for?" Andy squinted his eyes.

"Look here," Dr. Johnson drew attention to the butt and reserve tank to the super soaker. "This might be a water gun. It might be something a little more innocent, but the longer I have it, and it's moving around, I notice a very unpleasant odor. Chuck, do you want to tell us what they filled this water gun with?"

"It's my super soaker, and the guys and I filled it with pee. I would squirt Ethan and Logan on the way home, so they go home smelling like pee."

"The guys?" Dr. Johnson looked over at Chuck, hiding his face in his hands.

"I won't tell snitches to get stitches." Chuck was trying to hide his face from his grandmother. He could feel her eyes on him.

"Dr. Johnson, please give Chuck a break here. I will gladly step aside and have no contact with the family in question. I will also make sure Chuck follows any disciplinary request," Pam said as she shook her head at her now embarrassed grandson.

"This," said Dr. Johnson pointing to the bag, "Chuck will destroy on the loading dock. He will have detention since he has morning class. Would you both agree he can stay till his grandmother is off? He will help wipe things down and also work on extra homework. Not that Ms. States gives homework. He can write a letter telling Ethan he is sorry for getting him wet. After that, they might expel him from school, and you will have to enroll him down the street or wait one year to come back."

"Let's go destroy it," Chuck said with a sad face. They walked to the dock, and the principal grabbed a hammer and goggles. "Okay, Chuck, smash it."

"Let me empty it first." Andy went to empty it.

"No, Mr. Travis, he needs to destroy it. If he will soak other people in his friends' and his urine, then he can suffer the fate himself." Dr. Johnson crossed his arms. "Now, Chuck, put these safety glasses on, and I want you to smash this until it's broken and you can't tell what it is. Got it?"

"Yes, sir."

Chuck smashes the gun, and by the end of it all, he was dripping in the contents of his water gun.

"This does not feel good. Can I go home and change? Do I get to come back tomorrow to learn?"

"Son, you can. Andy, Pam, take Chuck home. I will see the two of you first thing in the morning. If he ever brings anything to school that breaks the rules, I will expel him from scout public." With that, Dr. Johnson walked back to Ms. States' room to explain that Chuck went home and would be back the next day.

CHAPTER 7

BOYS VS. GIRLS

The day-to-day things can be like a mountain in our youth, even though they are nothing more than a molehill in reality. School for the Chimera children wasn't much different than it was for any other child. While in Ms. States' class, the kids stuck together. Aurora liked to break away from her brothers once in a while, but she was quick to make friends with Betty and Clarissa. They were often found playing together.

One day they were all playing house while the boys were out on the playground.

"Aurora, can we get your brothers to play house with us?" Clarissa was looking right at Ethan as she asked.

Ethan looked to Logan for help and mind-linked his brother. *"Brother, these girls are crazy. They want to have a fake wedding with us! They are not our mates. Get me out of this."*

"You think they are crazy? Deven said Clarissa was his girlfriend all summer long, and he will beat up anyone playing house with her."

"Brother, get me out of here!"

Aurora joined the boy's link. *"You boys, leave my friends alone. You're smelly, and I don't want you near us, or I will tell dad."* Aurora sat with a murderous expression on her face.

"Okay, peace. I'll take Ethan with me so we can go play ball. We don't want to play your stupid girls' games, anyway." Logan and Ethan closed the link and took off.

"Hey, where are the boys going?" Betty cried out.

"Oh, they are going to play ball. We don't need them. Besides, they smell like dirty boys." Aurora turned up her nose.

"Smell? I don't smell anything." Betty kept staring at Logan.

Ethan went to play basketball while his brother Logan went to play dodgeball with his newfound friends. Ethan set up for a basket, missed it, and landed behind the basketball hoop in the grass. He was walking over to pick up the ball when suddenly Deven dived for it, snatching it up and starting to dribble like he was a big NBA star.

"Hey, I was playing with that," Ethan called out.

"Not anymore. It's my turn now." Deven smirked an evil grin.

"I had it first. You were playing dodgeball!"

"Yep, and now I am playing with this. Deal with it."

"Ethan, we need to learn to share, buddy. It's only fair. You and Deven can share the ball," Ms. States announced before turning to watch the kids play dodgeball.

"Well, can we play together then?" said Ethan.

"Nope, I need to practice becoming famous." Deven avoided Ethan, completely ignoring his pleas to play.

Ethan decided to walk away, knowing when to toss in the towel, but as he turned, Deven took the ball and checked it at his head. It hit hard and knocked Ethan down.

"That's for getting my friend into trouble and not staying

away from my girlfriend. You better not play house with her," Deven grumbled.

"Girlfriend?"

"Yeah, it's like a boyfriend, but only a girl."

"Who would be *your* girlfriend?"

"Oh, you're going to have a smart mouth on you. It's Clarissa, so stay away from her, or a ball hitting you will be the last of your worries." Deven flexed on Ethan, trying to intimidate him. "Maybe you are like Chuck's daddy said. Just like your daddy."

"You can have her. I don't want to play house. That's something the girls play." Ethan raised his eyebrows.

"Are you calling me a girl?" Deven picked up the ball, ready to launch another attack.

"Wait, what's going on over here?" Ms. States questioned Deven.

"Ethan wanted to learn to play dodgeball without worrying about everyone hitting him. So, I was showing him how to play the game, Ms. States." Deven laid it on thick and sweet.

"Ethan, is this true?"

Ethan looked over at Deven as he shot him a look, daring him to say otherwise. "Yes, Ms. States, it's my turn to get Deven."

"Okay, just remember to play nice and not hit people too hard with the ball."

"Yes, Ms. States," the boys said jointly.

"Get me if you can, Ethan. I don't think you will, but go ahead and try," Deven taunted with a superiority complex that only he knew how to toss the ball right.

Ethan picked up the ball, faked, then tossed it hard and hit Deven in the chest, knocking the wind out of him. Deven hit the ground coughing. Then, Ethan walked up and got level with his ear.

"You can have her because my girlfriend is in California. I get to go back to see her during break and over the summer. Never judge a book by the cover. I might seem meek and mild, but don't rattle the cage if you don't want to see the beast." Ethan stood up. "Ms. States, Ms. States, I think I tossed the ball too hard by accident. Deven is on the ground, and I feel terrible. I'm sorry, Deven if I hurt you." Ethan put on the best act Logan had ever seen.

"Deven!" Clarissa cried out and ran over to him, helping him up.

"Deven, are you okay? It was an accident, but I think we all should head inside," said Ms. States, blowing her whistle.

Once the class got inside, she sat everyone down for snack and story time, and the children started in line for their choice of juice or milk with fruit or gram crackers.

Deven was in line before Ethan, so he got the first selection. Once again, he did whatever he could to get to Ethan. First, he waited till Ethan went through the line to select his snack. Then, he knocked the juice over, knowing it was the last juice of that flavor, and Ethan would now have to drink milk.

"Oops, sorry Ethan, I bumped the table and now your juice is spilled."

"Ethan, go get another drink. I will clean this up." Ms. States wiped up the mess and turned to dispose of the towels. Just at that moment, Ethan reached over and smashed Deven's banana, so he was stuck with a mashed-up banana for his snack.

"Ms. States, can I have another banana?" Deven pleaded. "Please."

"Sure, Deven, everyone has had a snack. It's okay to grab

the last banana." Ms. States pulled out the storybook about a monkey and a key.

Deven walked up, took two bites of the last banana, and tossed it in the trash while Ms. States was getting the rest of the class ready for story time. Then he shot Ethan a look, daring him to say anything, anything at all.

"Okay class, let's gather around. Grab your rugs and find a spot, and I will tell you a story. Then we can have nap time. After nap time, we will move on to music class."

"Move. I'm sitting here." Deven pushed Ethan from his spot on the floor and set up a rug for him and Clarissa.

Ethan looked over to Logan and Aurora, while they all gathered and stretched out. Then, Ms. States read the story, and the kids were all asleep in no time. This was the time Ms. States would normally have her own lunch at the back of the class, which gave Deven the opportunity he was waiting for. He reached out and yanked on Aurora's tightly braided hair.

"Ouch," Aurora let out a yell that alerted the teacher, and she came running up to investigate, only to find Deven thrashing in his sleep and getting a hold of Aurora's hair for the second time.

"Ouch, stop it Deven. Quit pulling my hair!"

"Sweetheart, it was an accident. I think Deven was having a dream of some sort. I'm sure he didn't do it on purpose."

Aurora got up, folded up her rug, and went to practice her letters. Logan and Ethan got up and quietly played with the fire trucks and monster trucks. Deven peeked out and saw that he didn't get the response he was looking for, so he acted as if he had just woken up. When he saw the boys playing quietly, he joined them as Ms. States finished her meal and came over to monitor everyone.

"Give me the fire truck. I want it." Deven provoked Ethan by yanking the toy away.

Logan quickly mind-linked his brother. *"Dude, let it be. We can't get into trouble, and that is what he's trying to do. I overheard him tell his friends that the three of us will pay for Chuck getting into trouble."*

"Fine, but I won't let him push me around, let alone hurt our sister."

"Trust me, I know how to fix this. Just let me think of the best way." The link got severed when a bell rang, and the class looked over to see Mrs. Keys walk in with her music cart.

"Rise and shine my little stars. It's time to stretch and come to life. It's time to sing and learn about music," Mrs. Keys piped up.

"I got it. Follow my lead," Logan said when he had reestablished their mind link.

"Ethan, I think today we get to pick an instrument we'd like to try playing. Dad told me all about Mrs. Keys. She has this whistle that sounds like a train. It would help if you got that, and I will get those maracas. Maybe we can get Aurora to sing. I have been working on the railroad. We can do a group activity," Logan confidently whispered loud enough for Deven to hear.

Deven quickly rushed to the head of the class, cutting in front of Ethan and his siblings. Before the teacher could even start music class, Deven grabbed the train-shaped whistle and blew on it, then belted out, "I have been working on the—" before he could finish, the teacher stopped him.

"Deven, what on earth do you think you are doing? Did I say it was okay to take anything off my music cart? We don't do that. We especially don't use instruments that go into other people's mouths. You could easily catch a cold or get sick."

"But I was told by those guys that we could play instruments and sing songs today. I only love music so much that I had to be first. I'm sorry, Mrs. Keys." Deven pleaded guilty to doing something he knew was wrong.

"So, you knew it was wrong, yet did it anyway just to be first?"

"Yes," Deven submissively responded.

"All right, go to the principal's office and tell them why I sent you. After I am done here, I will meet you there to talk to Dr. Johnson," Mrs. Keys said, all the sparkle having left her voice.

"I only did it because Logan, Ethan, and Aurora talked about getting to do it. So why should they get to?"

Mrs. Keys looked over at the George-Blazek kids. "Explain, please?"

"I told my brother before Deven rudely eavesdropped on us, that dad mentioned how fun your class is. I was privately sharing with my brother a thought I had: if we could choose our instruments, what each of us would have picked. Since Deven was listening to a private conversation, I'm sorry if he didn't hear the entire story. I don't have anything else to say. I'm sorry my classmate acted without direction."

"Logan, right?"

"Yes, Mrs. Keys."

"Is it dad or papa for Danny? He's your daddy, the lawyer, right?"

"I call them both daddies. Aurora will call daddy papa when he lays the law down."

"Well, I appreciate the apology, but Deven should not have listened in on that private conversation and acted so poorly. Please tell your father hello now, I'm just trying to remember them properly."

"Mrs. Keys Logan, Ethan, and Aurora's fathers are Danny and Austin," Ms. States explained.

"Ahh, yes, Austin has an amazing voice. If only you were

biological children, you might have picked up on his naturally talented voice. But unfortunately, such talent you are born with; no amount of practice can get anyone to that level," Mrs. Keys reminisced.

Aurora linked her brother. *"If only? Okay, I know we need to keep our gifts under wraps, but a little singing won't hurt. We will take dad's poem, Class Time, and make it a song. Logan, you go low, Ethan, you go high, and I will sing. Listen to the cadence of my foot tapping."*

"Okay," both boys agreed. All the kids knew of Austin's book of poems that they sometimes played with to learn how to sing.

"Time
Tick Tock, the clock will never stop
Another moment has passed.
Tick Tock, another day at last
Tick Tock Birth
Tick Tock Elementary and a student
Tick Tock, you're in middle school now
Tick Tock High School on your way
Tick Tock Married with the baby on due
Tick Tock parenthood, the blessings it brings
Tick Tock, life is an endless clock
We're all born to live a life on this endless march
Through all of time and space,
Tick Tock Never will I doubt their love
Tick Tock Love is eternal and pure
A moment has passed.
Tick Tock, this love shall last."

The three stopped singing and looked at the teacher. "Mrs. Keys, our daddies are just that, our daddies. Our blood tells us so. We were born with every bit of their musical talent," Aurora said with a broad smile on her lips.

"Class Time is a song I had never heard of before, but the harmony and everything was perfect. You *are* Austin's kids. Anyway, give your folks my regards and tell them to keep up the lessons at home. Class today, we will learn how to do what they just did. Oh, Deven, please head down to the office. I will be there when class is over."

CHAPTER 8
KAREN

T he school bell rung, indicating the end of classes, and the kids gathered their things and filed out of the building. Some of the older kids came to pick up the younger ones, while parents and grandparents picked the others up from outside. Karen was walking to the pickup area for her grandson, Deven when she had a run-in with Danny.

"Oh, look who's here. Looking for a new boyfriend? These guys are young, even for you," Karen said, rolling her lip up in disgust.

"Excuse me?" Danny retorted.

"You know, I saw you with that kid just a few years ago. It didn't work out I take it, so you came back to the school to find a new one to corrupt with your immoral life." Karen placed her hands square on her hips.

"Excuse me, Karen. Are we going to have an issue?" Danny was in hushed tones now that the kids were filing out of the building.

"Oh no, your order expired. Besides, you don't live here, so why are you at this school? You know I should call the cops; student safety and all."

"We live here, Karen." Three merry children interrupted Danny.

"Daddy," Ethan squeaked.

"Dad." Logan fist-bumped Danny.

"Daddy," came the excited voice of young Aurora.

"Daddy? Oh, please don't tell me they allowed you all to adopt? Karen's eyes bugged out of her head with this statement.

"Adopt? Daddy, what is she talking about?" Aurora questioned.

"Sweety, adopt is where someone else raises you and loves you. Don't worry, you three already know who your daddies are, and that we love you," Danny said as he got down to her eye level.

"Grammy! " Deven shouted as he ran into her open arms. Austin walked up to the group, not sure how he felt about seeing Karen after all these years.

"Who's ready for ice cream?"

"Are you sure these men are your daddies? Are you safe? If not, I can help you get away from these evil dirty men?" Karen looked sweetly at little Aurora.

"What's with the crazy lady, daddy?" Logan pointed at Karen.

"Why the nerve? I see, Danny, you are not teaching these kids to respect anyone." Karen let out a huff.

"Karen, our children respect people that deserve it. Quit living up to your name. Leave my children and my husband alone." Austin looked Karen dead in the eyes and showed he was not afraid of her.

"Ha! Husband, now that's a hoot. Marriage is between one man and one woman."

"Kids, let's go," Austin directed the kids and his husband home.

"No! How do I know these are your kids? You can't leave. HELP. HELP someone. Anybody HELP. I think these men are kidnapping innocent children." Karen's voice got loud and carried across the playground, gaining the other parents' attention.

"Really, Karen!" Danny spit out.

"Austin, you always were a rotten apple. No need to ruin these innocent souls."

"Karen, do not talk about my husband that way!" Danny warned her.

"Oh, get over yourself, Danny! I am not afraid of you or Doug." Karen crossed her arms and stared down at the guys and the kids.

"No need to fear us, just respect us like you desire us to respect you." Danny tried to remain calm. After all, this was a perfect life lesson for the kids.

"Respect!? You don't respect marriage. You make a joke out of it. Your marriage is a real joke. Where did you get it done? Is it even real? I didn't think it was allowed. This is a good Christian country, isn't it?" Karen was getting more and more upset as she went on.

"Do we have a problem here, folks? What was all the screaming for help?" Pam questioned as she looked on at the boys with disdain.

"Yes, Pam, thank God another good Christian woman is here. Help me! These two deviants are trying to take children from the school. You need to call the cops right away," Karen pleaded with her church friend.

"What?" Pam had a lost look about herself.

"Yes, Pam. These kids—our kids—she's upset because

we're taking *our* kids home." Austin was seething mad and Trey was itching to come out and play Karen soccer.

"That's a laugh and a half." Karen rolled her eyes at Austin's claims to parenthood.

"No, they are the parents of those kids," Pam said in a soft voice.

"NO!" Karen placed her hands over her heart as if she had been told that a loved one had recently passed away.

"Yes, Karen, and they are married." It took all Pam had in her not to vomit on the words. "I don't know how, but they even have DNA tests showing they are both the biological fathers of all three children. I know Danny has money, but I recently found out that Austin found his biological family and he comes from money too. So, I guess when you have the money you can play God." Pam forgot she was still at school and needed to be careful about what she said.

Suddenly, the crowd that had gathered around the bickering ladies, and the George-Blazek family parted as the deputy strolled up and looked over everyone, trying to see why he had been called out to the school.

"Ladies, what seems to be the issue?" Deputy Derick Reed asked.

"These men are here, and I feel they don't belong. They are picking up little children. Look at them! They don't belong here." Karen pointed at the two.

"Well, they look normal to me miss," Deputy Reed started off.

"It's Mrs. Matheson, the mayor's wife," she said, placing her hands on her hips.

"Oh, Mrs. Matheson. It's nice to see you."

"What are you going to do about this?" Karen pointed at Danny and Austin.

"He won't be doing anything, Karen," Danny said, looking seriously cross.

"You shut your mouth. No one asked you a damn thing." Karen was red in the face.

"Now ladies, let's not use such adult language around the kids. I'm sure these gentlemen have a good reason to be here."

"Daddy, why is this officer acting like you're not our dad?" Logan asked, perplexed.

"What's that little man? Did you just call Danny your daddy?" Deputy Reed squatted down to Logan's level.

"They both are, and Ethan and Aurora are my siblings," Logan said, holding their hands.

"Pam?"

"It's true Deputy, Danny and Austin are the parents of these three students." Pam let out an almost inaudible sigh.

"See Mrs. Matheson, these children are safe. They are here with their parents, although it is odd two dads and all, but nothing illegal. So, this one is out of my hands. If the school has all the paperwork showing they are the parents, I can't stop them from picking up their kids anymore then I can stop you from picking up your grandson." Deputy Reed put on his hat as he stood up to face Karen.

"You are worthless. Wait till I tell Sheriff Tate what a joke you are. Wait till I tell my husband about this. How can this be okay? Why are we allowing our Christian morals to be wiped away?"

"Karen, the religious school is that way." Austin pointed to the Catholic school. "Please, we don't allow religion to be pushed on to our children."

"See, he admits he is not raising them right."

"Officer, are we free to go? Can we please leave with our children?" Danny inquired.

"You guys are free to go—"

Karen cut the deputy off. "They are not free to go. I want them arrested. They harassed me. I feel endangered. Why else would you be called out if someone was not in danger?" Karen glared at Danny.

"Karen, that will not work," Danny said with a smug smile.

"Oh, and why not smartass?"

"Because... well, just look up," Danny pointed to the security cameras.

"Why?" Karen turned and saw the security cameras with his company's logo on them.

"Officer, you need to call in for a warrant on those cameras. In fact..." Danny pulled out his phone."Dad, I need to have you draft up a warrant for the school's cameras. Karen is harassing us again."

"Thanks, dad. Yes, we will bring the grandkids over for you and mom. I'm sure they would love a sleepover. Don't forget Brian will stop by to pick up Aurora, so Phoebe can take her dress shopping. Yep, love you too, Dad. Bye." Danny hung up the phone as Dr. Johnson walked out of the school holding the George-Blazek family folder.

"Mr. Johnson, I do hope you are not about to share our family's file with the public like that. I believe it is a breach of the school's code of ethics." Danny looked over at the principal, daring him to play the game.

"I am only showing Deputy Reed that all documents on file show you and Austin are the parents and have full authority to be here. I'm sorry it came down to this and no need to get a warrant for the cameras. Officer, here is a flash drive of the events as Mrs. Matheson showed up and started the conversation with Danny."

"Okay, I will take this with me in case we need it. I will meet with Sheriff Tate and the mayor here soon anyway regarding the school parade tomorrow." Deputy Reed nodded his head. "Sorry folks that so much of your time was wasted."

"Karen, have a good night." Danny turned with Austin and the kids in hand, leaving her fuming at the doors to the school.

"Deven, let's go. Your father will want to hear all about this. Tell your grammy what school was like. Are you in the same class as those poor children?" Karen doted on Deven.

"Yep, and I hate all three of them. They got Chuck in trouble and it's not right. Chuck's dad said the whole family is homo." Deven stopped when he could feel his grandmother's eyes on him, and he knew he was in for it.

"No, go on. In for a penny, in for a pound. You are already in trouble, so finish."

"No, thank you Grammy, I'd rather not."

"So, how are they in class?"

"I don't know. I just don't like them because they keep talking to my girlfriend and I don't like that." Deven pouted, hoping his grams would forget about his word choice.

"We will have to see about making sure they don't mess with my little boy here, and I will let your little misstep on words slide this one time."

"Thank you Grammy." Deven smiled as he buckled himself in the car and they pulled out of the school and drove off.

Meanwhile, the George-Blazek family walked in the other direction to their house, already forgetting the troubles that Karen had started for them. Once home, the kids were eating a snack while Austin and Danny prepared dinner.

"After all these years, Danny, she still has it out for me," Austin said as he washed the lettuce.

"Baby, don't let that old demon woman get to you with her bible this and I feel superior attitude that," Danny said as he snaked his arms around Austin and kissed his neck, bringing him in for a kiss.

"Eww daddy and dad are kissing again!" Logan yelled out to his brother Ethan, who came in with a water gun and started spraying the guys down.

"You two better cool off before we call Grandma and Grandpa." Ethan pulled the trigger again.

"Oh, you think Grandma and Grandpa will save you. Keep it up. We will walk you to school on Monday in our pajamas and bathrobes," Danny joked.

"Honey, that would only make all the carpool moms a little too happy for my taste." Austin shot his eyebrow up and laughed.

CHAPTER 9
VENESSA

Venessa had had enough of the parents, so she went into her classroom to find her desk and put her head down. She was lost in thought when a man clearing his throat at the door startled her.

"Oh, Mr. Johnson, to what do I owe the pleasure?"

"Ms. States, no Venessa, we are both adults here. No need for titles and formalities, the children are not here. Please call me Alex," Mr. Johnson said while smiling.

"Okay, Alex. What can I do for you?" Venessa pried.

"Tell me what you can about your day-to-day dealings with the George-Blazek kids."

"Only them? I have twelve other children in my class as well."

"I'm sure all the normal children are fine, but I want to be sure the George-Blazek kids are not causing any more disturbances."

"Disturbances? Sir, I'm not sure I follow."

"I don't believe Deven needed to be sent down to my office the other day. They also seemed to cause issues with Chuck.

I'm this close to telling them they need to find a different school."

"Why, sir?"

"Is it not obvious? That family's alternative lifestyle is causing those kids to be disrespectful to their peers. Causing fights on the playground. Bullying other kids on the way home. Venessa, before that family showed back up, our school district never had this many issues. The last time we had a drama like this was when Austin was in school and he dated Danny."

"So let me make sure I am understanding you perfectly clear, Mr. Johnson. It's all the children's fault they have gay parents, and that does not sit right with you. So, the children must pay for your view of sins of the fathers?"

"Now, now Venessa, let's be reasonable. You know as well as I do those kids are different on another level. Did you hear what the music teacher said? With all that drama and these talentless little humans can suddenly make their own concert. No, no mam that's not normal."

"What does that have to do with them in class?"

"Everything. If they aren't picked on because they don't have a mother but two fathers, or it's teasing about their hair or what they wear and now it's about singing."

"The George-Blazek kids are resilient. They can handle a lot, and if this school would have tested them prior to school, you would have known they are already reading and writing on a third-grade level. Both Austin and Danny have extremely high IQs. Why do you think they have the companies they have? Over the summer, I was the remote teacher those kids had. I pushed the school board to test them and put them where they belonged education-wise. Austin and Danny both wanted the kids tested, and they got tested. I don't know the results other than that Austin warned me that the kids might get bored, and if they did, I should call him. He has tablets for them to work on if they get done with the classroom stuff. I do not understand how a man in your position can stand here saying they are here for the children, then talk out the side of your mouth and talk down about these kids." Venessa was now getting red in the face. She stood up abruptly, catching Mr. Johnson off guard and causing him to stumble backward.

"I don't understand why you would normalize that," he said, pointing to the family mobile of the George-Blazek family.

"Because, Mr. Johnson we are in a place called America, where we all have civil liberty and rights. Your opinions are best kept to yourself, or at the very least, not shared here at the school." With that, Venessa grabbed her bag and looked at Mr. Johnson.

"What?"

"I am kindly asking you to exit my classroom so I can lock it. I would hate to have the ongoings of my class spill out into the hall. Is this why my class has to keep the family project in the room, but Mrs. Samsung can have hers in the hall?"

"I. Ah. Um." Mr. Johnson stumbled over his words.

"I don't believe it. The nerve of this school."

"You know it goes both ways, Ms. States. If you don't like it you can leave as well. I'm sure I could fill your spot in a heartbeat," Mr. Johnson sneered.

"Lucky for me, Doug George is my lawyer and holds a copy of my employment contract with the town. He is no longer the town's lawyer, so I would think about that before you assume I will fold like a cheap house of cards." With that, she locked her classroom and walked out of the building.

Venessa was boiling over as she walked to her car and was about to get in when Eric stopped her.

"Ms. States, right?"

"Yes? Can I help you with anything?"

"Yeah, I'm sorry to say this, but I don't want my child to learn about that love is love crap. Leave gender and all that other crap they keep shoveling on the kids out of the class-room," Eric said, leaning on Venessa's car door so she couldn't leave.

"Eric, right?"

"Yes, mam."

"So, you don't want the subject of gender used in MY classroom?"

"Well, it's more a scout public classroom funded by us good taxpayers and overseen by the state." Eric grinned using the verbiage his mother told him to use.

"Until the school board gives the direction, then NO Eric, you will not control my classroom. Besides, I don't think you all have really thought this one out. Your issue is with the fact I have a family that has two dads and no moms, am I right?" Ms. States said, while raising her eyebrow at Eric.

"Hell, yes, that's not normal. It's unnatural," Eric boastfully announced.

"So, tell me Eric, what am I to say about your son? He only has a dad. We have no record on file about his mother. The only thing I got out of the records was from Ms. Strongburg, and she said the baby's momma wanted nothing to do with you or the crazy family. She then dumped the kid at your door and walked away. So, tell me again how fair is that to Deven?"

"You leave my boy out of this. What relevance do the issues his mother and I had back then have anyway? At least he has a mom," Eric huffed.

"One that no one can find, and it's clear that Deven has had issues with it in classroom discussions. We do not use gender as a weapon or a discussion factor. I use gender to separate the kids: boys to a boy bathroom and girls to a girl bathroom. The fact that the kids have two dads doesn't mean they like other boys. In fact, your son is upset because a girl he likes has been talking to one of the George-Blazek boys."

"Well, ah, um."

"Now Eric, if you have nothing more, I want into my car so I can leave. My day is done, and I have things I need to do."

"Yes, of course. I'm sorry."

Venessa got in her car and drove off, leaving a confused and upset Eric standing there as his phone rang. He answered it with trepidation.

"Yes, mom I tried to talk to her about it. She is as stubborn as you said, but she brought up Misty. Not by name, but Deven seems to miss out on not having her around. I know I need to go back to Colorado and see if I can find her. It's hard to believe that my camping trip from six almost seven years ago landed me in this mess. I have called out to the Rangers near Mt. Evens to see if anyone matching Misty's description shows up. I'm not holding my breath after all this time. Yes, mom, I watched Venessa drive away. She headed toward the supermarket. Why?"

"Mother, don't harass her. Let's give her time."

Before he could finish his thoughts to his mother, she hung up because she had just seen Venessa pull up. Karen waited until she was in the store, before she walked in and picked up a small basket to do some light shopping.

"Oh, Ms. States, it's such a pleasure meeting you here. You know, I think Keven has the best cuts in the meat department."

"Hello, Karen," Venessa said in annoyance.

"Ms. States, have you ever thought of having kids?"

"Yes, in fact I have kids."

"Oh? It's Ms. not Mrs., right?"

"Correct. I have almost twenty kids, Karen, and my time at the supermarket is just like yours when you're free from the kids and want nothing to do with talking about them. I love all my kiddos, but it's me time right now." Venessa picked up her pace.

"Just look at that." Karen pointed to the rainbow flag on a shirt.

"Yeah, just look at that, a shirt with a rainbow. You better write to the press." Venessa rolled her eyes.

"How would you feel if you ever had a child of your own and they—" Venessa cut Karen off.

"I would love them unconditionally. If you're using the bible to be cruel, think about all the verses."

"Okay, but what if?" Karen said placing her hand on her hip in usual fashion.

"I would still love my child because children are a gift from God. he helped make that child."

"But..." Karen's voice cracked and broke.

"Karen, what part of unconditional love does not make it into that head of yours? Why is this entire town so closed-minded? Let me give you a friendly piece of Christian advice. Read the book cover to cover; take your time. You should finish it in one year. Any time you come across a scripture you want to use to argue a point that you want others to believe—high-light it. Use say... yellow. Then we can meet up and talk the bible at, oh I don't know, let's say church. We can compare notes. Don't worry, my bible is already highlighted and divided into sections. So, until then, please let me unwind and shop in peace."

"Why the nerve? I am older than you and you talk to people this way. Wait till I tell my husband the cheeky new teachers they are giving jobs to."

"Karen, you do you. Sticks and stone break bones, but those who live like a princess should not live in a glass house and toss stones. I tried to be nice, but now you are pressing your luck. You come for me and my job like you have all the power when, in fact, I have a contract that can't be broken unless the town wants to pay me out like they did Doug George. You will step back with your cheap knockoff of a high-end designer outfit with blended materials. Take your shellfish and what is that, pork? to the checkout and make sure you pray that it's all okay. I don't like to bring children into this, but I know where you're driving your point, so let me be clear: sex before marriage? Children out of wedlock? When is the stoning party? You work your business from home, right Karen? And I believe I have seen you post your work on Sundays?"

"I don't! Whatever. Oh, my sweet baby Jesus, you need to get your head out of the clouds." Karen stormed off in a huff, leaving Venessa to finish her shopping.

Venessa took the next thirty minutes to finish her shopping in peace. She picked up a nice dinner and grabbed a bottle of wine. Then, as she approached the checkout, she noticed Deputy Reed and Sheriff Tate walking up to her.

"Ms., would you mind coming with us?" Sheriff Tate asked.

Elena happened to be in line just nearby and she overheard them. "Hey honey, what brings you into Big Ks? I told you I was shopping for our dinner tonight?" she asked Tate sweetly.

"Sweety this is official police business. I need to see this lady about her—"

She cut Tate off. "Love, Ms. Venessa States was in here shopping for almost forty-five minutes. That Karen, the mayor's wife, was in here harassing her, and I was about to step in when she left. Venessa here stood up to that bitch and she's lucky I didn't deck her for the way she was talking about mixed families." Elena gave Tate the look he knew to step down from.

"Ms. States, is what this beautiful young lady said true? Was Karen harassing you?"

"If it was not Mr. Johnson, it was Eric, then it was Karen.

Why can no one in this town leave the George-Blazek kids alone?!" Venessa said with an edge to her voice.

"Oh, that's the family that has the triplets. They are so sweet. How could anyone pick on them?" Elena pouted her lip and flashed her eyes at Tate, so that he became flustered.

"Well, I appreciate your candor, Ms. States."

"It's Venessa. I should say thank you to your girlfriend."

CHAPTER 10

SCHOOL CALLS

O nce Venessa had finished talking with Sheriff Tate, she quickly called up Austin and Danny.

"Sorry guys, I hate to be the pest, but I want you both to be aware something seems to be about to go down regarding the kids and school," Venessa confessed, walking to her car and looking to make sure she was not being followed.

"Venessa honey? Are you okay? What's going on that has you rattled?" Austin asked in rapid fire.

"Well, Mr. Johnson started in on me about the children when he didn't get the answers he wanted. Then I had a run in with Eric because of the boys' interactions with his son. He was pressing me to turn on your family. I left him behind and made it to the market, only to get broadsided by Karen."

Venessa finally took a breath, giving Danny the chance to speak up. "Venessa, it's fine. We will deal with them. Are they harassing you? If so, call Doug. He will take care of everything at no charge. We will cover any legal fees that come up, okay?" Danny said, while shooting a quick text to his father to start the subpoena process for the school cameras and the church across from the teacher's parking lot. He included in the list the supermarket cameras inside and out.

"Hey, Venessa, guess who is calling right now! Thanks for the heads up. We will keep you up to date." Austin bid her goodbye and answered the other line.

"Hello, this is the George-Blazek residence." Austin played it out like he didn't just see the caller ID.

"Oh, um, who am I speaking with?" Mr. Johnson asked, unable to tell if he was talking to Austin or Danny.

"This is both Austin and Danny, Mr. Johnson. You're on speaker," Danny said, loud and clear enough for Mr. Johnson.

"Well, I would appreciate if I was not on speaker."

"I understand your application of not being on speaker, but you called us so you will be on speaker," Austin said, smiling.

Danny shot Austin a look that he knew all too well as "play nice."

"Very well, we will just go about this a little differently. Instead of a simple casual phone call, let's do this in person." Mr. Johnson's voice cut off with static.

"Wonderful. We can be there at the school in just a few minutes. We just drove by and saw your car still in the lot. See you soon." Austin hung up before Mr. Johnson could object.

"Austin, what part of that look did you not understand?" Danny was cross with his mate.

"Kids! Come here. Daddy and I have a meeting to go to. I'm sending you to Grandpa and Grandma Blazek's. You all better be on your best behavior." The children nodded and lined up as Austin opened a portal door to his in-laws and Grandma was waiting with open arms. "Come on, kids, I have cookies in the oven."

"Mom, not too many sweets. The kids need to eat dinner first," Danny yelled out as his mother acted like she suddenly couldn't hear him.

"Danny, let's go. We don't want to keep Mr. Johnson waiting," Austin suggested, as he left the portal to his in-laws open, but closed the door to the pantry.

"Try to remain calm, Austin. I have things redirected to my cell, so as soon as anything pings for the security footage we will know," Danny said, taking Austin by the hand and walking onto the school grounds.

"Mr. Johnson, they're here," Pam said in her usual chipper voice.

"Thank you, Pam. You can go home. No need to keep you here for this." Mr. Johnson put on his best smile and encouraged her to go home.

Once in the office, the guys settled in at Mr. Johnson's desk, and unknown to Mr. Johnson, Austin started his recorder but set it out in plain view.

"Now Austin, you know in order to record me you must have my consent." Mr. Johnson smiled wickedly, thinking he had them by the balls.

"Well, Mr. Johnson, as a publicly paid professional working in your professional capacity, I have all the rights to record you while you are doing your job. You had the opportunity to keep this as just a simple phone conversation, I believe you said so yourself, but because it was on speaker so my husband could hear, you decided it needed to be more formal and here at the school. The school, I might add, has video and audio recordings in public spaces. One is right outside this very door," Danny said, folding his hands under his chin.

"Fine, record, I have nothing to hide. If it holds me accountable, it will hold you to the same standard." Mr. Johnson rolled his eyes, hating dealing with Danny, one of the town's best lawyers.

"Well, gentlemen, this meeting should come to you as no surprise. Let me be frank, this school district's vision is to prepare our students to make positive contributions to society and thrive in this rapidly changing world. Our core mission is for every student, every day, to be successful. If not only in their young minds but their hearts as well. Here at scout public, we aim to prepare the young minds sent to us to make ethical and moral choices during their time here. But we desire to leave a lasting impact far beyond our simple walls, by instilling in them the value of societal norms and how to keep life peaceful and valued. With that said, we have had severe issues arise since your children started school here. So, let's sit here and have a nice adult chat about what I, as principal, expect from your children, and from you going forward."

Mr. Johnson adjusted himself to a more comfortable position in his oversized office chair, while Austin pulled a pen and pad out of his bag and looked over at Danny.

"Now, in your start of term packets, you both received a copy of our code of conduct. As a reminder that a code of conduct is a set of principles, expectations, and/or rules that are given to students and parents to make sure that I clearly communicated the expectations that the school has for their behavior. I can clearly tell you it seems your children have no respect for our school's code of conduct." Mr. Johnson picked up a glass of water.

"Examples please, Mr. Johnson, and pray to tell why, if they have been in violation all year so far, why are we just now getting called into your office?" Austin asked as he tapped his pen on the notepad.

"Where would you like me to start? Let's start with dress attire. Young Aurora seems to be dressed beyond not only her age group, but dare I say overdressed. I have seen her come to school wearing clothes that cost more than some of the teachers earn in a month. I'm sure you can understand how flustered that makes her teachers. Moving on to the boys. I have seen them come to school in what I can only describe as 'high waters.' How can you sit there and not feel that your daughter is overly dressed? How are her peers to see her? Nothing more than daddy's spoiled brat?"

Austin couldn't help but let out a giggle as he remembered how quickly the boys were growing.

"Do you find this funny, Austin?" Mr. Johnson was getting red in the face.

"Alex, calm down. Since you are addressing me by my first name, we're done with formalities. My daughter can wear whatever my mother and father send to her from Colorado. Nothing my Aurora has worn ever violated the dress code. I am not sending her into a potato sack. The dynamics of my family are not your concern, so close your mouth before a fly gets sucked in. Second, if you have such a keen eye on my boys, you'd see that they have been growing a lot in these last few months. Moving on, what are your other concerns about the code of conduct? As you can see, I'm taking notes, so once we're done, I can compare them to our code of rules that I have right here." Austin waves the paper at Alex.

"Family dynamics. That's a good place to start, and how is it again? You both are the fathers of said children, and they were all born at the same time?" Mr. Johnson pressed on.

"As I stated, our family dynamics and how we came to be are neither this school's, nor your personal concern. Your job, Alex, is to provide a safe learning environment," Danny said through gritted teeth.

"We are overly concerned with Logan's behavior. He beat up a fellow student." Alex was showing signs of getting flustered.

"That happened off school grounds, off school property, after an issue raised by another student assaulting Ethan. Mind you, they only brought it up to the school's attention so you could monitor and keep our kids safe at school," Danny said, shifting in his seat.

"Regardless, we do not allow students to beat up other students here."

"So, what did you do to the student who hurt Ethan outside of school and then again on the playground?" Austin looked Alex dead in the eye, and he could not hold the gaze.

"I don't know what you're referring to, Austin. As far as I read in the report, the kids were playing dodgeball. If I recall, it was your boy that hit Deven a little too hard. Now I do not know what your family's issue with Deven is, but the bullying on the playground and then getting him into trouble with music class all seems a bit much. Some would say your boys are attention seeking. Perhaps it's just an unbalanced home life. The children's home life seems of grave concern," Mr. Johnson stated while adjusting his tie.

"Excuse you!" Austin exclaimed while bringing his fist down on the desk.

Mr. George-Blazek, I feel there is no need to be so aggressive and hostile," Mr. Johnson said, while holding back a smile.

"This is not aggressive, nor is it hostile," Austin glared daggers at the man, making him angry.

"Austin, let me handle this." Danny placed his hand on Austin, calming him instantly.

"Why? Is it because Austin and I are gay? Does this school have an issue with us being gay? Are you saying we're unfit because we're not the quote end quote normal household? I know for a fact several of your students here are from single-parent homes." Danny looked at Mr. Johnson, but he would not return his gaze.

"Gentlemen, let's be frank. I do not see how this school is a good fit for your children. They seem to fail at keeping up with the class. Several times they are off doing their own thing while the poor teacher is trying to teach a lesson." Mr. Johnson was looking at his notes, not looking up at the men across from him.

"I feel your children have a hard time keeping up, so they act out and start fights."

"No, my boys will just end them, not start them."

"Mr. George-Blazek, I don't agree with you on that. Regardless, your children are not staying with their lessons."

"No, according to their teacher, they are completing everything and also working well on the higher education lessons we have for them. Our children are above the average student," Austin said while digging in his bag for the children's IQ scores.

"Austin, every parent says their child is a genius," Mr. Johnson said, rubbing his chin.

"Well, these doctors back up what I have been saying. Our children are in grade K but are testing at the third- to fourth-grade level. The professionals say with time they are only going to be excelling faster. They estimate that by the time they hit sixth grade, they should finish high school. But to keep our kids humble, we have them going to class with kids their age."

"Austin, I don't believe these scores. They need to be retested. I can't take this paper as accurate." Mr. Johnson tossed the IQ test into the trash.

"No, it's clear to me this school has always sided with the bully, and that bully is Eric, his mom Karen, and now even you, Mr. Johnson. We provide you with all the paperwork this school has ever needed, and it seems like it's never enough," Danny growled out.

"Danny, what are you implying?" Mr. Johnson looked up over the brim of his glasses.

"I don't know, Alex, what does it sound like to you?" Danny crossed his arms and narrowed his eyes.

"It sounds like you are accusing me of being unfit to run this school?" Mr. Johnson put his pen down.

"Well, Mr. Johnson, are you?" Austin asked.

"Your son attacked another student. Your other son, we cannot prove it, but it seems he attacked one on school grounds. I truly feel the school down the road might be a better fit for this family." Mr. Johnson cleared his throat.

"No, we will not be going to a religious school that says we're going to burn for all time. You are so closed-minded. We are in a public school for a reason, and if you had anything on our children, you wouldn't be trying to intimidate us like this." Austin stood up.

Just then, Danny's phone beeped several times, showing email files coming in. "Austin, they heard us for now. Mr. Johnson, you can look forward to hearing from our lawyer. My father, Doug, will be in touch. Have a wonderful night. Austin, let's go pick up the kids before my mother completely spoils them with her cookies."

CHAPTER 11
GRANDPA DOUG

A
ustin and Danny returned home, and it was obvious
Austin had a lot of pent-up energy. Noticing this,
Doug stepped through the open portal.

"Austin, Danny, your mother and I will keep the kids
tomorrow, as it's a teacher's in-service day, and they have a
long weekend because Monday is a holiday. This will give you
both some quality adult time. Talk things over, go home, vent,
do whatever you need to do." Doug hugged both of the guys.
"Don't worry, I am already on the case. When I have something, I will let you boys know." Doug returned home, leaving
Austin half crying in Danny's arms.

"Austin, I love you," Danny said, picking up his mate and
carrying him off to their bedchambers.

Danny let out a low growl of pleasure as the sparks skipped
across his skin. The mate bond was one of Selene's most
precious gifts to all of them, and Danny was reminded of how
magical that feeling was. A smirk spread across his face as he
replayed his first moments with Austin, when Danny knew
they were mates, but he had left Austin to figure it out.

"Danny, what are you playing at?" Austin looked around to ensure Candy's cuffs were still in hiding. Danny must have read Austin's mind, as he could see that Austin kept looking around the room almost in a panic.

"Oh, trust me, I have looked for months for those cuffs so I could give you a taste of payback."

Danny chuckled as he laid Austin on the bed and turned off the lights so the room was pitch black—except for the glow of their eyes. Then, he pinned Austin down by placing his hands above his head. Austin knew better than to resist; it would only make it harder for him. Danny noticed his mate was not struggling, and smirking he said, "What's wrong, love? Realized I have you pinned?"

Danny let out a soft chuckle as he kissed and nibbled his way across Austin's body. He was stopping now and then to stare deep into the eyes of the one who owned his soul.

"No, sir, you're worshiping my body with kisses and grazing your teeth in all the right places. Why would I fight you on that?" Austin hissed as Danny dragged his teeth along the mate's mark.

"Calling me sir? Hum, stroking my ego won't help you here, Austin. You have been very naughty and very sassy. A simple time out won't be the solution this time," Danny growled in Austin's ear, and he nibbled from his ear down his neck to his exposed collarbone. "You taste so sweet, my love." Danny took Austin's shirt and ripped it off his body.

"Yum, it's been far too long since I had this much time with you, my mate." Adonis surfaced with his eyes two dark black pools of lust. The raw desire filled the room and only made Austin more aroused and ready for his mate.

"I understand, but you understand this is Danny's time." Austin looked deep into Adonis' sorrow-filled eyes, as he whimpered and receded, giving Danny complete control.

"What did you say to Adonis? He's pouting in the corner of my mind now. Danny said as he pulled Austin out of bed and up against the wall to dominate him further. He ripped the rest of Austin's clothes off, leaving him nude and helpless. Then, he licked his lips and bit down on his bottom lip to hold himself back from taking his mate.

"I only let him know tonight was our night. Adonis and Trey can have another night. As your folks said, they wanted them for the long weekend. This gives us more than enough time for everyone to get to enjoy their mate. I want some quality time with my husband," Austin said while biting his lower lip and looking up at his mate suggestively.

"Austin, I have warned you about biting that lip. That lip belongs to me, and only I may nibble on that soft, pouty flesh," Danny declared as he pinned Austin to the wall with just one hand. "Now, to the fun part." Danny's eyes turned jet black as he took in his prize, his mate, and how wonderful that night would be.

☽

Across town, Doug and his wife were planning their dinner and then family game night. Aurora was in the kitchen helping her grandmother prepare, as the boys were upstairs, going over what games to pull out of the closet. Doug meanwhile, was in his office, working diligently at his son's request.

"Yes I know, your honor, this seems a bit like overkill, but it's necessary. This is not the first time that family has put my family in danger, and now they are going after my children and my grandchildren, and now even their teacher, because she won't bow down to them. Karen is requesting not only her son but the principal of the school. We are doing our due diligence in collecting evidence before we proceed." Doug sat down at his desk and began looking at the files that the store willingly gave with no court order.

"Yes, your honor, I am still here. No, I don't need the order for the supermarket. Carol gave us the surveillance videos willingly. So, we need access to the ones around the school. I have reached out to Darrelle for access to the church surveillance."

"All right, thank you, your honor. Sorry about all the noise, I have the grandkids over for quality time. The boys are dragging all the old games out, and yes, they seem confused about how we all played games not run by power." Doug softly chuckled as he listened to the boys asking each other what they thought of the ancient games that Dad had to play growing up.

"All right, Nathen, I will talk to you later. Thank you for working with us on getting all this taken care of. I too, hope it ends up being nothing more than Karen being a little over the top, and I hope we can bring her down to Earth again." With that, Doug hung up and walked out to see a war zone. He looked to his left and saw two piles of board games. To his right were more adult games the kids didn't understand. It was then he got hit on the head by a beanbag... swish.

Doug looked up to see two more coming at his head. He dodged just in time to see the two hit the corn hole table. "Boys, that's an outside game. Please take it outside before you break something. You know how Grams gets when you break stuff." Doug warned the boys.

"Grandpa, what is this game then?" Logan asked as he shot a lawn dart at Grandpa, who caught it in the air.

"Another yard game is lawn darts, and do not even toss that horse shoot, Ethan; it is an outside game."

"Wow, no wonder Dad tells us to go outside. He had all these cool games," Ethan said, grinning at Logan.

The boys took all three games outside, and with Doug's help they made a game of their own combining them all together. The boys enjoyed guy time with Grandpa Doug, while Aurora enjoyed learning to cook with her grams.

"What are those boys up to?" Grams asked as she looked on with Aurora.

"Looks like you have to make twenty-one points with the beanbags to make so many points in lawn darts to play horse-shoes," Aurora said, rolling her eyes.

"Well, tell them to knock it off. The supper is ready. Make sure they all wash up, and that goes for your grandpa. Especially your grandpa actually. That man would be out playing with your father, and I had to fight them both to wash up."

"That won't be an issue for Ethan. He is a clean freak." Aurora rolled her eyes and opened the door, yelling at the guys. "You smelly boys better get in here right now. Get washed up or no dinner, and I will tell Dad on you!" Aurora turned and counted, "One, two, three..." Before she could even finish the word three, all the guys were in the house in a line to wash their hands in the bathroom.

"Aurora, why do you have to be such a telltale?" Logan looked up at his sister in defiance as she was sitting on the countertop.

"Hey, Aurora," Logan called out as she turned to look at her brother. He snapped a picture of her on the countertop. "Two can play at that game."

"You better delete that right now, or so help me." Aurora was about to pounce on her brother when Grandpa walked in and took the phone away. "We do not blackmail family, son." Doug took the phone and put it up where none of the kids could reach it.

"Aurora!" Doug looked over at his granddaughter.

"Yes, Grandpa?" Aurora put on her sweet voice.

"Cool it. As your grandpa, your dad set us both up with charms to prevent you three from getting us to let you do things you know you're not allowed. With that said, why are you on the counter? Get down now. Boys, help your grams get dinner set on the table. I will grab the meat out of the oven."

"But Grandpa, what if I need to get a hold of my dad's?" Logan pouted.

"Son, your dads are fine. They are having a date night. You all go back Sunday," Doug said, lifting the plate of taco bake casserole to the table.

"What is date night, and why do dad and daddy need it? If it is date night, why are we here all weekend?" Ethan said out loud to no one in particular.

"Yeah, what is date night, Grandpa?" Logan asked, raising the same eyebrow his father, Danny did when he was unsure of the answer but still wanted to know.

"Well, kids, we don't get to see you as often now that school has started, so we asked to have you here for this long weekend. I hope that is not an inconvenience for the three of you," Grams said as she placed two loaves of fresh homemade bread on the table.

"Now we need to eat up before the food gets cold. Doug honey, let's say grace." Grandma J clasped her hands together. "Yes, dear. Selene, precious Moon Goddess, thank you for this wonderful family, my beautiful mate, the children, and now the grandchildren you have blessed us with. We pray for you to bless our family and our packs with continued peace and prosperity."

"So may it be," Aurora praised.

"Amen," Logan quipped out.

Ethan responded, "If it pleases you."

Both Doug and his wife, Julia said in unison, "Amen."

"Grandpa, you never told us what date night is." Logan pressed the issue as Grandma put servings on his plate.

"Date night is where two adults spend time with each other and do not allow the outside world to interrupt them. So, whatever your folks want to do on date night is up to them. They could be off in the woods on the pack grounds, letting their wolves out. We don't know, nor is it anyone's business," Doug said, helping plate up Ethan. Aurora had already helped herself. She may have been the last one to hatch, but she knew her way around the kitchen and how to serve her plate.

Just as the family was settling in, a sharp knock on the door came startling them. "Doug, who could it be at this hour?" Julia was rightfully upset as they had finally just settled down for dinner. Doug got up and walked to the door. "I will find out, sweetheart, and send them away as fast as possible."

The laughter and fun all stopped when Doug opened the door to find Sheriff Tate there holding his hat. Doug could smell vampires on Tate, and he knew it had to be the vampire princess he had fallen for. *I hope this human knows what he has gotten himself involved with*, he thought to himself.

"Doug George?" Tate asked, unsure how to proceed.

CHAPTER 12
CHILD PROTECTIVE SERVICES

"The nerve that these disgusting men have to destroy those children's lives. Yes, Eric, your father already told me to leave it alone because Doug is snooping around. Well, I don't care! I am a concerned citizen and mother. So, once I have enough, I'll call Darla over at CPS. She agrees no gay couple should raise three kids." Karen's voice grew raised with anger.

Eric let out a very unhappy sigh. His own mother could tell even he was not for her snooping around the yard of the thorn in his side. He had hated Austin since high school, all because Danny had managed to get his mother banned from the school. She had never let Eric live it down that she missed prom and graduation and every school event he was involved in.

"Then you know you better be damn careful. I don't have bail money for you," Eric said while shaking his head, thinking of his mother wearing an orange county jumpsuit.

"Why would I need bail money from you? I have plenty of money, and I have your father that I can call if I would ever need him." Karen was getting more upset that her son lacked faith in her resolve.

"Because, Mother, they have an eight-foot-high privacy fence and all the gates locked. They have clear and visible no trespassing signs posted in all the right places. Danny owns one of the largest security companies in the world. The security cameras are no joke, Mother." Eric's voice was straining as he tried to reason with her.

"No, son, they need to be careful! They don't realize it yet, but they have no leg to stand on." Karen smirked as she looked at Danny and Austin's house from across the street with a deeply satisfied sigh. "Well, I have to let you go. It's time to show these little boys you don't mess with a momma bear." With that, Karen hung up on her son and quietly slipped out of her car with her camera.

"Well, look at this broken sidewalk. Better take a picture of this. Ah, look at this old half-dead tree, that can't be safe. All these toys tossed around; someone could get hurt tripping over this stuff. Look at the locks on the fence to the backyard, that has to be a safety risk. It's locked from the outside. The fence is way too tall. A normal person has no need for a fence taller than six feet. What happens if they lock the kids in the backyard and have a fire? For having an up-to-date security system, they leave windows wide open. I see candles everywhere that seem to be a fire hazard. This is only part of it. Therefore, I brought my camera so you can see what I see every day. Look! Look at those bottles of wine and no kids. I bet they sent them upstairs and locked them in their rooms. Those poor souls." Karen continues to narrate her little movie on the George-Blazek house.

Slowly, she made her way from one side of the front yard to the other. Unknown to Danny, she had found a way around the system by wearing a heat necklace that blotted out the face of the one wearing it. It was as if she wasn't there. The system picked up movement, but due to not being able to determine if it was a human, the cameras didn't alert. They recorded, but they sent nothing to alert Danny.

Karen moved to the other side gate and found yet another lock. She noted it, but she temporarily shut down her camera as she picked the lock to the gate. Once in, she recorded. "What the heck is this place? Look at all this junk. It's like a wild man's gym, or that gladiator sports show. I pray he doesn't make those little ones go through that obstacle course. Combat weapons! Oh my God this family is full of freaks." Karen's attention was drawn away as she saw movement in the house. She slowly approached, only to see Danny lifting Austin, pinning him to the wall, and ripping his clothes off. This was just too much for her and she ran out and forgot to lock the gate.

Karen stopped the camera once she was back in her car and called Darla. "Darla, pick up, pick up, pick up."

"Hello, Karen. How are you?" Darla started off in a chipper voice.

"Stop right now, Darla. Where are you? Oh my God it's so much worse than I thought," Karen let out an emotional sob. "They are having sex and one has the other pinned to the wall and is ripping his clothes off. I can't tell if it's consensual or if it's rape. I don't think that is a safe environment for children to be in."

"Are you talking about those two gay guys we were talking about this morning?" Darla asked with extreme loathing in her voice.

"Yes, the same!" Karen was on the verge of tears.

"Would you say you feared for the general safety and welfare of the children in the household?" Darla asked in a serious tone.

"Yes, I fear for the safety of the children of that home." Karen addressed in more of a professional manner.

"Thank you, miss. I take very seriously all safety concern calls and will look into it. For the security and safety of our alerters, no records will show your name. We will send Sheriff Tate over to do a full investigation, and I will meet with him to do an investigation with the children."

"Thank you so much. If you need a video, I have it for you." Karen offered over the phone.

"Yes, miss, please send that to, Darla.Charelston@NECP-S.org. We would appreciate all the evidence you want us to consider." Darla cleared her throat. "Have a wonderful and blessed day."

Darla hung up and texted Karen, *"We will get those bastards."*

After the phone call, Darla waited for Karen to send the video via a cloud link. Once Darla saw the video, she wasted no time in calling the Sheriff.

"Sheriff Tate, we had a safety concern and a request for a welfare check to be done at the George-Blazek home. Tate sat there dumbfounded at the fact he now had to go investigate a family that had not even had as much as a moving violation. With all claims, he had to investigate, and he was listening as Darla droned on about the possibility of what was going on at the house. Drinking, open flame, erotica, and rape.

"Darla, Darla, can you wait about thirty minutes before you head over there? I have to swing by my place and pick up some gear. You know if it's as bad as your informant's complaints, then I need to swing by and get the big guns. The more I can defend you and those children, the better, right?" Tate played her like a fiddle.

"No, you're right, Tate, please come prepared. I can meet you at the George-Blazek home in, say, forty-five minutes."

"Perfect Darla, we will get to the bottom of all this. Child safety is one of my major concerns." Tate hung up the phone and turned his car away from the station and over to see Doug, so he could ask him some preliminary questions. If he was going to walk into the lion's den, he wanted to be safe. It doesn't take much for an educated person to put things together.

Tate quickly pulled into the George family home, knocked on the door, and waited, thinking about how he was going to present this to the man who used to defend the town against any lawsuit. As a man came to the door, Tate took his hat off and asked with uncertainty in his voice, "Doug George?"

"Yes, Sheriff, I'm Doug George. What seems to be the problem?"

Tate took a deep breath and bit his lip while Doug seemed to size him up. "Sir, I need your help. How would you say is the proper way for me to go about an investigation? I feel perhaps it's fabricated?"

"Are you seriously showing up at my door at this hour for advice about the town I don't cover anymore?"

"Sir, maybe if I tell you who the complaint is about." Tate bit his lip again. He always seemed to bite his lip when he was worried.

"Well, I'm listening to you, Sheriff. I don't have all night."

"Sir, no, sir. I don't want to take too much of your time. It's just that someone wants a welfare check done, but the things the parents are being accused of sound more like a wine dinner and making a little love."

"Karen, that bitch!" Doug roared. Doing so got the attention of those at the table and the children came running to see what had Grandpa so mad.

"Who are these little guys? Oops sorry guys and gal," Tate said, looking over the well cared for children.

"Tate, these are my grandchildren. Their fathers are having a date night at home, so yes, Karen seems to be out of hand," Doug said through gritted teeth.

"Wait, so these are the children," said Tate in surprise. He was not expecting to find them there.

"Yes, Tate, when my son informed me that tomorrow is teacher's in-service and Monday is a holiday, I reminded him it was our turn to have the grandchildren. He jumped at the chance to have husband time with his love. Is that somehow illegal now? A grandparent can't take the grandchild over the weekend?" Doug was now shaking. "By the way Tate, please find out how Karen, no wait, *the informant* could get all this to you. My sons have video monitoring equipment, and an eight-feet-tall privacy fence that is locked on the two gates. Not to mention several no trespassing signs."

CHAPTER 13
DARLA

With Doug's last words still echoing in his head, Sheriff Tate took the short drive over to the George-Blazek house. Unfortunately though, he was unaware of the betrayal that was already afoot, seeing as Darla had arrived well before him so she could talk to Karen. They had met up a couple of blocks down the road from their target house, and Darla had arranged all the paperwork so that no one could trace it back to Karen.

Karen walked her through all the safety concerns and some code violations, including the town ordinance violations, she believed were on the property. Darla then gave over the video in-person to be reduced in edits to credit the report. As Darla was quickly working things out, with buffers and changes to the voice on the video, she looked up and noticed the time.

"Karen, you need to go. Sheriff Tate is on his way. We don't need him to see you with me. He's such a pain in my ass for these service calls. Trying to make sure no criminal justice is being given out when in reality, monsters like them don't deserve children." Darla finished the edits and reports just as she spotted Tate down the road. "Karen, go now. He's just down the road. Quick pull out."

Karen waved as she pulled out and drove away, while Darla waited, then slowly got out of her car and walked down to the house in question. As she approached the front of the house simultaneously with Tate, he cocked his head at her. "I prefer people not to know what I drive, retaliation and all." There was only one reasonable excuse offered by Darla.

"Darla, let's talk about this," Tate tried to reason with her without tipping his hand, but Darla walked past him with a clipboard and started muttering to herself as she took notes and used an audio recorder. "Sidewalk appears poorly cared for by lack of being maintained. As a result, I see several tripping hazards."

"Sidewalks are due to be fixed. They already have informed the town, and the contractor's permit is approved," Tate offered, but it fell on deaf ears.

"Toys are everywhere. Someone could fall and break a neck. Do they not have these kids clean up? Suck a pig pen. I wonder how bad it will be inside?" Darla asked herself into the recorder while scribbling down some notes.

"Sheriff Tate, do you see my badge? Do you see what it says? Do you know my job? I can tell you don't, so stand there and do your job. We are going for a wellness check. I have enough proof this family may very well be questionable." Darla puffed out her chest and raised her chin.

"Darla, do you see my badge? Don't pull that crap with me. Your name is Darla, but if I didn't know better, it should say Karen. I already know more than you think, but if you want to fool yourself and your department, feel free. I will do my report as required by law. No, we will not sit down and chat and compare notes. I know you sometimes did that with the last Sheriff, but not this one."

Tate crossed his arms, and his lips created a fine-pressed line.

"Shut your mouth! I will file a complaint about unprofessionalism!" Darla's lip quivered with anger.

"You do just that, and I will submit the Freedom of Information Act on today's events," Tate smirked.

"We will redact some things for privacy's sake. You will only see what I put in this report." Darla smiled back.

"Well, that would have to include the evidence that brought you to a conclusion to do a wellness check." Tate waved his finger in the air, pleased he remembered how Doug told him to say things.

"Sheriff, just do what I tell you to do." Darla picked up her pace and looked for reasons to complain.

"This is so wrong." Tate shook his head, knowing this would not end well or as well as Darla had planned. "Darla, look." Tate pointed out the many no trespassing signs.

"So, does that prevent me from doing my civic duties?" Darla continued on her checklist.

"I count eight of them, Darla, and they are at the legally required height and all clearly visible. So that is going in my report. Something tells me whoever gave you the tip was trespassing."

"So what if they did? This could save three children's lives?" Darla's theatrics were lost on Tate. He knew better than to fall for her act.

"Oh, what's the excuse for a locked fence that is of this monstrous height?" Darla pulled out her tape measure.

"Town charter or city code. However you want to dice, it allows up to ten feet tall fencing with a permit. The George-Blazek family has an eight-foot-tall fence, and they have the permit on file with the courthouse. You know Doug would not allow his son to make a mistake like that. Also, the gate is locked because of the expensive equipment and a pool in the backyard. Yes, signed off on and approved by the zoning board, as were about thirty other homes, Darla." Tate took notes, knowing this would be a shit storm.

"That's odd, the evidence I got..." Darla trailed off, trying to backpedal.

"So, your complaint trespassed. I believe that evidence is called forbidden fruit, and I will toss your claim out in court. You are using illegally gained prevalence." Tate took note and watched as Darla squirmed in her shoes.

"Who is saying they illegally got it? You don't know that." Darla pressed her luck, knowing she needed to watch it around this new Sheriff.

Tate walked over to the other gate, noticed it was unlocked, and took a picture with his cellphone just as Danny came out in a pair of gym shorts, followed by Austin, who was also in shorts and covered with hickeys and love bites.

"Sheriff, glad you are here. We had an uninvited guest. Unfortunately, someone picked the lock." Danny said, pointing to the lock.

"Oh, how convenient. Mr. George, Mr. Blazek? This is an official wellness check. I am here to inspect the home and ensure a safe environment for the children here." Darla pulled her pad closer to her face to hide the blush. Regardless of them being gay, she found both of them strangely attractive.

"That will wait. First, I'm talking with Sheriff Tate about the break-in of my property," Danny said, turning his back to Darla and setting her off in a rage.

"NO, it will be NOW. Sheriff Tate, I have my orders to do a wellness check!" Darla screamed.

"Darla." Tate shot her a glance to warn her to watch how she acts.

"Can they at least have the decency to have proper clothes

on? This is disgusting." Darla was writing a mile a minute on her notepad.

"Guys?" Tate bit his lip. "Can we work together on this? Danny, I will work on your trespassing case. But first, let me get my state-issued camera and fingerprint kit. I know you will review the security film and send it to my office."

"Is that necessary?" Darla let out a huff and tried to walk past the wall of sexy man-god bodies.

"Darla, ask them your questions while I do my job. That's an actual crime." Tate walked off to his SUV to gather his kits.

"Such disrespect. I'll make sure you will not be re-elected as Sheriff." Darla defiantly took more notes, before starting, "Mr. George..."

"That's Mr. George-Blazek. I took my husband's name, and he took mine," Danny said with smug smile.

"Yeah, you are *married*." She said the word as if she didn't believe in it, or at the very least like she wasn't much of a fan of the law that allowed it to happen. "Anyway, how long have you been a parent? No, I'm sorry, an adoptive parent, because I see no mother listed on the children's birth certificates," Darla said, pulling out copies of the birth certificates.

"This shit again!" Austin spit out the words in a rage.

"I won't take that kind of talk." Darla shot an evil eye at Austin.

"Then I suggest you look around, wench. You're on private property, currently trespassing, so unless you have a court order, you can kick rocks. Last I checked, your feelings don't trump my rights or my husband's. We are both the genetic fathers of those children. If you bothered to look outside your little bubble, you would see who you're talking to." Austin glared daggers at the woman he would rather set on fire in that moment. His face was turning red and he was shaking.

"Babe, I'll talk with her. But first, go grab us a couple of shirts." Danny leaned over, giving a well-planted kiss on Austin's lips.

"Only shirts. I don't want you coming out with any weapons. Sheriff Tate is here. I won't hesitate to have him protect me." Darla was worried about what these guys could be up to.

Austin rolled his eyes and walked in to grab a shirt for Danny and a tank for himself. Then, he blew out the candles, since no one was around to enjoy them anymore, before picking up his laptop and cellphone and heading back out to find Danny. When he arrived back outside, he gave Danny his shirt and watched as Darla stared at his mate getting dressed. Then he turned and walked over to the glider and looked over maps of the town. Austin was sick of all the haters and was planning a way to fix it quickly. Pulling out his phone, he hit send once he had found who he was looking for.

"Austin, what's up, son? This is your weekend with Danny. Why are you using it to call home?" Daniel asked his son with a deep, questioning tone.

"Dad, something has come up, and now I feel like doing some work." Austin's voice was flat and emotionless.

"Shit, this must be bad." Daniel motioned for Amy to come over.

"How about I buy up some property here for NRG?" Austin tried to change gears back to his proposal and not deal with the unknown family drama.

"It's your company as much as mine, son. What do you have in mind?"

"We have thermal energy. What about the use of hydro-electric and even using wind power?"

"Go for it. Son, it sounds like a wonderful opportunity for the company to experience some growth."

"Perfect. I will buy up some open land. Then I will purchase back owed tax land, and we will get a tax certificate. Then, we can apply for a clear land title if they cannot pay it back with interest. By that time, we will have all our permits in hand."

"Okay. Who pissed you off, son?" came Amy's voice.

"Someone broke into the backyard. Now CPS is here. The kids are at Doug's."

"Let me guess, you plan on buying up a third of the town?" Amy questioned.

"Or more," Austin smirked, even though he knew his folks could not see it. "I'll send a map for approval before I go forward." Austin emailed his parents.

Austin started looking at the realty he plotted out for his folks. Blue was a clear buy, and red was a tax certificate purchase. They desired yellow for the wind turbines. The locations with an X were not open and were to be left alone. That land was designated for parks, schools, hospitals, and significant buildings.

Danny walked over to his busy mate. "Okay, Austin, play nice. She has questions for you. Yes, you can use it. But first, the fourth hell, I don't care if you toss the constitution at her. I already got a link from Dad, and he's working on this on his end. What are you doing now?"

"I plan on buying up half the town for NRG."

"Oh."

"Here, look over the footage. Whatever or whomever they are, wearing a thermal neckless has blurred out the face. Work your magic and see if you can get anything." Austin handed over his laptop to Danny.

"Oh, Sheriff, any luck?" Austin asked, walking in earshot of Darla.

"Yep, I'll need your family prints to rule out sets, and I found several. But I'm hopeful. Besides, they left in a hurry. I found their tools on the ground." Tate smiled up at Austin.

Meanwhile, Darla heard this and she quickly texted Karen, *"Karen, please say you didn't pick the lock and leave your tools. They found them and have Tate dusting for prints."*

"Shit," was all Karen responded.

"All right, let's get this circus over, Darla. You know you have no grounds for this as well as I do." Austin crossed his arms.

"We will see. Let's start with your family history. It shows here they found you abandoned as a child. That had to be very difficult. So why did they abandon you? Did you ever find out after hunting them down and finding them after thirteen years? Hmm, family abandonment issues. Psychological processing of trauma." She continued talking and taking notes, but without asking direct questions.

"So, your foster father, Joe? He made you run as a punishment? He made Danny the enforcer, and now you two. Hmm..." She continued to write notes. Darla pressed her lips into a thin line, not looking up to see the scowl on Austin's face. It appeared she was only repeating whatever Danny said or what was common knowledge in town.

CHAPTER 14
DEVEN

After what seemed like a lifetime, but was in fact only twenty minutes of Darla's chatter, Austin had had enough. He stood up, looked around, and then he looked right at Darla and cleared his throat.

"Excuse me, since you are doing all the talking and answering your own questions, I'll say this is no longer, and has never been, consensual. That's it, Darla, we are done here." Austin gestured for her to get up and get off his property.

"Mr. Blazek, we are far from done here. We are done when I say we are done, not you. I am the one in charge, not you. I am the one in power and I have complete control of the situation." Darla glared over her glasses at Austin.

"Listen and listen well, my husband is a lawyer. My name is Mr. Austin George-Blazek. I am a father of three with my husband. The time is now nine o'clock at night. You said you needed a wellness check because of the information you received. Illegally got, I must add. I have identified your informant." Austin smiled with deep satisfaction, knowing this witch hunt was soon over.

"Not possible, Mr. George-Blazek, as you so claim." She clicked her pen, crossed her legs, and leaned over into a broad smile. "Your husband made it clear. I heard him tell that joke of a Sheriff Tate that the trespasser's face is hidden."

"Yes, but that was before NRG and WIZ combined forces. So, we have buffered, and filtered and now have a face to go with the fingerprints on the lock and the tools that were used to pick the lock. They found hair in the rosebush and a small footprint. That bitch stepped in my rose bushes." Austin puckered his lips in anger, narrowing his eyes.

"Hmm, name-calling. Hmm bad habits the kids have no doubt picked up from you." She scribbled more notes.

"Karen needs to remember that my husband's security company and my family's energy company supplied this town with new streetlights. They also equipped those lights with cameras to deter anyone from going into cars at night and rummaging. All it takes is Danny's security firm clearance and Sheriff Tate's log-in. We could download the street lamps in a three-block radius of the house." Austin crossed his arms and locked eyes with Darla.

"Oh my, a conspiracy theorist next. You'll say aliens killed the president, and Big Foot is real. You are shaping up to be a real nut, an easy open-and-closed case of poor parenting." Darla smiled while packing up her notes.

"Look for yourself." Austin pointed to Danny holding a tablet showing Karen coming onto the property, then activating the light color to hide her face. She stepped in the roses and caught her hair on the thorns. "That's just the beginning. We see the two of you conversing down the way, and she gave you something." Austin looked over at the now furious woman.

"She is a concerned parent!" Darla screamed.

"Her son is of age. Eric has a son in class with our kids. I believe he is what you would call a single father. His son's name is Deven," Danny said, amused that Darla was now upset.

"Your point being, Mr. George?"

"Well, I'm not trying to be petty here, but he is a single father," Austin said while raising an eyebrow.

"Nothing on the books says you can't be a single parent, Mr. Blazek." Darla shifted uncomfortably.

"I believe my husband has corrected you enough as I have when you spoke with me." Danny's voice came across as gruff and full of authority.

"Sheriff Tate!" Darla screamed, causing Tate to jump.

"Well, Miss Darla, you wanted to stick your nose in a hornet's nest. I tried to help you out, but you insisted you were in the right. I can't help you now since you got stung. Your feelings are all hurt. So, pull up those big girl panties." Tate stood next to Danny and shook his head.

"I demand to see the kids right now!" Darla stomped her foot several times, having a little fit that she was being made fun of.

"No," came Austin's quick reply.

"N-O get the picture?" Austin was getting sassy, and Danny knew how dangerous Mr. Sassy could become.

"You cannot deny me. This is a fair check for the children's safety." Darla poked Austin in the chest.

"We can, and we are, because the grounds you used to get the fraudulent check are based on illegally obtained information from our private property. I would strongly suggest you not to poke me again. That's considered assault and battery. Besides, you can't see the kids because they are away on holiday," Austin growled out.

"There is no holiday right now," Darla said. "So, I will repeat it. Bring me the children."

"They are not home," Austin said, standing taller than he once was.

"Oh, I get it. So, you let the children run wild and do whatever they want." Darla pulled out a pen and paper to take notes.

"No, Darla, they are at a relative's house." Sheriff Tate spoke up.

"Take me to them right now. I am placing all three into the town's emergency protective custody."

Darla pulled out her phone to make a call to get the orders to pull the children.

"No, you won't," Doug said, walking up to the group holding papers freshly signed by the judge. Doug handed over the documents to Darla. "This is your copy. It's already on file with the courthouse, and they have uploaded it to our cloud account. This letter is from Judge Hammon. It will stop you and all actions against the George-Blazek family at once. Afterward, you must turn over your notes and badge to the Sheriff."

"I cannot believe this! How is this right? I am now under investigation for allegations of fraudulently getting children." Darla looked up and was way beyond pissed. She stormed off the property and headed to her car.

"Gentlemen." Tate nodded and headed after her to collect the notes and her work badge.

"Mind explaining why you brought Deven up?" Austin asked Danny while pulling him into an embrace.

"Karen is the issue. Eric is the son of that issue, and he is the current issue because his son does not get along with our children," Danny said in a cold, matter-of-fact tone.

"I feel sorry for Deven," Austin said, letting go of Danny and sitting on the house's front steps.

"Why?" Danny looked at Austin, knowing his love had always been a bleeding heart.

"Doug, pull up a chair. Danny, have a seat. Let me tell you what I have known for a long time." The guys looked at Austin and quickly took a seat. "Deven's mom is not around. We haven't seen her for six years."

"Yeah, she had the kid, and I bet Karen ate her for dinner one night," Danny joked.

"Eric has always been an outdoors kind of guy. Well, before you got his mom banned from school, he always loved to go hiking. He took a hiking trip while we were settling down." Danny cut Austin off.

"So, wacky job likes to go hiking. Remind me to check the woods for some girl's body." At this, Austin struck Danny in the chest. Whack, the loud sound of skin on skin echoed around them.

"Eric went to Colorado. He went hiking and camping because he knew it was the one chance he had to be away from his mother, who, unless it was some five-star resort, was not going. While camping near Mt. Evens, he ran into a beautiful girl. They hit it off and hooked up every night for three weeks. One morning he woke up, and she was gone with no note, not even a trace of her. He came home brokenhearted, thinking he had found the girl to bring home to his parents. Nine months later, that girl showed up at Eric's front door. She had baby Deven with her, wrapped in a baby blanket that had little nature scenes on it. The woman handed Eric this little bundle of life. She cried, telling him Deven was his son, and that she could not keep him. They had instructed her to take him to a nearby orphanage but she could not pull herself to do so. Eric begged her to stay, but she denied him and told him her parents forbid her to see him again. They did not like Eric and didn't approve. So, she had to give up her baby and the man she fell in love with." Austin took a deep breath and let it out nice and slow.

"How do you magically know all of this?" Doug asked what the lawyer in him had to know.

"Trey, being a magical wolf, sometimes crosses over to speak to Selene and even goes for guidance. He came back to me one day about a month or two ago and told me everything he could that Selene had told him. But, even with that wall down, it limited them to how they interact with us." Austin took a moment to look over Doug's and Danny's expressions.

"Since Selene is the one that told Trey about this mystery girl being around your family's clan grounds around the same time you all conceived the grandkids, am I to assume she, too, is magical somehow?" Doug asked, while scratching his chin.

"Doug, I believe so. I also believe Deven is a halfling. Half-human and half-Fae. I planned on heading to my folks later with the kids for a holiday, but now I feel we should go sooner rather than later."

"You think she could have been one of Tatian's Fae clan?" Danny sat up with a more serious look on his face. "Baby, I'm so sorry. I feel like a complete dick right now. Deven is innocent in so much of this. I should not take my anger out on him. It's Karen. I know Eric is only the way he is and only acts the way he does because of Karen."

"Well, I'm glad to see you're coming around. I need you to stay here with the kids while I go see our Fae queen Tatian." Austin stood up and hugged his father-in-law. Then he turned to his husband, kissed him, and walked into the house.

"Austin, before you go..." But it was too late. Austin had turned the front door into a portal, walked through, and closed it.

Meanwhile, just across town, a little voice piped up.

"Daddy."

"Yes, bug," came Eric's reply as he helped dry his son off after his bubble bath.

"Why is GG so mean to Ethan's daddies?" Deven's little voice broke as he spoke.

"Your GG is very traditional. Why do you care? I thought you didn't like those kids, so why would it bother you how grandma treats their dads?" Eric now held Deven wrapped in a towel close to his chest. He could smell the Colorado wilderness and the faint smell of roses on him. No matter what soap or cologne he used on his son, he always smelled of the Colorado wilderness. He smiled down at his son; the best thing to happen to him. Eric kissed the top of his son's head and thought back to the beautiful woman who gave him this gift.

"Dad, I don't hate them. I am just jealous." Deven sighed in his confession.

"Why are you jealous little man?"

"They have two dads. Everyone in my class has two parents. I have only you." Deven looked at his father as a single tear ran down his little face. "Was I not enough for mommy to stay? Why don't you ever talk about mommy? I don't even have a picture of her."

"Neither do I, Deven. Trust me, I know your mother loves you. She just couldn't stay." Deven wailed and struggled to get free from Eric.

"Mom's dead! So, I will never get to see her!" Deven broke free and ran to his room, leaving Eric holding a towel that smelled like the woods in Colorado.

Eric put the towel up and turned out the lights. Taking a deep breath, he walked to his room. He walked into his closet and pulled down a box. Then, smiling, he walked over to his son's room.

"Deven, I'm coming in. We need to talk."

"Why? What's the point?"

"I have something to share, and I think you're old enough."

Deven cracked the door open and looked up at his father holding an old shoe box. Then, eyeing it and his father suspiciously, he slowly opened the door.

"Have a seat on the bed, son. I will tell you all I know and share what I have about your mother."

CHAPTER 15
HARMONY

"Dad, I can't believe he just up and left me here! We always do things together. We are a team." Danny growled out while Adonis was fighting to come to the surface.

"Danny, son, sometimes a man needs to do things independently. Austin is going to his clan's territory. That Fae queen lives in his territory. Perhaps it's best to let him deal with her," Doug suggested, trying to calm his son down.

"Would you be okay with it?" Danny trailed off.

"Son, your mother is already getting the kids ready to come home. After Sheriff Tate showed up, we already figured it would cut the trip short," Doug said while a deep sadness settled in his eyes.

"Sorry, Dad." Danny bit his lower lip, looking at the vanished portal and longing for his mate.

Suddenly the front door burst open, and the kids came running in with Grandma George. Danny rushed over, scooping his kids up in his arms.

"Daddy, why did we have to come home so soon?" Aurora cried out.

"Because daddy got lonely butter cup." Danny kissed Aurora on her nose.

"Why? Where is dad?" Aurora strained to get let down so she could look for her dad.

"He had an emergency and had to see his mommy and daddy princess."

"Oh, are Grandma and Grandpa B, okay? So, it's not Great-grandma or Great-grandpa B?" Aurora's voice gave way to a little catch as it quivered.

"Yes, honey, everyone is fine. Let's settle in. Did you all eat yet?" Danny asked his children with his eyes shining brightly. Seeing them settled both his and Adonis' nerves.

"NO! We're hungry," cried Logan and Ethan together.

"Danny, don't let those boys fool you. They had dinner. They have you and your father wrapped around their little fingers. Austin and I are the only ones to see when they are up to no good. I made dinner, so if they chose not to eat what I made for them... you know the rule in my house, Danny," Julia scolded while monitoring the children.

"All right, mother, I understand. Now boys, when your grams makes you dinner, you eat it, period. Got that?" Danny gave the boys a cross look and they bowed their heads in submission.

"Yes, father," they declared in unison.
"Now that's settled. Since your daddy and I didn't get to have our dinner, want to help me eat some perfect food, kids? Mom and Dad, you're welcome to stay. I need all the company I can get right now." Danny stood up, looking into his parents' eyes.

Next, Danny directed the children and his folks into the

dining room where a full spread of delicious food was already on the table. Lobster tails with king crab legs were ready for eating, with rich, sweet butter sauce. Prime rib cooked to perfection with a nice thick creamy horseradish sauce. There was a hot steaming dish of vegetables with a dab of butter on top. It was enough to make any grown man's stomach rumble in hunger. Seeing the food and being a werewolf family, everyone made room for a second meal. Danny's folks stayed for dinner and decided they could wait for the weekend while Austin was away to keep the house in order and still have time with the grandchildren.

Monday came around, and still no Austin. Danny was really worried but he knew he needed to get the kids to school. He woke each of them with his mother's help, while Doug was baking breakfast; the little Chimera Clan was well on its way to getting the day started.

"Danny, is it always this backed up?" Doug pointed out across the street in the child drop-off lane.

"Nope, it's usually quick in, drop, go." Danny scanned the crowd till he found the issue. "Figures," he huffed out.

"What am I missing here, son?" Doug asked, as they approached the crosswalk and waited for the guides to tell them when they could cross safely.

"See that devil?" Danny pointed out to Karen and rolled his eyes.

"Looks like she is not alone, son," came Julia's response.

Looking closer, Danny discovered it was Karen and Darla, and they were inches away from Venessa. Both seemed to be harassing Venessa, while Dr. Johnson stood idly by watching it all happen.

As Danny and his family approached, the sound of the argument kept getting louder. Aurora broke free from Danny's grasp, ran up to Venessa, and hugged her tightly, trying to shield her from the mean adults. All the while, a silent tear ran down her cheek.

"See, she even knows she should have a mommy and a daddy," Karen exclaimed, looking down her nose at the crying child.

"Karen, leave my daughter and her teacher alone," boomed Danny's voice from across the parking lot.

"Oh, look, it's Mr. Sinner himself." Darla looked smugly over her glasses at Danny.

"Darla, are you on official duties regarding my children? Do I need to have legal representation? Does Ms. States? Mr. Johnson, why are you standing there with a thumb up your ass doing nothing while you have these two harassing her? Karen is a grandparent, not a parent. Darla has no say; she has no children in Ms. States' class."

"Mr. Blazek, I have made my point as clear as I can. Karen is an adult addressing a grievance with the teacher of her grandson. She is showing her concern about the LGBTQ+ or whatever you call yourselves these days. With you pushing your ideas and agenda onto our youth." Mr. Johnson gave a cold and dark stare at Danny.

"Well, lucky for us, current law protects the LGBTQ+ from being discriminated against. So please tell me how we're pushing our agenda? Is it because I have a husband, we're both men, and our children are happy and content?" Danny gave an equal stare in return.

"See, my grandson doesn't need to be exposed to such trash. It's not right. It's a downright abomination," Karen screamed out while pointing a long, thin finger in Danny's face.

"Seems to me, Karen, you broke a nail. Perhaps it matches the one you left in my backyard while trespassing." Danny smiled and returned his gaze to the principal.

"Stop it! You all are naughty. You need to be nice!" Aurora screamed out.

"Hush, child, adults are talking. It would be best if you had learned you never interrupt adults. Go sit down and be quiet." Karen spat out her words so fast, it was as if her mouth was moving faster than her brain could think.

With that, Aurora shook in anger and began humming. Gradually, the low hum got louder, and turned into song. Danny realized what his sweet girl was trying to do, but he knew she hadn't been trained yet, so he scooped her up. Being her father, he was immune to her gifts, as were her brothers.

As Danny stopped her from using her powers, he felt a sharp burning pain in his arm. Looking down, he saw the trident on his arm pulsate like a heartbeat, but he knew he was too far from Austin to mind link. Nevertheless, the pain in his arm was telling him all he needed to know.

"Since you ladies cannot be civil and behave, my children will take a home school day. Ms. States, call me later. My father has paperwork for you to sign and fill out. Now that he has seen it first hand, I'm sure the judge will sign off and we can set a meeting up with the board of education for next week," Danny said, picking up all three children in one swoop.

"Mr. George, excuse me, Mr. George-Blazek, you cannot pick when children attend school." Darla looked so excited that she may have justification for taking the kids into her custody.

"I can if I feel they are not in a safe environment. But you can bring this up in court, because the summons is on its way. Enjoy, ladies." Danny smiled and walked away, leaving Karen and Darla spitting mad as Doug motioned over Sheriff Tate to deliver the paperwork Danny had mentioned.

Once off school grounds and out of earshot of any humans, Danny set the children down and looked deep into Aurora's eyes to see the light inside still playing about. "Aurora, honey, were you trying to sing the harmony song Grandma Blazek was teaching you?" Danny lifted one eyebrow, and the kids all knew the truth had better come out when that went up.

"Yes, daddy, please don't be mad at me. All those big people were so mean, and the poor Ms. States was getting yelled at, and her boss was doing nothing." Aurora's eyes filled with tears, and she softly sobbed, thinking how even though what she felt was right was wrong.

"Sweetheart, don't cry. Daddy is not mad at you. Your heart is very much like your father's. It is in the right place, but you need to play it safe until you have more practice and can do it without the humans knowing. Okay, pumpkin?" Danny wiped away his little girl's tears.

"How am I going to get more practice, daddy? With dad gone, we don't live with Grandma and Grandpa B anymore." Aurora stuck out her pouty lips and looked up at Danny, trying to understand how she was to act.

"Well, sweetheart, thank you for your attempt. We just need to get you more practice. Since I pulled you out of class for the day, how about we go home and see if we can pay a visit to your Grandma B? How does that sound, kids?" Danny took the kids by the hand and walked them home, where Doug and Julia were waiting patiently.

"Take a long way home, or did you just get lost, son?" Julia joked.

"I had to sit little Aurora down because she tried to use a Siren's song at school," Danny said, beaming ear to ear.

"Son, that is not something to encourage. She lacks the years of practice necessary to pull that kind of thing off. Something terrible could have happened," Doug chastised Danny.

"Well, dad, I already have the kids packing. We were going to the Mt. Evens Clan. I know Austin needs me." Danny rubbed his arm as the painful burn had returned.

"What makes you feel that way, son?" Doug looked at his son with a mild dose of fear in his eyes.

"Father, he is too far to link, but they connected us on a different level. See this tattoo? It is no normal tattoo—"

Doug cut Danny off. "Son, I know the Sea Queen put those on you both. What is the point you're making here?"

"Dad, mine has been burning since we were at the school. It's pulsating like a heartbeat. It's like he's calling out to me differently."

"Well, what are you waiting for? Go to him." Doug urged his son on.

"Kids, are you ready to go?" Danny yelled out.

"Wait, why are you taking the kids if you feel Austin is in danger?" Julia questioned as she placed her hands protectively on the children's shoulders.

"Mother, you know what happened to Austin as a child. I agree with him we never want to be separated from our children. They are coming with me." Danny looked at his mother and then at her hands. She released the children.

"Okay, guys, are we ready?" Danny asked the excited children.

"Yes, let's go get daddy!" Logan opened the door to the basement revealing a portal to the Mt. Evens Clan.

"All right, guys, remember to hold hands and stay with me, understand?"

"Yes, Dad."

"Yes, Papa."

"Yes, sir."

With that, Danny and the little Chimera Clan walked through the portal to find the Mt. Even Clan.

CHAPTER 16
EYES WIDE OPEN

O nce across the gates to the portal leading to the Mt. Evens Clan, Danny could see why his trident tattoo was burning and pulsating. The clan was on fire. Danny pulled the trident from his arm and scooped the children into his arms, looking for the surrounding danger. Then, he set the kids down again and took a deep breath.

"Daddy is going to change into his big blue dragon. I need you all to get into my hand and hold on tight. I need to take you to the hatchery where you will go in and lock yourselves in the family room. Got that?"

"Yes, daddy, I will make sure they all get to the hatchery," Logan piped up. He was taking Ethan's hand in one hand and Aurora's in the other. Once Danny had shifted, the kids climbed into one hand while his other held a trident that grew with him.

Danny launched them into the air when suddenly he saw a fireball flying right for them. Using the trident, Danny summoned a wall of water to surround the fireballs, snuffing them out. As soon as his feet touched the hatchery, the attacks stopped. Someone well knew that the hatchery or nursery of any creature is sacred and taboo to touch.

Danny kissed his children goodbye, and launched back into the battle at hand, linking to his mate.

"*Austin! Austin!*"

Austin was quick to reply. "*Danny? What are you doing here?*"

"*I could tell you were in danger, so I had to come.*"

"*Where are the kids?*" Austin screamed in Danny's head.

"*They are safe. The kids are in the hatchery.*

The hatchery is off all limits by the laws we all abide by."

"*Thank God, no, wait, not so much. After we left, a wonderful trickster was wreaking havoc and causing all the tribes to fight.*" Austin was getting upset, and Danny could tell. "*I just wish everyone could get along again.*"

"*That's it, Austin.*"

"*What is it?*"

"*Our little princess is too smart for her own good.*"

"*You are just now figuring that out? Heaven help us, but what does that change, Danny?*"

"*Easy! Where are the sirens?*"

"*Most of them are in hiding. Why?*" Austin asked as he homed in on his mate's location and flew to him.

As soon as Danny and Austin were together again, they landed and changed back into human form, still holding their tridents. Austin asked Danny again, "Why do you need sirens?"

"The siren song of harmony. We need help projecting it on everyone to stop the fighting," Danny said as he pulled up plans to amplify the song using the clan's announcement system.

"Danny, you're a genius."

Soon the great hall filled with anxious sirens, a little fearful of a room full of dragons and two Chimeras.

"All right, everyone, we need to work in harmony. We need to sing the siren's harmony song.

Once we get everyone calmed down, we can try to solve the issues the trickster fired up," Austin explained, and Brandon took the group of tritons to patrol and ensure the safety of all those trying to bring peace. Soon the air filled with a low hum that resonated off the mountain rocks, and the course was coursing through the veins of the land. Everything stopped burning and returned to life, and those who were fighting became friendly once more.

Danny walked over, turned off the recording device, and set it up to loop play to keep everyone at peace and give the sirens a break so they could recover.

The different leaders from all the factions living on Mt. Evens Clan lands had a meeting set up the next day. Meanwhile, Austin retrieved the children to have them stolen away by his parents when he walked in the door with them.

"Hey, now those are my kids. I was away from them. Can't I get a little time with them?" Austin winced as his mother brushed him off and started babbling to the children about how crazy it was, and now that things had calmed down, she was so glad they came.

"Looks like your mother won again, Austin," Danny joked as he pulled Austin close to his chest and took in the scent of his mate.

"What are you doing? Danny, I smell terrible. I haven't showered in three days. I'm a hot, sticky mess." Austin put up a fight to push Danny away.

"Oh, no, you don't. You're my mate, regardless of whether you're clean, or a hot, sticky mess. So here, let me draw you a nice warm bath, and then we might get back to our date night." Danny wiggled his eyebrows, then picked Austin up and carried him off to their room where he set him down next to the tub and turned on the water.

"Now, Mr. George-Blazek, it seems you have too many clothes on, and you are filthy. It would be best if you got cleaned up at once. I wouldn't say I like to brag, but I have been told I give amazing baths. Here, let me help you out of that." Danny reached up and ripped the torn, sweat-stained shirt off Austin's sore, muscular body before running his nose up his neck, pausing briefly over the mate's mark, causing him to shiver.

"Get me in that bath before you get too turned on, Mr."

"So I can get you clean to make you dirty again?" Danny smiled at the invite, and his eyes turned jet black.

"Adonis, no, bath first, dinner second, and if I'm not too tired, maybe then and only then will I consent to playtime."

"Party pooper," Adonis growled out and faded back into the recesses of Danny's mind.

"You know you hurt his feelings. He has been worried about you and Trey, and here he was, giving you love, affection, and attention, and you shoot him down faster than... Awe heck, I can't think of how fast." Danny smiled as he lifted Austin and removed the rest of his clothes in one swoop.

Austin looked down at the heap of shredded clothing on the floor. "Gee, I'm glad it was nothing valuable I was wearing." Austin poked Danny in the ribs as the two sank slowly into the hot, steamy water. Then they filled the tub with suds and a gentle fragrance.

Soon after their bath, the two called it a night and just fell asleep cuddling. It was not until the following day that they had a quick round of tag in the bedroom before a shower. Then it was off to the meetings of the clans.

"Something has changed. Why are hybrids and tribrids

getting pushed around these days?" Austin said, standing up and adjusting his gaze.

"After you left, Austin, this is how we have been treated, like we're even lower than second class," Envy said as she crossed her legs and flashed a smile at Austin.

"Well, if you were not a dirty mix, maybe you would be of some use to all of us," Piper said, while adjusting the shells in her hair.

That is about enough of all of this treating each other like trash. I thought we were over this since that last titanic battle with the vile creature that sought to destroy life as we know it.

"Austin," came Grandpa Zacks's voice, "perhaps a minor break from all of this is in order. Sirens, it's time you return to the sea. Give it a few moon cycles. If you want to return, we can look into that. Werewolves of the Blue Sapphire Pack, please go home, rest, and enjoy your on-pack lands again. If you choose to visit after a couple of lunar cycles, that's fine. Dragon Clans, let's step back and check out our homelands and give ourselves some alone time. Fae folk, we share common land, and I am happy to continue this, but let us not step on any toes."

"That's fine by us Fae as long as the sacred rose bushes from Eros remain untouched. That is on our land." Queen Tatian said while adjusting her gown.

"All due respect, Tatian, you know the bush belongs to Danny and me," Austin said, standing up.

"Indeed, we have maintained it for you, but while you were away, someone tried to poison the bush to sow the seeds of chaos." Tatian looked over at Austin and smiled at her old friend.

"Well, with that, everyone is dismissed. I need to speak privately with Queen Tatian," Austin said, standing up and dismissing the rest of the party.

Once the room was clear, Tatian explained, "Oh, I'm so

happy to see the two of you. This all started when the God of Chaos surfaced and was not pleased to see everyone living in harmony, so he started little fights here and there. That is until he discovered the rose bush from Eros and lost all self-control. He has continued trying to poison the bush."

"Well, I guess I needed to come home," Austin said, looking at his old friend deep in her eyes, almost pressing into her soul.

"What brought you home?" Tatian asked in shock.

"Oh, a little boy by the name of Deven. Deven is the same age as our kids. Only his father is human, and I have reason to suspect his mother is Fae."

"Show me his picture, Austin. What you are saying is a serious accusation. Fae do not walk away from their children. But on rare occasions, we might not have a choice." Tatian pursed her lips while waiting for Austin to pull out his phone and show her a picture of Deven.

"It can't be! He looks just like her, Austin. Are you positive this child is alive?" Tatian had a worried expression on her face.

"Yes, this child bullies my children, and I don't blame him. His grandmother was a pain in my ass when I was dating Danny. Her son picked on me because she made him. But I know that hate is a learned behavior, and little Deven is learning it from his grandmother and his single human father." Austin took back his phone from a shocked Tatian.

"So, with your expression Tatian, I assume you know the mother?" Danny questioned.

"I know the mother, but I don't understand how it happened." Tatian sat down and placed her head in her hands, shaking her head in disbelief.

"Remember back when we first got her to Mt. Evens? Then Eros blessed us with a seed, and we planted it, making that rosebush, and it blessed the land and so on." Austin gestured with his hand, rolling it, implying everything that came after the rose bush grew. "Well, around that time, Eric came out this way camping, and he ran into Deven's mother, and sparks flew. I guess from what Trey told me from Selene, it was a magical trip for Eric. Eric fell in love with this girl. He was ready to—" Austin stopped in the middle of his thoughts, looking up to meet Tatian's gaze.

"No."

"Yes." Tatian looked up with tear-stained eyes.

"But Tatian, how?"

"It's not me, but my twin sister, Rebecca," Tatian whispered.

"What, when, how?" Danny stammered out.

"Do you remember the triplets I was to have shortly after you had your eggs? I was due two weeks after you. I was not married or mated. Nor was my twin sister. She was wild and carefree and used magic to create a placement here. It forced me into my pregnancy with the roses from Eros. My sister is a free spirit in every sense of the word. While exploring, she found a young man, and it was like fireworks when they touched. It was so magical for her, and she spent more time with him than she should have. Fae can become pregnant quickly, and we give birth faster than most species, but we can hold back the pregnancy if we need to. Our kind can birth non-magical children, but it is looked down upon. When the Supreme King, our father, found out she too was pregnant, he forced us to give birth in this form. With no magic, and no medications to ease the birthing pain, I carried all three children to a term like a human woman as punishment for not telling our father of her actions with a human. Rebecca carried her one child. Once they were born, I could see none of them. I was never told what happened to them." "Then how did she just drop Deven off at Eric's door?"

"My father must have made Rebecca give up her child in person, the most embarrassing thing for a Fae to do. I would never give up my babies, yet to this day my father has kept them from me. It is a punishment for failing my duties as a queen and a sister." Tatian put out her hands. "Can I see his picture one more time?"

CHAPTER 17

DATE NIGHT

"Danny, let's leave Queen Tatian to process all of this. No point having her relive the pain." Austin's voice was practically cracking.

"No, please don't go." Tatian begged them to stay.

"Tatian, where is Rebecca?" Danny asked in a stern voice.

"She isn't far away. My father wants to offer her to the nearby king to be his queen. The only problem is, she already has a child. So, my father is unsure if the king will take her as a bride." Tatian let out a stifled sob.

"We want to see Rebecca. Please inform your father that I request his and her presence. I will try to be as diplomatic as possible, but we have a halfling in my world who, when he comes of age, will have powers and no idea how to use them. I will not allow someone to grow up without parents." Austin stood, and Trey's eyes showed through.

"Austin, Trey is at the door knocking. Mind telling him to calm down?" Danny said, putting his hand on Austin, and instantly calming his mate.

"Of course, Austin. I will see Rebecca tonight and will

speak to our father come tomorrow's light. Can I take Deven's picture to Rebecca?" Tatian asked as she tucked the picture into her dress. She took her leave and quickly retreated to her home under the rosebush. She was leaving Danny and Austin to sort through the emotions and reality of what awaited them back home.

"Austin, if Deven is half human and half Fae, why are we only just now figuring that out?"

"Danny, one thing Fae do is hide in plain sight. Besides, since he is half human, those human genes can dominate, and he might show no magical gifts. For those gifts to be put to good use, he needs guidance." Austin stood up, reaching his hand out to Danny.

Danny took his hand and pulled Austin to him, holding him in a tight embrace. "I love you, baby," Danny whispered into Austin's neck, peppering it with kisses.

"Austin, don't forget your mother has our children. We can get back to date night, you know?"

"Well, let's get home first. I need to settle a few issues. Then I might let you take me out." Austin looked down at Danny with a sheepish grin.

Austin and Danny made it back to the Dragon Master's house to see the kids playing with Uncle Ente and Aunt Rose. The children didn't even know their parents were there until Logan looked over and saw them standing in the doorway.

"DADDIES!" squealed Logan, and he ran to the guys as the other two turned and tried to outrun each other to see who could get to them for the first hug.

"Austin, thank you for coming when you did. We were at our wit's end as to why the fighting started. I can't believe it took just you singing a song to calm everyone down. Sadly, we had to separate. I thought this would have worked out for the best." Ente shook his head.

"Boys, please, it's like you never had fights with family. That is all we are. We're kids, and each is a brother or sister. But, of course, we will have times when we fight. We all have growing pains," Rose said as she walked up to young Aurora.

"Auntie Rose!" Aurora squealed as she turned into Rose's open arms. "Can we finish my hair?"

"You all look exhausted. Let's get you three settled in for the night. I know we will have a slumber party tomorrow. How does that sound?" Rose said, peering down at the three excited children.

"Rose, thank you so much for taking the kids to bed. I need to feed this man before he looks at me like I am his next meal," Danny said as he pulled Austin in from behind.

"Look here now, old man. You are in my daddy's house. Don't make me get my dad," Austin teased as he squirmed to get out from Danny's tight grip.

"Oh, so Mr. tough guy is not so tough? Do you need to run to your daddy for help? By the way, when did I become this old man? You speak so highly about Mr. George-Blazek." Danny teased, nibbling on Austin's neck on his mate's mark, sending shivers down his back.

"Would you two stop already? If you're going to play, take it to the woods or up to your room. We don't need a show of your lovey-dovey. It's enough to make me sick," Ente teased while poking Austin in the ribs. "Why Ente, are you jealous? you have your mate, don't you?" Austin teased while raising his eyebrow.

"Danny, you better take that man out on a date. He is looking a little thin around the middle."

Ente winked and started rubbing an invisible baby bump.

"Ente, I swear on Delphine, if I end up..." Austin gritted his teeth. "I swear you will have diaper duties until they are potty trained. I'm already having my hands full at home with Karen, the teachers, and some downright stupid simple-minded people." Austin was about to cry, but he took in his mate's scent and began calming down.

"Karen is a story for another night. You two go out to your date night. The cook has prepared a basket for you guys. Enjoy, and let's hope the peace lasts now that everyone has, mostly, gone home. Like I said before, our land is open to everyone who wants to be here, but they must maintain peace.

All these nations we brought together are fighting over your Chimera Clan, Austin. Some feel it's an abomination. Others desire to join your clan. Some are only halflings and fear you would reject them," Grandpa Zack replied, walking up to the group.

"Grandpa Zack!" Austin pulled his grandfather into a warm embrace.

"So, it takes a minor war to bring my grandson and great-grandchildren home for a visit. I need to start a war when I want to see these sweet children. Come now, kids, I think if we're lucky, GG is making cookies." Zack took the kids by the hand, leading them away from their parents.

"I guess that is that. Show up, and your grandparents kidnap our kids," Danny said while holding Austin tight to his chest, thankful that he was alive and safe.

"That leaves us no choice. It looks like we're getting our date night after all," Austin said with a big smile spreading across his face.

"Then we're going home, Austin. I have everything we need for date night at home." Danny's voice was low and deep, and Austin knew by his tone there was no changing his mind.

"Fine, I will open a portal, but you better make it worthwhile to have missed out on the wonderfully packed basket." Austin waved the basket under Danny's nose.

"Bring it along. That smells amazing!" Danny caught a whiff of the sweet delights awaiting in the basket.

"Okay, Mr. George-Blazek, here we go." With a wave of his hand, Austin opened a portal to their backyard.

Once in their yard, Danny and Austin heard voices out front, so they crept around to see Sheriff Tate and his girlfriend leaving a care package on the porch.

"Hello, Sheriff Tate! Austin said, coming around the corner of the house.

"Oh, um, ah. Hello fellas," Tate paddled on with a nervous tick.

"What my sweet Tate is trying to say is we're sorry if we disturbed you. We both know Karen has been a handful. She has caused a lot of stress for your family. So, we took it upon ourselves to put this together. We love you as part of our community. There are cards from the town people. We are collecting for you as the parents of your children at the school. We have some fun things in it for the children. I got a few gift cards for that gaming place down the road. I believe you know the gracious lady, Candy, who works there. Once I told her what we were doing, she was stuffing the basket so full we had to beg her to stop." Elena let out a gentle laugh. You could almost forget she was a vampire.

"Yeah, my Candy Cane rock star can go overkill with the kids. That doesn't surprise me." Austin smiled and shook his head.

"Oh Danny, you and your father run that big law firm in town, right?" Elena said as she tapped Tate on the chest.

"Yeah, that's right. Danny, mind if I pick your brain for a minute?" Tate pulled Danny to the side.

Elena walked up to Austin. "Austin, I know you are the Chimera Wolf. Thus, this is your clan. I am a hybrid myself. I don't fit in with my people, and I am not part of his world," she gestured to Tate. "But believe it or not, I love that man. We vampires have our own fated mates. He is mine. I am his. Please allow me time to introduce him to our world. All I ask is if I have children, would you and Danny help us protect them?"

"Elena, I can tell you and your hunk of a mate have done everything, but you have yet to mark him. You don't mark him because he would then become a vampire. He would lose his humanity. Are you afraid he would turn away from you in anger? Or are you afraid of blood lust? How would he live as a vampire without Candy's help? I know you are not your brother and had nothing to do with Grandpa J's death, but I'm still unhappy about your family coven being so close to town. I suppose it was due to your excellent skills of smooth-talking a deal with Danny and the werewolf council. I'll say this: I'd rather have you here and not your father. So, as long as Malcolm keeps his fangs in line, you will have no fear from the Chimera Clan. We are open to all hybrids. I knew this day would be coming," Austin said, fishing in his pockets.

"You did? How?" Elena questioned.

"Elena, you think I only look this amazing? No, girl, don't worry, Candy and I already had this talk. So here you go, one white witch daylight ring. Not some gaudy old tacky thing. It has your initials engraved on the infinity symbol. I ask you to be honest with Tate, Elena. Does he know you are with child? Does Malcolm? I know he would not allow you near Tate alone for the longest time." Austin raised an eyebrow.

"No, and that is another reason I am so scared." Elena looked around for any of her brother's spies.

"So, it appears our date might need to be a double date, sweetheart," Danny said, smiling, knowing the dirty filthy night he had planned out for him and Austin was now shot.

"Oh, no, please don't. That was not our intention," Tate processed.

"No, I insist," Austin's eyes glowed. "I, Austin George-Blazek, welcome and invite you, Sheriff Tate, and Elena, into my home."

Elena knew instantly to take the invite and step inside. "Thank you, kind sir, for your warm, welcoming invitation."

"Danny, ensure someone has adequately cared for our invited guests. I have some unfinished business to attend to in the garden." Austin was on top of the vampire spy hiding in the thick bushes with Chimera speed. "Give me one damn good reason I should not send you into the beyond!" Austin growled in the intruder's ear.

"You have no power over me, little wolf," the pompous voice of Malcolm rang out.

"For a vamp, I expected you to have more common sense, but at last, you don't. I am no simple wolf. I am a Chimera. You are on my property, and under vampire law and the law of the treaty you are violating, I have every right to rip your dark heart from your chest."

"Temper. Are you still mad about that pathetic old man?"

"That old man, as you call him, was Grandpa J, you bastard. You and your idiot blood suckers killed him." Austin's fangs were out. "You understand a Chimera's bite is worse than the wolves?"

"Austin!" Brian called out as he walked into the bushes. "Danny said you needed help to show some blood-sucking bastard off the property." Brian locked eyes on Malcolm and let out a low, guttural growl.

"Brian, no bloodshed. Malcolm here is just leaving with a reminder of the pact that he and his kind on this side of the river are part of, in which not a single drop of human, witch, werewolf, or any other species' blood is allowed to be spilled within a 600-mile radius of the center of town."

CHAPTER 18

MALCOLM

"You heard my brother, you blood-sucking leach, get your ass moving." Brian shoved Malcolm out into the street.

"Brave man from the little flee bag hiding in the vents. Why only now are you so bold? Did your balls finally drop?" Malcolm said with a wicked smile dancing on his pale lips.

"If you don't shut your mouth, I will be happy to shut it for you." Brian balled up his fist preparing to fight.

"You are human. The only reason I don't drain you like the blood bag you are is that stupid treaty." Malcolm struggled to free himself from Brian's firm grasp. "How is it you're stronger than me?" Malcolm worked to free himself from Brian's hold, which only seemed to become tighter and tighter.

"What makes you think I am only human? One of your many mistakes." Brian looked down at Malcolm with a sinister smile.

"I know you took a silver dagger for that mutt." Malcolm gestured to the house since Austin had walked inside.

"What did you call my brother? Did you call him a mutt?"

Brian twisted his grip, and Malcolm's eyes narrowed as the pain became noticeable.

"Oh, you don't know, do you?" Brian let out an evil laugh. "The Moon Goddess, Selene gave Ted back to me recently, and he is dying to kick your ass for killing our grandfather." Brian's eyes turned black as onyx.

"Right. Take me for a fool, do you? Once you lose your wolf, you don't get them back. It's unheard of." Malcolm let his fangs extend.

"One, two, three," Brian counted.

"So, the fleabag can count; you passed first grade." Malcolm reached for Brian's shirt collar.

"I am going to let you go. You better make your getaway and stay away from me, my family, and our territory." Brian let Malcolm go and stayed fixed in place, locking eyes with him.

"Fleabag, I want my sister. You will fetch her like the dog you are. Do you understand?" Malcolm picked Brian up, tossing him to the foot of the steps of the house. "She belongs to me!"

Meanwhile, inside the house, Austin pulled Elena aside. "Elena, he's here."

"No!" Elena gasped in shock, holding her belly protectively.

"My love, Elena, are you okay?" Tate came running to Elena's side.

"Tell him." Austin looked deep into the eyes of a woman scared for her life and that of her unborn child.

"Elena, tell me what?" Tate asked, eying her until the puzzle clicked in his head. "Are you? You're sure. I am going to..." Tate trailed off, all the color washed out of his face. Then came the sweetest sound to Elena's ears from his lips. "Elena, this is not how I had this planned. I am not doing it now just because of your condition. I had this day planned in my head from the first day I ran into you at Peg's." Tate reached into his pocket.

Suddenly, the loud crash of Brian flying through the front door got everyone's attention. "Tate, I will deal with this. Finish talking to Elena." Austin's eyes glowed.

"What the hell?" slipped from Tate's lips. He turned to see Elena's eyes giving off a light glow. "My love, it must be because of your pregnancy, or I don't know what, but your eyes are giving off a light glow. Austin's eyes on the other hand were out and out glowing."

"My love, do you love me?" Elena asked fearfully.

"Yes, what kind of question is that?" Tate looked at his love, shocked, and continued to take one knee.

"I, Tate Stone, herby am professing my undying love for you. Elena, will you be my wife?" Tate pulled out a diamond ring. "I want to hear you call my name every night by my side for all eternity."

"Yes, a thousand times, yes. I will, but before you put that ring on my hand, I have a confession that you need to know." Elena took a slow, deep breath.

"What that you're half immortal? Elena, I would be a poor Sheriff if I failed to know the woman of my dreams is half vampire." Tate grinned ear to ear.

"Wait, you knew?"

"Elena, do not let that man fool you!" Danny tossed out, trying to hold back a deep laugh. "He pulled me aside to confirm he was not sure of anything," Danny said, shaking his head.

"I knew enough to see you are a werewolf!" Tate said, pointing at Danny.

"Fair enough." Danny raised his hands.

"Elena, I know you want me in the best but worst way." Tate wiggled his eyebrows. "I don't know how this will work, but I want to be with you all the time," Tate said smiling, holding his ring again for Elena.

She held out her hand, and he placed the ring on it and kissed it. "Baby, I will cook and clean—" Tate was cut off by Elena's slender finger to his lips.

"No, my love, we will do the cooking, cleaning, and everything in life together. But if I mark you as mine the way our people traditionally brand our mate, you could become one of my kind. So, until then and after that day, you must keep this ring on. It will help keep your humanity where it is now. I cannot risk turning you into a blood-lusting monster." Elena let a single tear run down her face.

Tate took the sterling silver ring with an intricate design cut into it, exposing the blue moonstone underneath. "Elena, I love it," Tate said, smiling down at the ring.

"Once it is on, it won't come off unless you take it off, Tate. They cast a spell on it to protect you, so no harm can come to you. But don't think I won't be able to kick your ass," Danny teased.

Tate allowed Elena to place the ring on his hand. "I will save my bite for another night." Elena looked out to the front door.

"Elena, I demand you come home at once!" Malcolm's voice rang out.

"We have invited her. You are not welcome here, Malcolm. It is best if you leave now." Austin pointed down the road, while standing next to Brian and providing a shield for Elena.

"Dogs, step aside. I will go in and get my sister." Malcolm balled up his fist.

"Sorry, not sorry old boy, rules are rules, and I know you cannot enter without permission, and you'll never get that from us." Austin crossed his arms, and his eyes glowed brighter.

"She is my sister. She belongs to me. I say when she can marry and who she can marry," Malcolm hissed out.

"Is that so, Malcolm? The mate you took is a werewolf from my pack. She is your mate, and you saved her from slaughter. Her mate knows the risk and happily takes it on. Do not provoke me." Austin's eyes danced with a lightning storm. He covered the trident in his arm with his hand, calling it forward.

"So, the mutt is truly beloved by the old gods. Sheriff Tate's days are soon to be numbered."

"What did I tell you about calling him a mutt?" Brian ground his teeth as his wolf edged closer to the surface.

"I take it Ted has finally settled in?" Austin said, turning to his brother.

"He has and comes with a blessing upgrade from our lunar mother." Brian's eyes danced with a newfound fire from within his soul.

"Fool, you think the moon is only yours?" Malcolm pointed up to a full blood moon. "This moon belongs to my people. It is a sign we can move against our enemies, and if you keep this up, you will be at the top of my coven's list."

Suddenly, the ground was covered with a dark mist dancing in the moonlight and Selene appeared with a handsome man. Danny and Austin instantly bowed to Selene and she returned the bow. Then, the man walked away from her and sized up the guys.

"These two are the ones we owe everything to?" he asked Selene.

"Yes, Absalom," Selene said with a smile on her lips.

"Sir, Austin, I presume?" Absalom looked right at Austin. "Could you kindly put that away?" Absalom pointed to the trident.

"Very well. Only because you came with Selene. Other than

that, I do not know who you are in all of this." Austin returned the trident to his arm.

"Young Chimera, my name is Absalom. I am the first Strigoi, more commonly known as a vampire." Absalom turned to look at Danny. "A fine mate you have. I want to thank the two of you for setting us free. As for you," Absalom turned to face Malcolm, "I am ashamed of you. You found a wolf mate. As you know, it is rare to change one supernatural into another. I won't give my blessing and change her from being a daughter of Selene. Instead, I will help your sister and her mate be happy. Interfere with her destined mate, and your mate will become a widow. Do I make myself clear, fledgling?"

"I am no fledgling," Malcolm spat out.

"To me, you're a fledgling, and that behavior confirms my beliefs," Absalom said, shaking his head. Then, turning to the house he said, "Child of mine, bring your mate."

Elena came out without hesitation while Tate took a protective stance on his soon-to-be wife.

"Elena, my child, your mate is human, and I will bless him with our gifts but without the curse of the blood lust. He will live a long life with you. He will have our strength, but he will still be human. As a hybrid, he will age like you. Do you accept my wedding gift?" Absalom asked with a smile on his lips.

Elena turned to Tate. "My love, the choice is yours."

"I have made my decision long before his offer. You are my bride, my life, and the mother of our unborn child. Nothing will take me from you." Tate kissed her as Absalom placed his hand on Tate and Elena. "By my powers, I declare you two a mated pair. Elena, you can mark him without fear of turning him into a full vampire. The white witch did a good job with the ring. Keep it as added protection." Absalom looked at Malcolm. "Interfere with their life, and I end yours."

"My lord, why? Why dilute our blood and our power with that of this human?" Malcolm asked with an edge in his voice.

"All things will come in time, Malcolm. It's time you returned to your coven. Since we're no longer restricted, our powers don't weaken, and I advise you not to test my patience. You are standing before more power than you have ever known. Some do not yet realize the power they hold." Absalom looked out the corner of his eye at Austin and Danny.

"Now, my queen of the night, shall we return to our evening?"

"Absalom, you might be the king of the undead and the night, but I am not your queen. Don't give these boys the wrong idea." Selene half-heartedly backhanded Absalom to his chest.

"Yet. You're not my queen yet," Absalom teased.

"In your dreams, boy." Selene let out a bubbly chuckle, and she vanished.

"Elena, you are with precious cargo. Do you know the name? Wait, don't tell me. Let it be a surprise." Absalom faded into the shadows and dissipated under the light of the full blood moon.

"Brother, you have heard from the highest of our kind. This union is blessed, and Tate is my mate. We are with a child. Neither you nor father will be interfering." Elena stood to her full height, and power rolled off of her.

"Then, what is this?" Malcolm gestured to this wave of power emanating from Elena.

"That is called the power of a mother. I advise never again messing with a woman who is with a child. They will kick anyone's ass," Danny said, holding back a wicked laugh, remembering when people tried to mess with Austin.

CHAPTER 19
PAPERWORK

"The coven will not stand for this. I should never have allowed you to entertain the thought of being around this fool. Come home now, dear sister." Malcolm's eyes glowed red as he tried to pressure Elena to return to the coven.

"Malcolm, get lost. Elena is going to stay with me. I don't care if you don't like me. Hell, it seems your father of all vampires doesn't care for you. So, I kindly ask of you to shimmer away." Tate stood by his bride's side.

"Fool, you stand by her side. She needs to be behind you. Men are the superior sex." Malcolm laughed at Tate for his foolish action.

"Not in today's age, pal. Men are not superior to women. Your sexism is really showing," Austin said, stepping off the deck and getting face to face with Malcolm.

"I cannot guarantee this flimsy treaty. With so many vampires, it's hard to keep them all in line, especially when I can't even keep my sister from getting in bed with the enemy." Malcolm spat at Elena and Tate's feet.

Austin opened a portal behind the angry, childish Malcolm and pushed him into the vortex, depositing him into the muck pit outside the coven territory.

"You bastard, how dare you touch me!" Malcolm continued to spew insults, but Austin closed the portal and returned to his guests.

"Tate, it's obvious Elena cannot return to her coven home. So, what are your plans?" Austin raised an eyebrow.

"I plan on taking my queen home with me. She is already pregnant with my child. What do you say, my sweet Elena?" Tate took Elena's hand and pressed it to his lips.

"Tate, take a deep breath. I will count to three, and we will be in your condo. One, two..." and on three, they shimmered out and were gone, leaving Austin and Danny to their date night again.

"Well, one shoe had dropped. So, I am waiting for the other to fall," Austin said, turning to face Brian and Danny.

"On that note, I feel bad being the one to give you this notice that was on my door, hell, everyone's door in town, but I don't see a notice on your door." Brian handed over the notice.

Austin read it and his eyes became engulfed in flames. Danny watched as he saw Austin's eyes flicker across the page. Each word seemed to enrage his mate that much more. By the time he was done, Austin was shaking, and Danny tried to calm his mate down by pulling him into an embrace.

"Austin, sweetheart, what could have you so upset? I can tell you are moments away from torching this town to the ground, but you know we can still make it. I see the meeting is not until 6:30 tonight." Danny tried to calm Austin down while running his hand down his back.

"We must go now if we are to make it on time. Forget it! We're using a portal. Karen is behind all of this." Austin flicked his wrist, opening a portal to an alley next to the school board office. Danny grabbed the notices to read for himself:

MEETING NOTICE

Scout Public School Board

3609 Cyrus Blvd

Date: Tonight, October 5, 2022

Time: 6:30 p.m.

Emergency meeting called with the mayor, the town council, and the school board.

Topic: Where do we stand on same-sex parental rights in our schools?

Who, if anyone, is at risk where it concerns parents and their children?

The floor will be open to discussion. Please remain civil.

Danny quickly linked his father. *"Dad, did you get the notice about the emergency school board meeting? The only way we found out was because of Brian! He got one on his apartment door. So, we're headed there now. It looks like we will need a protection order for the kids. Karen must stay away from the kids, and I don't want that Darla near them either."*

"Danny, Calm down. I have already got those orders. We can serve them tonight at the school board meeting, making it more than necessary publicly. Have it noted the courts served them." Doug's reply seemed rushed.

"Dad, you all right?"

"No, son, I have a million irons in the fire, and my son wants to dance around in my head. Let me get this stuff filed, and I will see you and Austin soon. Please make Austin behave." Doug quickly ended the mind link, leaving Danny to catch up to Austin and his quick-tempered march.

"Austin, I talked with Dad. He is taking care of some things and will be here soon. Please take a deep breath." Danny looked up to see why Austin suddenly stopped walking.

"That bitch." Austin let out a low growl.

Danny saw that the entrance had a rented cop covering it, checking people's licenses.

"Austin, take a deep breath. I will do the talking when we get to the door."

"Gentlemen, we need to see some ID."

"Why?" Danny asked with a smile.

"Sir, don't give us any attitude. Do you want to come in? We are requesting ID."

"You can't do that," Danny said, trying to walk past.

"Sir, I will not ask again. NOW! Or you will not enter."

"Why am I being forced to give my identification up? It seems you are preventing the public access to a public event that you put notice out for us to attend." Danny showed the letter.

"What is your reasonable, articulate suspicion to demand ID? You understand the color of the law won't save you, Mr. rent a cop," Austin piped in. "If you're going to be a rent a cop in our town, it's best to know who the town's top lawyers are."

"Well, if that's the case, present ID, and you can be on your way."

"Excuse me, just show the guy your damn ID, the rest of us want in as well," A sassy middle-aged woman yelled from the back of the now gathering crowd.

"Nowhere on your statement, or in the history of this school board have any of us been required to show ID and we are not starting tonight. It seems to me you are trying to prevent someone from attending a public meeting, so tell me who is on your list that you keep looking for so intently as you look at people's driver's licenses?" Danny's eyes narrowed in on the rental cop.

"Just a pair of guys. It's no big deal. The mayor and school board want to avoid drama."

"So, they are deliberately trying to exclude people to make it seem like it's a one-sided issue."

"I don't know, and I frankly don't care. Now sir, one last time, give me your driver's license."

"Babe, gather evidence," Danny said as he stepped up to the much shorter officer.

Austin snatched the clipboard out of the officer's hands and took the paper:

"Under no circumstance allow the following people in: Austin Blazek, Danny, and Doug George. Signed Mayor Matheson." Austin quickly folded it up.

By this time, Doug had arrived and served the cops a complete stop order, confiscating all body cameras and paperwork stating who not to allow into the meeting.

"Thanks, Dad," Austin chirped, as he walked past one of the guards who was texting someone quickly.

"Who are you—" Before Austin could finish, he heard the scream telling him who was getting texted.

"NO. NO. NO, they can't be allowed in. We must stop them, lock the doors, and make this a private meeting. We can't allow them in here." Karen Matheson, the mayor's wife, was screaming.

"Too late, Karen." Austin held out the bag full of body cameras still on and recording. "So, did you have them deliberately skip our house in hopes we wouldn't know of the meeting?"

"Damn right, I did. We don't need your filthy, sinful kind in our schools, let alone here, while we make rules and policies up. So, get the hint and get out of our town." Karen's face was beet red, and she was shaking with fury.

"Karen, sit down and shut up. It's over. They are here. We will deal with it all later," Mayor Matheson said through gritted teeth.

"All right, folks, let's start this meeting. We called you all here tonight because of concern for your children's welfare," Karen stated from the podium

A hushed murmur ran through the townsfolk at what she said. "I feel it is my duty as the wife of the mayor of our fair town to bring to your attention how our school is currently being run. We have same-sex parents ordering principals around like they own the school. We are telling them what is and is not acceptable documentation for the parent of a child. These two fathers have lost touch with God for the far left. It is basic biology 101 folks, it takes one male and one female to make a baby. Thus, a mother needs to be listed on the child's birth certificate. Those are necessary to document the child attending school in our district. These fly by the seat of their pants parents want to come in here and tell us how it will be. I say no, sir. Our school needs to go back to how things were not so long ago, with proper paperwork, and I, as a grandmother, should not have to explain to my grandbaby why someone has two daddies. I can't even bring myself to say, dads. It is just downright wrong. I tell him one is the dad, and the other is the daddy's friend." Karen pounded the podium with her fist.

"These delusional people come into this town and get people fired for doing their job. Darla was a CPS agent until a few hours ago when the state let her go. They said her investigation of charges was called into question. The investigation was for one of those abominations. I say we vote now as a town and school board not to accept paperwork unless it's properly filled out." Karen turned to face Danny and Austin with a smug smile.

Austin stood up and walked to the podium. "Excuse me, sir, what makes you feel you can talk here tonight?" one of the board members spoke up.

"Well, since my tax dollars and my company's tax dollars

are tied up in this town, I think I have a right to talk, especially when you're addressing my family. Now, Karen is right. Darla got let go, but it's Darla and Karen's fault. Doug, if you would please." Austin gestured, and Doug served them both with paperwork. "Karen, Darla, consider yourselves served with a no-contact order for our children. My husband and I have three wonderful children, and I want you both to stay away. I will summon Karen for trespassing, breaking and entering in our backyard, evidence tampering and the list goes on. You will explain the charges to the judge. As far as the paperwork goes." Austin spun to face the school board. "Here are copies of each of our children's enrollment paperwork. Please note my name for the record is Austin George-Blazek, CEO of NRG Energy Source. My husband is Danny George-Blazek, the Owner of TEC WIZ and that is not all. He is also partners with his father, Doug, the former town lawyer. Doug left after the event last year. But anyway, all of our papers are legal and up to code. We are both biologically the fathers of these children. But to make your small town minds more understanding of everything we had," Austin did air quotes, "adopted each other's children. Nothing in the law books or town charter prevents that. This seems like a meeting led by a leader full of hate."

"Big words come from a boy serving the mayor's wife with papers for the second time." Karen waved the bundle of papers Doug had given her.

"So, Austin, tell us why we have to recognize your situation. What makes you two so special?" the board president, Jefferson asked with a considerable distance in his voice.

"Well, Mr. Jefferson, not recognizing our joint parental rights is comparable to the school only seeing your wife as the parent of your three boys. Say Jane went to see her folks in Kansas, leaving you with the boys. The school could not call you if they got sick or in a fight, or even allow you to pick up the children on school grounds. Now, since your boys are in grade school, they may not leave unless picked up by a parent—"

Danny was talking but he was cut off by Karen. "Or, OR a guardian. Why can't one of you freaks be the parent as we listed the other as a guardian?"

"Because we are both parents of those children, Karen. Since you want to pull the rug out from under us since birth certificates need parental names, what about Eric's boy?" Danny let an evil smirk fill his lips.

"Leave my son out of this, please." Eric stood with a pained look in his eyes.

"Austin?" Danny gave Austin a look. "Are you going to tell him, or am I?"

Austin stood up. "Yes, sorry Eric, forgive us. Sadly, Deven's mother has not been listed as Karen requires, but lucky for Eric and little Deven I know his Aunt Tatian, and she is getting a hold of Rebecca." At the mention of her name, Eric rushed to Austin.

"You know where to find my Rebecca? My love. The air I breathe is nothing without her. So why did she leave me with just our son?" Eric sobbed.

"When you hurt us, you could end up hurting one of your own. But Mr. Jefferson, do you see our point with the example of you and your boys?"

"That won't fly while I am on this board, Karen. This meeting is over. You have misguided this town, and this board of education, and I am truly sorry for ever entertaining your madness." Mr. Jefferson banged his gavel down hard.

Austin turned to a crying Eric and lifted him up. "Eric, you know more than you let on. I know better. Bring Deven to our house in fifteen minutes, and I only want you and Deven to come."

"Why?" Eric asked as he wiped away tears.

"I know someone who is dying to see her family. I got a message from Tatian just now. She found her twin sister Rebecca and they will be at our house within the hour." Austin went to turn away when Eric reached out for him.

"You better not be pulling my leg. I can't and won't risk getting my boy's hopes up," Eric said, while clenching his jaw.

"Deven smells much like his mother Colorado wilderness and a hint of rose," Austin said with a raised eyebrow.

The look on Eric's face was all it took. He swallowed hard and nodded his head. "See you in fifteen." Eric rushed to flee his pleading mother, desperate to stop him from leaving.

"What did you say to my son!" Karen yelled at Austin.

"Only what he needed to hear. Now maybe he will see we have never been enemies. It's only you and that bitter party, for one. Goodbye, Karen." Austin pushed past her, with Danny and Doug following close behind.

CHAPTER 20
ERIC'S AWAKENING

Austin and Danny arrived home with enough time to look around at the night that was planned but never going to happen.

"Austin, every time I try to have a romantic night for us, something comes up. I'm sorry." Danny looked into Austin's eyes pleading.

"Boy, stop. This is not your fault. We already knew our lives were going to be... crazy. To top it off, we moved back to this place." Austin pointed in the air with his index finger and made a circle.

A soft knock came at the door, making Austin jump.

"Jumpy, are we babe?" Danny teased.

Austin shot him a brief scowl and rolled his eyes, as he walked over to the door and opened it to see Eric standing there with Deven fast asleep in his arms.

"Eric, you're early," Austin said while directing Eric to come inside.

"Sorry, I just didn't want to run into my mother. Austin, if this works out..." Eric trailed off before clearing his throat. "If this works out, and you're not pulling my leg, I would like to start over. I know I haven't been very nice to you or Danny."

"Let's leave the past in the past, Eric, but I think we should talk. How about letting Deven nap on the couch, and we can go to the dining room and have some coffee?" Austin said cheerfully.

As Eric walked into the dining room, he let out a low whistle. "Someone was having a good night."

"If only," Austin said as he cleared the table. "We had plans for tonight, but a little drama stopped it. No, not just the school board, but family stuff came up. As parents, we are accustomed to putting our plans on the side to help others."

Eric took a seat and hung his head low in shame. "I'm sorry about tonight. My outburst, it's just you talked like you know Rebecca, and that just ripped off the bandage to an old wound that won't seem to heal."

"I don't know Rebecca. I know her sister, Tatian." Austin corrected him.

"Oh." Eric's voice broke as he spoke.
"Eric, correct me if I'm wrong, but around the same time I left this godforsaken town about, oh, five or six years ago, you yourself took a break from the town and went to Colorado, didn't you?"

"Yeah, why?"

"You went camping near Mt. Evens?" Austin asked while taking the fresh cup of coffee Danny brought into him. Danny placed a coffee in front of Eric.

"Yeah, I did. What, let me guess, you had things investigated, and that's how you put all this together. You know what? If you were going to fake it this entire time just to get your way at the school board meeting, that is low," Eric said with an edge to his voice.

"Eric, I will let that slide because I know you're hurt. But my birth parents live on the privately owned land that is most of Mt. Evens," Austin said, standing up, walking to the fireplace, and blowing on the logs to start a fire.

Seeing this, Eric jumped up from his chair, "What on God's green earth!"

"Calm down, Eric, my friend. You have stumbled into a world that is mostly unknown to the outside world. Now you are only being told what you need to know for right now. The land you went camping on, was that part of one of the public camping sights, or did you find a more suitable spot, say on the private land?" Austin said, raising his eyebrows.

"Well, I... I started off booking a spot, but thistle overgrew the area. So, I crossed a little creek, and I found this amazing little clearing that had soft grass, a wonderful tree line, and the best view of the stars." Eric smiled, remembering his trip.

"That sounds like Apollo's Clearing." Austin pulled out his phone and showed him a map of Mt. Evans. "Is this the spot?" he asked, pointing to the map.

"Sure is! Do you know of that place?" Eric questioned.

"Yes, because it's on my grandfather's land. I'm having a cabin built there right now for my family," Austin said, looking at Danny.

"Is that why you and your father and grandfather were in a rush to keep me out of the clearing?" Danny smirked seeing the anniversary present was now given away.

Austin just looked over at Danny and stuck out his tongue, causing both Eric and Danny to chuckle at his display of immaturity.

"Well, I know it's a little late and all, but I'm sorry that I trespassed. Then a g a i n , who knows if I would have found Rebecca? Is she related to you? And what is this world you are talking about? How did you get a fire started with no match?"

Eric's brain finally caught up to his eyes, and the questions fell out of his mouth.

"Eric, take a deep breath." Austin attempted to calm him down.

"What are you?" Eric narrowed his eyes.

"I am a Chimera," Austin said with ease.

"Like Greek mythology, a lion, eagle, or snake?"

"More like a werewolf, triton, or dragon," Austin said in a hushed tone.

"Werewolf? Now that is a joke and a half. What, do you howl at the moon too? I have no clue what a triton is, but you said dragon? What like puff the magic dragon? Come on, Austin, I thought this talk was going to be serious. You shouldn't mess around like this, because it makes me doubt you know Rebecca." Eric was beginning to get annoyed.

Danny let out a low growl and rolled his eyes at Eric being like that so close to his Austin.

"Oh, are you in on this as well, Danny? What are you, part Pit Bull?" Eric let out a laugh at his own joke.

"No, I am a purebred werewolf. I am an Alpha at that." Danny let his eyes flash to onyx black.

"OH SHIT!" Eric shouted and leaped from his chair, only to be caught in Danny's grasp.

"Sit down, calm down, and I will let you go. Do you understand?" Danny whispered into Eric's ear.

Eric nodded and relaxed.

"So, this is all real?" Eric looked around.

"Before you run out of this house and start ranting and raving about something you would have a hard time proving, know that your own son is at risk of exposure," Austin said, bringing the coffee cup to his lips.

"My son is not one of you." Eric trailed off in fear of choosing the wrong words.

"But he is of the supernatural world, Eric. Do you not know Rebecca that well?"

"Well, when I first met Rebecca, she was down by that pond in the clearing. I didn't notice her at first, and I stripped to take a bath in the pond when she appeared out of nowhere. We hit it off. It was like fireworks when we touched." Eric smiled, remembering that night.

"Mates." Danny said to Austin, raising his eyebrows.

"Mates? Is that some weird way to say, did we have sex? Obviously, we had a lot. I became a dad because of it." Eric chuckled.

"Eric, in our existence, when you are with the one destined to be your other half, you feel sparks or fireworks when you touch each other. That crosses all divides: race, gender, species."

"Race? Gender? Species?" Eric repeated each, as if it was their own question.

"Race as in race, Eric. It's not rocket science. Gender." Austin pointed between himself and Danny.

"Now, species is the one I think I would have to explain. So, shifters are human and then something else. Like a werewolf, werebear, dragon, phoenix, that sort of thing. Some species are like Fae. They are humanoid but are more fairy. They can take on a full human body, but they don't change into an animal."

"So, what is my Rebecca?"

"She is Fae," Austin replied.

"My Rebecca is like Tinkerbell? Now that is rich. What is she going to sprinkle some dust on me and fly me to some alternate reality?" Eric's voice had an edge to it this time.

"Well, I believe she did that enough at the camp sight Eric, hence why you have a little boy sleeping on the sofa," Danny said with a stone-cold look on his face.

Eric's face turned beet red as he got quiet, knowing what

was just said to him was not only meant to put him in his place, but to kindly remind him of the events that transpired.

"Okay, say for a minute I believe in all of this stuff." Eric made an open hand gesture to the room.

"Where does that put me and my son?"

"It makes him what most of the supernatural world calls a halfling." Austin explained when Danny piped in, "Sadly, some will call your son a mutt. I hate that word so much." Tears welled up in Danny's eyes as he looked at Austin.

"Wait, that's what Brian always called Austin. Now it makes sense. It is rude as fuck." Eric turned to look at his sleeping boy, hoping he didn't just hear him cuss.

"We do that too Eric, sometimes our adult mouths run before we realize there are young ears around us." Austin looked at Danny, this time causing his face to become flush.

"All right, am I going to wake up one day and he's going to have wings and be two inches tall?" Eric asked, never taking his eyes off his sweet boy.

"Since I am not Fae, I cannot say for sure. We will have all our answers once Tatian and Rebecca show up. Now, when they show up, you need to know a few things. Eric, I need you to look at me when I tell you this, because I need to be sure you understand." Austin's voice and tone made Eric break his gaze and turn to face him.

"Shoot," Eric said, winking at Austin.

"Tatian and Rebecca are twins. But both are not your soul mate. So, do not get any hair brain ideas you get to have two women in your life."

"Hell, dealing with my mother was bad enough. Having a destined wife and my mother, my hands will be full as it is. I don't need to make it three ladies trying to control me," Eric said, putting his hands up in mock surrender.

"Eric, serious. Even as twins Tatian was born first, thus, she got birth right as firstborn. Tatian is the queen of the Fae on Mt. Evens. Rebecca is still a princess. So that—"

Austin was interrupted by Eric. "That makes my son a prince." Eric's tone was flat, like he was just reciting lines.

"Yes, he is a prince, only he is not supposed to exist. Because of Fae laws, Rebecca could not give birth to Deven as a Fae. It forced her to carry him to terms of human birth. She couldn't keep him as well. That's why Rebecca was forced to give him up to you. He was to live his life without knowing his past. Lucky for you, I know his aunt and I dug around. Now doing so has stirred the pot. It would not surprise me if the king, well the old king, shows up in a huff. Tatian was pregnant as well and had to suffer the same fate as her sister for not telling on her. Tatian's children were taken away as punishment."

"This old king sounds like a right ass to me." Eric's face contorted, thinking he caused not only the loss of a child to his Rebecca, but that of her sister.

Suddenly, a loud banging come from the front door. The men all looked at each other as Austin looked at the clock. "It's not Tatian or Rebecca, Danny." Austin looked at his husband.

Danny walked over to find Karen at the front door.

"GIVE ME MY GRANDSON!" she demanded in a loud voice.

"Mom, keep it down. You will wake my son. He is taking a nap on the sofa. We're both fine and you're not allowed here. I saw the court order." Eric was now red in the face.

"Don't tell me you are falling for their bullshit," Karen hissed.

"Mother, you need to leave now!" Eric demanded.

"Why I never—"

Danny cut her off. "Aww, somebody call the waambulance, because Karen's feelings just got hurt by her son becoming a man," Danny sneered.

"Dude, I like that. That shit's funny: waambulance. I will have to remember that next time a guy gets butt hurt because he has cleaning duties." Eric's face was red from laughing so hard.

"Eric, come home right now and bring me my grandson. I will not allow the two of you to be corrupted by these demon spawns." Karen had a grip on the door, ready to force her way into the house.

"Karen, get off my property and let go of my door. We will meet any attempt to enter my home with equal force to keep our home safe," Austin said, walking up to the door.

"Austin, don't," Danny said, knowing Austin was moments away from opening a portal to hell to show Karen what a real demon spawn looked like.

"Fine, she needs to leave. Our guest will arrive and she cannot and will not be here." Austin turned to walk away.

"Yes, turn and run little fairy boy. Run along. I'm going to collect what is mine," Karen said, smirking.

"ENOUGH MOTHER!" Eric ripped the door from her hands as he charged out of the house like a crazed bull.

"Mother, I moved out years ago. I am not your little child to manipulate. I am a grown man and you will not bully me or my son. Get out of here. I don't need you. I don't want you around. My son will leave here when I'm good and ready. So, get the hell out of here." Eric now had his mother pinned to her car. Her expression was one of pure fear.

"Eric, what have they done to you, my sweet boy? You never were this aggressive to me before, why now?" Karen's lip was trembling with fear.

"Mother, I know you love me and my boy, but if you don't leave right now, you will never see us again. I will take my son and move far from here. Thanks to my newfound friends, I am learning a lot, and it is no thanks to you." Eric stepped back to give his mother a chance to get into her car.

"Eric, please think about what you're saying. What are you doing? I won't allow you to take my grandson from me. I can easily make it hell for you like I am doing for those delinquents. My son is unfit with no wife in his life. I guess I will just have to ask the courts for custody of my poor grandson, Deven. Only a good Christian family of one man and one woman can raise a child, right?" Karen said smugly as she opened her car door.

Hearing this, Austin snapped. In a flash, he was closing her car door with her just inside. "Listen to how you talk to your own son. Don't you see the hate you have in your heart, Karen? Just because he won't get in line with your views, you will attack your own son. Hum judge, the woman in question seeking custody raised the man in question. Are you sure she is more fit than the birth parent? I'm sure the judge will love the way Danny and Doug will spin it and use every legal resource to keep Deven with Eric. Now get off my property." Austin spat the last words out with such animosity that Karen knew it was time to leave.

"Eric, just wait till your father hears of this. I swear you turned your back on us. Be prepared for us to return the favor." Karen quickly left, heading back to her house to complain to her husband about how rude she was treated.

"Bye-bye now. Bye-bye," Eric said in a cheeky, high-pitched voice.

"Eric, care to finish our discussion in the house?" Austin ushered everyone back inside.

"What's the rush shortie? I was having fun sticking it to that pain in the ass mother of mine." Eric seemed lighter, like an immense weight had been lifted off of him.

"Because we have a lurking vampire." Austin turned to Danny.

"Vampires are real too!" Eric sat down with the recent news, trying to wrap his mind around things.

"Danny, do not kill, but detain him in the shed. I'm sure we can get intel from him." Austin smiled wickedly at his husband, who was all too eager for a fight.

Then they heard a brief struggle, followed by a high pitch cry for help.

"Keep quiet. I don't need you waking the young one," came the gruff voice of Adonis.

"Who is that?" Eric asked in shock.

"Adonis. That is Danny's wolf. My wolf has a name as well. It's Trey," Austin said, taking another drink of his coffee.

"All right, so since you are a Chimera and have three parts, the name Trey totally makes sense. Does it get confusing on who's talking? How does it work with your wolf and his?" Eric was once again full of questions while monitoring his sleeping child.

No sooner had Danny walked in the door when the grand-father clock chimed, and Austin looked at his watch and nodded to Danny. "Eric, it's time. I hope you are ready."

CHAPTER 21
HYPNOS AND MORPHEUS

A soft knock brought the guys' attention back to the front door again.

Austin walked over and took a deep breath before slowly opening the door, unsure how this was all going to play out. Once the door was open, they saw two tall men standing guard on the other side.

"Hypnos? Morpheus?" Austin asked in shock.

"Yes, we're here and we came with more than you planned for here tonight," Hypnos said, rolling his eyes.

"Dad, knock it off. You know you wanted to bring the kids back. I believe you even begged Daniel and Amy to let you bring them home," Morpheus said, grinning ear to ear as he called his father out.

"You brought my kids home? I thought they were going to stay for a week. Did they annoy my parents that much?" Austin looked around to see three sleepy-eyed kids standing behind the two giant men.

"Really, Hypnos, you have my kids half a sleep? I could have just got a call and opened a portal. In fact, if they needed to come home, they have a private portal in my old playroom. Something is fishy and you will need to fill me in later. Danny, please put the kids to bed. Hypnos, Morpheus, where are they?" Austin raised one eyebrow.

"Damn Dad, you were right, that totally looks like a brat tamer," Morpheus joked as he stepped aside to help Danny get the kids in the house.

"Sorry about all this, Austin and Danny. We did this as a favor for Tatian and Rebecca," Hypnos was saying as two golden orbs buzzed into the room and hit the floor. Soon after, two beautiful women stood before them.

Danny walked back in to see Austin being embraced by the ladies and he chuckled. "If I was a jealous wolf..." he started off.

"Oh, but you are Danny Mc Fussy fanny," Tatian teased as she left Austin to hug Danny.

"Uncanny!" is the only thing that dropped from Eric's mouth. "Eric!" Rebecca shrieked and ran into his arms.

"Becky? Is this really you? Please tell me this is not a dream!" Eric cried out as he grabbed a hold of the mother of his child.

"Boys." Tatian shot Hypnos and Morpheus a look.

"Yes, Queen Tatian, it would be our honor." Both men started off on a low hum and waves of power emanated off their bodies.

"What are they doing?" Eric asked, stepping back only to get pulled close to Becky.

"My love, I know you got a crash course on some things. Hypnos and his son Morpheus are putting the town all to sleep safely, so calm down Austin." Rebecca shot Austin a look like, yeah, my sister warned me.

"Tatian?" Austin's voice did a little uptick.

"Easy Austin. Hypnos is putting them to sleep, and Morpheus is giving them all wonderful, happy dreams. We need to make sure no one interferes, especially since Karen is his mother." Tatian shot Eric a look.

"Hey, no skin off my teeth. You can keep her asleep for all I care. She has made my life hell, and I ended up taking it out on Austin unfairly. But I hope this means Austin has forgiven me because he helped me get Becky back." Eric kissed the crown of her head as she melted into his arms.

"Okay princesses, you have about an hour before our magic goes noticed," Morpheus commented.

"Please tell me everyone and thing is asleep. We have a problematic coven of vampires," Austin started in when Tatian put up her finger to his lips.

"Those were the main reason we brought backup. We don't need one of them getting a hold of a Fae folk." Tatian turned to Eric. "Where is my little nephew?"

"Daddy?" came a little sweet voice as Eric turned around and saw Deven staring at two people who looked like his mommy. The look of shock on his face... then panic. "D-d-d-daddy, why are there two people that look like my mummy?"

Rebecca squatted down. "Deven honey, I'm your mommy, and that's my twin sister. It's kind of funny she had to copy me in all my looks, but the one thing she has never been able to copy is you. That was all my pleasure."

"Daddy?" Deven put his hands up to get picked up.

Eric quickly got on the floor next to Rebecca. "Squirt, this is your mom. Scout's honor. Her sister is friends with Mr. and Mr. George-Blazek."

"WHO?" Deven asked, wiping the sleep from his eyes.

"Logan, Aurora, and Ethan's daddy, buddy." Eric said, holding back a soft chuckle.

"Oh." Deven's eyes lit up. He pulled free from his dad and ran up to Austin, wrapping his arms around his leg and looking up. "Thank you, mister. You brought me my mommy and now my daddy won't be sad." Then, just like that, he let Austin go and ran into the loving arms of his mother.

"Easy killer, don't squeeze your mother too tight. We don't want you to break her now, do you?" Eric teased.

"Mommies are magical. She can't break," Deven responded, wrapping his arms even tighter.

"But we can break, my love. Mommy was heartbroken all these years you grew up without me," Rebecca said while taking in a deep breath and relishing the sweet boy's scent.

"He smells just like you, Rebecca. I don't know how, but I am so grateful I went camping in a restricted area." Eric looked up at Austin, biting his lip with guilt.

"Eric, that look might work for Rebecca, but not me. I am immune to those looks," Austin teased.

"Say what?" Danny gave his best sad puppy dog eyes.

"Grr, Danny, don't give me that look. I have done nothing wrong. You're not being ignored, so cool it." Austin chastised Danny with a smirk on his face.

Suddenly, the door burst open, and a red orb shot in as a large billow of red smoke filled the room. Once it had cleared, a furious man was snapping his fingers at Hypnos and Morpheus. "What is the meaning of this? How dare you help my daughters sneak into the human world!"

"Fae king or not, you do not own us, and we owe you nothing. Need we remind you we are the gods in the room, not you?" Hypnos spat out.

"Rebecca, Tatian, we are leaving right now, but before we go—"

"Sir!" Eric stood up to address the angry man who appeared to be Rebecca's father.

"That is Mr. O'Brien to you, human."

"Mr. O'Brien sir, Rebecca is my fated mate. I know of Fae law. I am human, yes, but Rebecca and I have had a child together." Eric was standing tall and firm in his resolve. He had lost Rebecca once, and he wasn't losing her again.

Deven wiggled out from behind Rebecca and walked up to O'Brien. "Are you my grandpa?"

"I have not..." his voice faltered once he'd looked down into Deven's eyes. "Young man, I don't..."

"Mr. O'Brien, as you are very well aware, I am the Chimera wolf. All half breed or mixed breed species are under our protection. That includes this child. Any thoughts you had of erasing memories or making him disappear are hereby void. You know where I get my powers from. I helped them break free. Many of the old gods have no problem coming to my aid. I only need to ask for it." Austin's eyes flashed with power.

"Yes, yes, I know what you are." O'Brien started in, but he had a hard time pulling his gaze away from the young child. "Boy, what is your name?"

"Deven," he replied, looking down at the ground under the glaring stare of the stranger.

"Austin, can we put Deven to bed, so us adults can speak?" O'Brien asked with an abundance of kindness in his voice.

"Baby, I will take him to the boys' room. He can sleep in Logan's bed," Danny said as Deven ran up to him and passed him on a dead run to the boys' room.

"Slumber party! Thank you, Daddy. Thank you, Momma. It was nice meeting you, Grandpa." Deven was gone before O'Brien could say another word to him.

"Rebecca, I will give you seventy-two hours with Eric and Deven to prove to me you are, in fact, destined mates. If you cannot provide proof, I will pull you both apart so fast and you will be forced to marry the prince of the southern province," O'Brien announced.

"O'Brien, here, have a drink of some of the Fae wine from

my mother's home." Austin handed over an ancient bottle covered in old shells from the ocean floor.

"Ah yes, young Austin your mother is half wolf, half siren." O'Brien poured himself a tall glass.

Danny got the picture once he walked back into the room; it was mingle and talk time to get people to calm down and let down their guards. It didn't take long before O'Brien was handing an empty bottle back to Austin. "Do you have any more?"

"Sure do. Here you go, sir." Austin gave him another bottle. "I have more in the basement. Just ask and I can have it right up, O'Brien."

After O'Brien had polished off his third bottle, his lips loosened up. "What? How? How does that boy have Petra's eyes? He has my beloved Petra's eyes." He seemed to be talking to himself, but loud enough for everyone to hear him. He looked up with hurt in his eyes. "Daughter, why did you not tell me he had your mother's eyes?"

"Because you made him go away when he was only a baby. You took him away from Rebecca and you took my triplets away, father. Give us back our children. You are not the leader anymore, I am. You took your grandchildren away only because you don't like their fathers. Rebecca had a human mate and mine is not of noble blood." Tatian shot daggers at her father as her words fell upon his ears.

"Father, my destined mate is human. I will not leave him or our son again. Banish me if you must, but I will only be with Eric and Deven."

"Deven, who named him that? I like it. Tell me something young man." O'Brien looked at Eric. "Does he ever get into trouble but with a simple look melt your heart so much that you forget *why* he is in trouble?"

"All the time. I swear he has to get it from his mother

because I am sweet and innocent." Eric smiled while looking devilishly at Rebecca, whose face turned red.

"Now, now there will be no talk of banishment for my daughters. Tatian, do you really like Jack that much? I swear he is a complete nit whit. But I suppose if he's your mate, it's for a reason. When we get home, I will have your boys brought home. I will tell you this for your ears only girls. You have made me a proud grandfather enough already."

"We will decide if you get more grandchildren, father. You're blessed so quickly because of that bush on Mt. Evens." Tatian crossed her arms, looking down her nose at her father.

"I was only saying, dear, that I have four very handsome Fae grandchildren. Rebecca, I can already see this human. What is your name, son?"

"Eric sir."

"Eric is, in fact, your mate. But I require we keep his lineage from him till he is older. He has a human in him. Sorry, no offence son. Last time humans really knew and believed in our existence, our people were imprisoned and vampires highly craved for our blood, and you seem to have a starving coven not too far from here." O'Brien looked at Austin for an explanation.

"Mr. O'Brien I already know about the vampires. They will not harm Deven.

"They better not. Now I want to hear about his upbringing. Has he shown any powers?"

"Dad, we used magic to hide him from the vampires and it blocked his powers. The only way to know is to take the binding spell off. As long as he keeps the charm I saw him wearing, it will protect him from the vampires." Rebecca looked at her sister.

"Let's give him time before we pull him all the way into this world, sister." Tatian looked warily at the clock.

CHAPTER 22
UNEXPECTED ENTRANCE

A ustin was about to ask Tatian why her attention was drawn to the time, but then just as the clock struck midnight and was chiming its last chime, the hall closet gave off an eerie glow.

"What is this? It's a trap. Girls hide!" O'Brien cried out with panic in his voice.

"Calm down, father. It's only one of Austin's portals," Tatian explained with a crisp annoyance at her father's cowardness.

The door handle turned, and there was a gentle click as the door slowly swung open, revealing Bou carrying a siren in his arms with tears in his eyes and panic on his face.

"Austin! Please help. They attacked her. We were by your salt lake in the mountains, when two tritons from a southern tribe arrived unannounced and came out of the water. They called her a traitor. They attacked her for no reason other than she was walking with me and holding my hand. Please help. These wounds are bad enough that I can't help my mate!"

"Mate? Bou, you found your mate!" Tatian exclaimed but

P.A. POWER

held a puzzled look on her face seeing the siren in his arms clutching his chest.

"Oh my Goddess, what happened? Bring her over here," said Austin.

"I thought?" Tatian still looked puzzled as Bou sat his mate on the couch.

"It's okay. Brandon had the hots for me, but I think he just wanted me for my body." Bou flexed and showed off his smile and cute dimples. "But no, seriously, Austin, she is my mate. I know it in my heart, and her scent of fresh rain drives my wolf crazy."

"Danny, go to the pantry. I need a few of my mom's herbs she sent for the kids." Austin pointed to the kitchen.

"I'll know which ones to get, how exactly? Never mind, I already figured it out." Danny's words trailed off, showing he disapproved of what was to happen next. Austin let out a low growl as his eyes gleamed emerald green.

"Austin, you don't need to give Danny a hard time." Rebecca walked with Danny to the pantry.

"Don't worry, Danny, I will help you. I am a Fae after all. I'm sure I can identify what herbs you need."

"It's not that, Rebecca, it's just that Austin promised not to do the return to sender with me in the room. It gives me flashbacks to when he got beat up when we first started dating," Danny explained as he opened the fridge, pulling out a beer.

"Return to sender?" Rebecca said as if they were foreign words, strange and unknown to her tongue.

"Okay, Boo Bear?" Austin called out from the living room.

"Thank you, sugar lips, but I still knew what you were doing!" Danny stood up, took a gulp of the beer, grabbed a couple more, and walked out to the living room. "Catch." Danny tossed a beer to Eric and one to Bou. "Sorry, O'Brien, you got the good stuff already."

180

"Oh, it's all right. I will take sea Fae wine over land folks' beer." O'Brien smiled wickedly.

"What is a return to sender?" Rebecca was still fussing over the words, trying to understand the big deal with Danny.

"You'll see." Danny pointed to the siren on the sofa.

"Oh my stars in heaven! She doesn't have a scratch on her!" Rebecca cried out.

"Bou? Where are we?"

"Hush Lexi, my love, you are safe." Bou's voice took on a dark, sultry feel that made all the ladies swoon.

"Wait, you know..." Lexi pointed to Austin. "You know the Chimera!" Lexi sat up and pulled back from Austin.

"I told you—"

Bou was cut off abruptly by Austin. "Is my brother bragging about knowing people again?" Austin smiled and winked at Bou, teasing him.

"Brother? Wait, does that make you a Chimera? Why are you unable to come to the sea again? I saw you at the victory party." Lexi winced her eyes, trying to remember the night she first set sights on Bou.

"He calls me brother, but it's not by blood. Family is not always by blood, it's whom you make it with," Bou said while kissing the top of Lexi's head.

"Oh." Lexi looked on wide-eyed.

"After finding him abandoned and abused, my father gave me a brother. He became part of our family when we found him wandering in another pack's territory. Lexi, my name is Austin, not the Chimera. That is more like a title, and titles can be more for the books and not for my future sister-in-law." Austin smiled sweetly at his brother's destined mate.

"So he told you I'm his fated mate? Are you okay with that? You won't attack me as those southern pod tritons did on Mt.

Evens?" Lexi's breath caught as she remembered what had happened moments ago.

"Lexi, you're safe here in my home. No one with half a brain cell in the supernatural world would dare to come into this home and cause any harm. My mother is half siren and half wolf, so yes, I'm okay with the two of you being mates." Austin pulled both Lexi and Bou into a tight squeeze.

"Austin, you are squeezing a little too hard, bro." Bou struggled to break free of the iron grip that Austin held them in.

"Sorry, tell me why the southern water tribe attacked you and what tribe they belong to; what is it like, sixteen southern tribes?" Austin looked only at Lexi and ignored everyone else in the room.

"I don't know. These men had tribal tattoos on their left side of a sea turtle chasing a serpent from the shoulder to the elbow." Lexi illustrated it on her arm as she described the tattoo to Austin.

"Rita's tribe! I'll send them a message later, but first Danny will take the love birds to the spare room. So, Bou, you two settle in. We can talk in the morning. Lexi, if you need a salt-water dip, let me know. I can turn the large tub into seawater for you." Austin got up, walked to the fireplace, and faced the old weathered mirror.

"Show off! She's my girlfriend," Bou teased as he jokingly boxed Austin.

"Yeah, so what? I am the one with the gifts and talents," Austin teased back.

"You can keep your talents, brother. I got the good looks," Bou joked as he walked back over to Lexi and picked her up bridal style to carry her off to the spare room.

As the two followed Danny down the hall, Rebecca asked in a hushed tone, "What happened to all her wounds? I know shifters can heal fast, but that is far beyond any healing I have seen."

Austin turned to the old mirror over the fireplace. With a flick of his wrist, the mirror had ripples like a puddle of water. "Rita! We need to talk. NOW!" The waves in the mirror rippled with the flux of anger rolling off of Austin.

"Not now, Austin! My boys have fallen under dark magic! They were at supper when an unseen force attacked them out of nowhere." Rita came near the portal looking stressed out.

"It is called a return to sender, and it's not dark magic," Austin said, crossing his arms and looking down at Rita.

"Wait? What? Return to sender? How would you know that this is not dark magic?" It took Rita a moment before she realized. "It was you! You did this to my boys. Why Austin? We have done nothing to you or your family. Why would you attack us? I thought you were all about keeping the peace. Are you trying to test us for weaknesses to attack us and take over our territory?"

"Rita, those boys are suffering from return to sender. Think about that for a moment. They would have to have been the initial aggressors for my siren song to return to the sender. But they used one of my portals on Mt. Evens and attacked my soon-to-be sister-in-law." Austin was calming down as he explained things and noticed Rita's expression was calming too.

"How? Who?" Rita still had a blank stare on her face, unsure of where Austin was going. "Austin, you are an only child, so how would you have a soon-to-be sister-in-law?" She rested her hands on her hips.

"Lexi, from my mother's tribe, is the fated mate to my chosen brother. The adopted werewolf brother that worked the lookout point when we battled to save my mother." Austin took a drink from his beer and shot Danny a look as he walked down the hall from the guest room. "They taunted her, calling her a traitor, and attacked her using the sea portal on my family's lands." Unfortunately, Austin was cut off when one of Rita's boys came into the frame.

"That is because she is no better than a sea slug to muddle her blood with a flea bag."

"Jared, hush your mouth!" Rita attempted to hush her son.

"Why? He's no better mother. He is a mutt, and the only good thing is he can't have kids to spread that illness." Jared sneered at Austin.

"Austin, please don't take offense. I will work with him on correcting that mouth of his." Rita snatched her son up by the scruff of his neck. "Wait until your father hears of this. Austin is the Chimera wolf. He has power granted by the old gods, and you want to stand here and insult him. You attacked his family. You are lucky he only did a return to sender." Rita bowed her head.

"Austin, you're not taking this to the council of tribes, are you?"

"Rita, punishment has been served. I will take this no further. Please educate your boys. Enter my land and attack any of my pack, clan, or tribe again, and return to sender will be the least of your worries." Austin lifted his arm for them to see as he pulled at his trident tattoo, drawing out the physical trident.

"Yes, of course. Thank you for your leniency, Austin. My boys will receive punishment. I will not allow this to happen again. Once again, Austin, I'm sorry for their behavior. I hope your sister-in-law, Lexi, is going to be okay. Congratulations on the addition to the family. See that, Jared! I warned you the Goddess of the Sea blessed him." Rita smacked the back of both her son's heads, and they both looked at each other and bowed their heads to Austin.

"Sir, we are sorry. We will not trespass again on your lands or attack anyone without proper provocation," AJ said in a strained voice.

"Thank you. Sorry our visit couldn't have been under better circumstances, Rita," Austin said, bowing out of courtesy.

Moments later, the mirror was glass again, leaving the Fae speechless. Then, finally Austin turned in time to see the look of awe and complete shock on their faces.

O'Brien shuddered. "How?"

"I have more power than I allow people to know, sir. Rebecca, now you know what return to sender is; it inflicts the pain and torment back onto the assailant." Austin crossed the room to find Danny sitting in his oversized chair, pouring himself a tall glass of bourbon.

"That looks like it would be a handy siren song," Rebecca mused as she looked at her father, shooting daggers at him, remembering her childhood.

"That it is. Only hubby here doesn't approve of me using that song." Austin sat on Danny's lap and looked into his lover's eyes playfully, trying to look innocent.

"Sorry Austin, but it just feels wrong. I get it that people are being unjustly hurt all the time, but two wrongs don't make a right." Danny took a swig of his drink and started drawing circles on Austin's back.

"Danny, you know I only use it when I need to. I feel we should only use it when things like this happen." Austin nodded to the room between Lexi and Bou's room.

"My dear boy, I agree with your mate." O'Brien huffed and puffed out his chest, trying to regain his composure.

"Wait Austin, have you ever, you know, used it on Danny?" Rebecca smirked, thinking of all the things she would have used that gift to do to her Eric.

Before Austin could answer, Hypnoses cleared his throat

and spoke. "Well, it appears to be about that time, so we must get going."

Morpheus took a deep breath across his teeth. "Well, those vamps are going to be cranky. We have kept them asleep this long."

"It doesn't matter what they want, like, or feel. The blood-sucking leeches can return to being the undead and far from here." Hypnoses looked at his son and then at the door.

"Will there be any backlash from Absalom for doing this tonight, fellas?" Danny questioned, fearing the answer.

"I'm not worried about Mr. blood and fussy pants. Besides, he is too busy trying to court Selene."

Hypnoses made a gagging sound, showing his opinion on the bloodsucker trying to get with his oldest friend.

"That should prove interesting," Austin smirked, knowing Selene would have nothing to do with Absalom. "She is making him work for her attention."

"Hey, do I need to coax you to bed later, Austin?" Danny was now rubbing his hand up Austin's leg, more out of desire than just a casual touch.

"Never. You belong to me, Mr." Austin let out a low growl and leaned over to nibble Danny's bottom lip. "But right now, we have company, and you need to behave."

"Well, daughters, that is our cue. We need to let these fellas get some sleep." But, of course, O'Brien knew it was anything but sleep that Danny wanted at this very moment.

"But father—" Rebecca protested.

O'Brien raised one eyebrow at Rebecca, daring her to question his authority. "What is it, Rebecca?"

Rebecca took a step toward Eric and grabbed hold of his hand, blushing. "I just got him back, and you even admitted he is my mate. I want to go home with my boys." Rebecca smiled sweetly.

"Rebecca, I can't allow you," O'Brien chastised.

"Daddy," Rebecca whined.

"Sir, please, I want Rebecca as my wife. Please let me show her the home I've built for our son," Eric pleaded.

"Well, I..." O'Brien wavered.

"O'Brien," Austin teased, looking up at him while sitting on Danny's lap.

"Fine," O'Brien scoffed.

"Let's grab our boy, honey," Eric said joyfully, picking Rebecca up and spinning around the room.

"Better yet, Eric, I know he doesn't get to have many sleep-overs. How about Deven stays here tonight? You and Rebecca can pick him up in the morning. I'm sure the two of you need to get reacquainted." Austin gave a devilish wink.

"Thanks, man. You would do that for us?" Eric smiled ear to ear.

"Why not? You're practically part of the family now, Eric. Just don't expect me to forgive your mother." Austin's expression turned to stone.

"Wait, are you related to my Rebecca?" Eric looked on, confused.

"No silly, part of the supernatural family, and because your son is a hybrid, he falls under Austin's protection," Tatian chimed in, smiling. "Everyone in the supernatural world knows not to cross the Chimera.

CHAPTER 23
BOU

"Son, it is time we leave. He has toiled long enough." Hypnos nodded at his son and they both shimmered out of the room, leaving the house quiet until Eric felt the electric touch of Rebecca brush on his arm.

"Austin, thank you again for watching the little one. Now that we have fixed our issue, I hope the boys will get along. To be honest, I think my little boy has a crush on your little girl," Eric said, grinning.

"Oh, no. We cannot allow that to happen. She is my little princess. No boys, at least till college!" Danny growled out.

"Babe, stop. They are in grade school. Besides, if it's fate for them to be mates, then that's just how it is, so you can stop being a grumpy old man." Austin playfully backhanded Danny's chest.

Danny let out a playful growl. "Easy tiger, keep that up and we will end up with a new pup in the house."

"Well, on that note, Eric and Rebecca, have a good night. Don't do anything I wouldn't do," Austin said with a cocky grin.

"Austin, I have going on six years of being a good old boy to play catch up on," Eric said looking at Rebecca, who could only blush.

"Do you need a quick retreat home, Tatian?"

"Would you?" Tatian asked as she pulled her father to the closet door while Austin opened it to see the back gardens of his family home.

"Now wait just one minute," O'Brien started in, when Tatian pulled him into the portal to take him home, leaving his objection to fall on deaf ears.

"All right farm boy, how about we go for a roll in the hay." Rebecca smiled, poking Eric in his ribs.

"With pleasure," Eric replied, picking up Rebecca and walking out of the house, so that Austin was left to the whims of his mate.

"Well, would you look at the time? All of our guest have left. The kids are all tucked in. I think I will turn in for the night." Austin went to leave the living room when a powerful pair of arms grabbed him, pulling him back and tossing him onto the couch.

"Did I say you could leave, boy?" Danny growled into his ear as he pinned Austin down.

"Excuse me?" Austin said with a smirk.

Danny gave Austin a firm smack on his ass as he picked up his mate. "Excuse you for not addressing me properly? Perhaps, but you will still get spanked boy. You can pout all you want. I have put up with you and your constant games of turning me on and leaving me like a hot teapot. I am all steamed up and ready to shout." Danny seductively growled in Austin's ear as he had him lifted, and Austin wrapped his legs around Danny's waist.

"I think my husband has been singing songs with our daughter too much, you're saying them, and I love you for it, but it's not sexy." Austin looked into Danny's eyes while biting his lower lip.

"Stop biting that lip boy, it belongs to me." Danny quickly latched onto Austin's lips and started passionately kissing them.

Under protest from Austin, Danny carried him to the master bedroom; the furthest room from the children. "No need to have Deven woken up to our little antics," he said as he dropped Austin on the bed and ripped off his shirt. Austin took this as his chance to make a dash for the master bathroom, but he was not fast enough. Danny reached out and slapped his ass hard and firm.

Once Austin was subdued and laying down, Danny yanked him across the bed by his ankles.

"Shameful, my mate. Do you not love me?" Danny flipped him over to show his doe-eyed expression and make a mockery of his pouty lips.

"Don't you go start that again. You're the one who got all horned up." Austin teased Danny, running his finger along his clenched jaw.

"Excuses. Excuses. Austin, this was our date night. Your folks were to keep the kids. I don't care if our nest has children in it. I want quality time with my mate, and Adonis does as well. Trey needs to come out and play with his mate."

"You know as well as I do, those two can't be out with kids in the house," Austin chastised Danny lovingly.

Danny pushed him onto his back, and grabbed his ankles, licking from his ankle to his deep inner thigh. "Umm, you know the saying if you lick it, it's yours. Well, I have already bitten you, so this belongs to me." Danny gave a hard bite into Austin's deep inner thigh.

Austin buried his face deep into the pillow, stifling a soft moan.

"No, no, that won't do at all." Danny pulled the pillow away with a gentle growl, while his eyes turned deep onyx black. "I earned those moans. I want to hear them as I make you squirm while putting this mouth of mine to use."

"Danny, please," Austin whimpered as Danny ran his lips closer and closer to his groin.

Danny grasped the sides of Austin's boxers, looking up at Austin with an evil grin, and with one swift move, he ripped them off and tossed the scraps to the floor. Then he stuck out his tongue and ran it around his desired target, causing Austin to arch his back and grab the bed as shockwaves of pleasure ran over his body.

A loud cough suddenly caught the two off guard and Danny paused, looking at Austin, and trying to remember who was in the house. "Austin?"

"I told you," Austin sassed.

"Oh no, I wouldn't be a brat, Mr. you know what the punishment will be." Danny took Austin by his wrist and pinned him to the bed.

While the sounds were muffled, they could still be heard throughout the house. Lucky for the lovebirds though, the children were fast asleep and the only ones hearing the muffled cries of pain and pleasure were Bou and his destined mate, Lexie. Bou was in bed holding his mate to his chest, kissing the top of her head.

"I'm sorry Bou," Lexie whispered, as she held onto his arms that were wrapped around her snuggly.

"Why are you sorry, Lexie? You have done nothing wrong," Bou whispered sweetly in her ear, as he placed a kiss on her temple.

"But I have, because the first time we share a bed and it's like this." Lexi gestured to their fully clothed bodies.

"What, because we are at my older brother's house?" Bou evaded her intentions.

"No," Lexie whined.

"Because I can hear them going at it?" Bou pointed his thumb down the hall to Danny and Austin's room.

"Well, no. But really, you can hear them? They are going at it while they have a kid sleeping over and we're down the hall?" Lexie turned to face Bou with a questioning look.

"Yeah, you can't hear that?" Bou raised an eyebrow, questioning his mate's genuine lack of knowledge of werewolves.

"No Bou, I'm on land. I'm as good as a human. Now if we were underwater, you would be the one at a disadvantage. Besides, you're going to pick on the girl who was just beat up because her man is a sweaty, smelly werewolf?" Lexie pouted out her lower lip. "I'm still shook up, Bou."

"Lexie, you are my destined mate, like Danny is Austin's destined mate. We are a match for our mates. You are mine," Bou gently growled out. "You are safe in these arms, my little siren. I don't need to mate and mark you right away to be protective of you." Bou tilted her face to look him in the eyes as he placed a kiss on her quivering lips. "After all, like I said, you are MINE. Anyone touches you; I will snap them like a twig. Austin and Danny have taught me how to fight for what is mine."

"Bou, it feels like you're purring a little." Lexie smiled and nestled into his chest.

"Love, I'm a werewolf. We howl and growl, and we can bite and play hard. We don't purr," Bou growled out with a clenched jaw. Then he began playfully nipping at his mate's neck.

"Tell me, Bou..." Lexie gently whispered while running her hands along his arm.

Bou pulled her tighter into his embrace, kissing her neck and then her temple.

"Tell you what? How much I already feel about the mate bond? The pull of your soul to mine? How I feel as if time has stopped and I am the luckiest man alive?"

"Are you upset with me?" Lexie winced in anticipation of his response.

"After I just professed my love, you think I'm mad at you? Madly in love, yes, but mad at you? No Lexie, I'm not mad with you." Bou looked perplexed, as he tried to figure out what was going on in that beautiful head of hers.

"But Bou." Lexie pressed her back into Bou and could feel his arousal.

"Do you have seaweed in your ears?" Bou whisperingly growled while nipping her lobe. "Again, no, my little mate, I am not mad. But if you want this, wait till I put a ring on it."

"Bou, I've seen you naked before, when you shifted in front of me. Goddess knows you don't need a cock ring!" Lexie blushed, remembering the day Bou had shifted from a wolf into a man by the lake.

"Ha ha," Bou chuckled out. "Wrong kind of ring, but thanks for noticing."

"Wait, you're saying no sex till we're married?" Lexie sat up, looking at Bou in disbelief.

"Hey, call me old-fashioned. Most of the slutty werewolves take for granted the mate bond, but I am not one of them. I want more than just fate written in my heart to be yours. I want the world to see our ceremony, so everyone knows you are mine. Besides, with the two of us being from separate shifter worlds, the customs are bound to be different." Bou propped himself up on one arm, looking back into Lexie's eyes.

"I have no problem with waiting." Lexi kissed Bou on his

nose and snuggled back into bed so he could wrap his muscular arms around her.

"Little one, that will not sway me. Besides, I thought you were sore and tired." Bou nestled up to her, breathing on her neck.

"I'm just snuggling. It feels so safe and warm in those arms."

"In my arms, you will always be safe." Bou gently placed a kiss on her neck, taking a deep breath and breathing in her scent.

"So, Bou, the Chimera is the protector of all who are mixed species. Our kids will be..." Lexie trailed off in thought.

"Well, my love, you're already talking about pups! We have yet to even have a lot of time together. Regardless, it warms my heart. You're already talking about giving me pups. To answer your question, Lexi, you're pure mermaid, I am pure werewolf. So our kids will be blended, but what powers manifest as dominant I do not know. Austin is my adopted brother, but our pups will be as much of a priority as his own. He is very protective with children. Yes, as blended children they fall under his protection. When the gods of old were free from their prison, they gifted him and Danny with powers beyond a normal werewolf couple. But with that great power came the responsibility of protecting those who cannot protect themselves. It was very much Austin's idea."

"Well, that is good to know." Lexi let out a deep, gentle sigh.

"Now, I know that's not everything in that mind of yours." Bou drew circles on Lexi's arm while his eyes danced over her body.

"Well, erm. Can..." Lexi paused briefly before blurting out, "Can you tell me about your family?"

"Austin?" Bou arched his brow questioningly at his mate.

"No. Not Austin. Your other family. You know your birth parents?" Lexi turned and laid flat on her back, looking up into Bou's eyes.

"Okay, yeah. I don't call them family, though." Bou half heart grinned, wondering where his little mate was taking the conversation.

"I know it's a sore subject and all, but I would like to know more about your past. We share a destined future. Don't you think I should know all I can about you?" Lexi pouted, batting her long lashes at Bou.

Bou took a haggard breath before he began. "I am originally from a pack near the border of California and Mexico. The pack I was born into seemed quite content with being, for lack of a better term, pirates. They used to roam around and raid other packs. Some folks would say that that made them rogues, but it's not true. Rouges, my little mermaid, are wolves who can't conform to a pack and follow wolf law. My pack was indeed a pack, but a pack of outlaws. They were cruel, and anyone who would not partake in their thievery and down-right criminal behavior, got beat up. The Alpha of that pack considered himself a king more than an Alpha. Our pack land was covered in traps and hidden underground networks of caves and tunnels. I could never prove it, but I think the Desert Shadow Pack worked with a drug cartel. All the males were separated from their families by age six and forced to train every day. They turned the girls more often than not into..." Bou's voice cracked, as he didn't want to finish his thoughts.

"Bou, you don't have to finish. I knew a leader who treated his female pod members like they were second class." Lexi brushed her palm on Bou's cheek.

"When the females came of age, if they were lucky and found their destined mates was one thing, but any she-wolf who was unclaimed by the age of twenty was forced into the brothels. I was just a teen when I ran away. I couldn't do it anymore. They wanted us to fight to the death because someone spread a rumor that a male was born that would one day take Zeek's kingdom from him. Oddly enough, I had drifted onto Danny's pack territory when Daniel found me. He adopted me on the spot, stopping the pack from taking me and locking me up as a runaway, or worse, a rogue. So my love, that, in a nutshell, is my life before Austin and Danny. Don't worry, I have not heard from Zeek or that horrible pack since then. I'm sure they all assumed I died in the desert." Bou kissed the top of Lexi's head and snuggled in for the night.

"Oh Bou, I feel terrible that all of this has happened to you. You went from that pack, to part of a crazy, multiple breed family that ended up battling a Devil and his supporters. Not to mention dragons and gods of the old world." Lexi gently rested her hand on Bou's chest, feeling his heart race under her touch.

"Don't." Bou paused, biting into his lower lip as he felt the electricity of the mate bond dance upon his skin.

"What? Wait? Why are you?" Lexi pulled back to look Bou head on.

"Don't, Lexi. All that shit happened for a reason. If not, then I never would have found you. Now put your head down and go to sleep."

"Bou, are you?"

"Yes, Lexi. At the moment I am resisting plunging my raging bone deep into you till you're screaming my name. So please forgive me and my massive hard on." Bou tried to scoot away because he could feel the heat radiating off her core, and her flower was giving off such a delightful scent, making the ache in his groin that much harder to ignore.

"It feels so big and so tempting to stop pulling away," Lexi said, blushing.

"Lexi, Stop. I am warning you. Besides, you have already seen me nude." Bou scoffed, remembering the time he had shifted in front of her and had to cover his package.

"Can't blame a girl for trying." Lexi traced her way from Bou's lips, down to his chiseled chest, and across his nipple.

"Keep it up, my naughty little mate. I'll make you wait longer," Bou growled huskily into her ear.

"Do you think I can't take matters into my own hands?" Lexi put her two fingers together and put them under the sheets when Bou grabbed her hand.

"Bad girl, did Daddy tell you that you could release the pressure?"

"Umm, no Daddy." Lexi became turned on even more now by her werewolf mate.

"Then be a good girl for Daddy and go to bed. You don't want me to spank you. Not this kind of spanking. Come now, let's go to sleep. The George-Blazek home wakes up early regardless of when you go to sleep." Bou nipped at her ear as she settled in for the night.

CHAPTER 24
PROTEST AT SCHOOL

While the world slept, Karen lived out a never-ending nightmare. She watched as her worst fears kept coming to life repeatedly. "Mr. Piper, would you?" Karen stopped mid-sentence as she caught Mr. Piper, the English teacher, making out with Jack Fanning, the new fire chief. "NO!" Karen let out a blood-curdling scream.

"What the actual fuck, Karen?" Jack spat out after pulling his red puffy lips out from Derik Piper's teeth.

"You. You. The two of you. You are filthy unholy." Karen shuddered as she fell backward.

"We have been together for years, Karen. What does it matter?" Mr. Piper questioned her biblical ramblings.

"This is blasphemy," Karen started out. "I will condemn you to all eternity in the fires of hell."

"Well thank *God*," Jake sarcastically emphasized *God* just to watch Karen's face turn a deeper shade of red, "I know how to manage fires."

"You think you're real funny? You will be out of a job."

Karen poked her finger into Jake's chest. "You won't be teaching much longer, Mr. Piper. You and your whore of a fireman would be better off leaving this town. We are a good Christian town. We have no place here for your kind."

"Our kind? Funny how that little black book is a weapon of war when you deem it necessary, but when others bring up verses you choose to ignore—"

Derik cut Jake off, placing his hand on his shoulder. "It's pointless. This woman is the queen of cancel culture in this town. Let's not fight." Derik took a deep breath and let it out slowly.

"See Jake, why don't you run along and listen to the teacher while he still has a job? It's a hard lesson, but I run this town. People like you and people like this..." Karen poked Derik hard in the chest.

"Bitch, hands off my lover." Jake reached out for Karen's hand.

"People like him should never be allowed to teach." Karen's hand was ripped away from Derik's chest by Jake, who shoved her away.

"Don't you have a fire station to be at? Oh wait, not after you caused a scene by performing what looked like lude activities here in a public park. Not to mention assaulting the mayor's wife, who was only asking you to stop and not do this in public with children around." Karen smiled a malicious smile, letting out a dark, evil cackle.

"That's not even how it happened, Karen," Jake protested.

"Really? That's how I saw it happen, and let's face it, who are the people going to believe? Me..." Karen placed her hand on her chest, smiling. "Or a pair of sexual deviants that should be locked up for the rest of their lives."

Karen turned to call over one of the officers to arrest the

men for their lude activities and for the assault. Her eyes were about to bug out of her head as she watched her pastor making out with not one but two of the police officers. "Father Myers!" Karen screamed out.

Karen woke up screaming, looking at her bedside clock as it read midnight. Her husband burst into her room with a bat, ready to strike whoever must have broken into their home to scare his wife.

"Honey, what's wrong?"

"Oh Jack, I had the worst nightmare. We got a new fire chief. I picked him because he was qualified, of course, but he had the same name as you and he was strong, and I just knew I could set him up with Tammy from church."

"That doesn't sound bad. What happened? Did he die in a fire?"

"No, he's gay!" Karen wailed.

"So, you want to hire another gay guy to work in the fire department?" Jack asked, confused more than before.

"No, I caught him and the English teacher, Mr. Piper, making out at the park. I warned them that that behavior is not fitting for our town and it needed to stop post haste. Jake did not like that and he shoved me to the ground. When I could get up to find an officer, I found two making out with Father Myers!"

"Now, now. You know Father Myers is far from gay, and I highly doubt he would make out with two male cops. Obviously, you have had a lot to go on today. Let me tuck you in and try to get some sleep."

"I'm worried that they will overrun our town with those people." Karen bit into her lip as flashes of her nightmare resurfaced.

"Oh, dear, try to put it out of your mind. Get some rest. We have work ahead of us if you and I are to save this sinful town." Jack kissed the top of her head.

"Jack."

"Yes, my love?"

"Don't go." Karen's eyes pleaded with him to stay.

"But I thought my snoring kept you up at night? That's why I have slept in the guest room for the last ten years." Jake looked down at his wife lovingly.

"I don't care about the snoring; I just want to wake up in the arms of the man God gave me." Karen pulled back the sheets to invite him to bed.

"I would love to join you in bed tonight dear. First thing in the morning, we will call all your sewing circle ladies, and we will start a campaign to ban the gay lifestyle. It is unholy, and we can't have them take over our town." Jack climbed into bed, kissing his wife and snuggling next to her for the first time in ten years.

The night was fleeting, and Jack's moment of bliss holding his beloved Karen was over with dawn's early light. He quietly slipped out of Karen's arms, made her breakfast, and brought it to her in bed. "Wake up sunshine, we have a lot to do today if we're going to get our town back on track with good family values," Jack said while setting up her breakfast tray.

"Jack, sweetheart, you are the best husband a woman could ever ask for. You made me feel safe last night, and now you made me breakfast," Karen said while sitting up, looking at the French toast and two poached eggs on her plate.

"Anything for you, my love. Now, let's get those freaks out of our town," Jack said while walking up to the closet to get dressed.

"Where do we need to start?" Karen said, taking her first bite into the French toast.

"I called your friend, that Darla lady, and she is getting a few of the church ladies together. We're to meet up at Sister Patterson's house to get the protest signs ready. I have already signed an approval for the group's protest. We put it in Sister Patterson's name so as not to draw attention to ourselves. Can't have the folks think I am playing favorites." Jack struggled with his tie as Karen walked up behind him to help him tie it.

"You were never any good at these things," she jokingly scoffed.

"And you, my wife, have magical hands that can make this crazy mess look right. I guess we're just made for each other." Jack turned and kissed her on the forehead. "Okay, you're all finished, so I will run the dishes down, take a shower, and see you downstairs in fifteen?" Jack raised an eyebrow at his wife.

"Very well. When wicked is afoot, one cannot drag their feet. Hurry along Jack, I need to shower. Go on, get, and stop staring at me like that," Karen blushed.

In one hour's time, the protest group had grown in numbers. Almost all the church members came together to support the cause. Within the second hour, they launched the protest onto school board grounds. Protesters held signs declaring war on sin.

"Pray. Pray. The Lord knows, the sinners got to go," the group chanted as they marched up and down the block surrounding the scout campus building waving signs saying "no gays here."

Meanwhile, as the town was waking up, the protest showed on the news, the news that Danny and Austin had just turned on while the family sat down to breakfast.

"Today in local news, we are standing here, outside the scout campus office, as a massive protest wraps around the block. It appears they are protesting the school allowing same-sex couples access to the students. Let's see if we can get an interview." The news reporter walked up to Darla.

"Ms., can you tell us what brought this on?"

"Yes, yes, I can. I have been part of this community for a long time, and I have fought and fought against the system that has become plagued with sin and sinners. We have people parading around as married couples, and they are two men or two women, and they say they are both parents to the same student or students. NO! The school needs to enforce the policy one mother and one father. They should also not allow PDA. I have seen couples kissing. It is wrong. We do not need to have two men kissing in front of the students. Nor do we need to have teachers teaching and having their same-sex partners' pictures on their desk. We are corrupting these children." Darla finally ran out of breath.

"So, this protest is against same-sex couples?"

"Yes, I would think the signs and our chant made that clear."

"Crystal."

"Well, if you will excuse me, I need to get back. My sisters and brothers need me in this fight for morality." Darla turned curtly and walked away, joining in the endless chants.

"It appears this has not gone unnoticed. We have Sherriff Tate on scene."

"Folks, do you have a permit? Yes, you have the constitutional right to protest, but the town charter says you need a permit for a crowd this size," Tate said, ignoring the television crew.

"Here you go, Sherriff Tate," Karen said, waving the permit at him like she was waving scraps at a dog.

"Karen, I should have known," Tate said smiling.

"Sir, whatever do you mean by that? I am just a God-fearing woman, and I have taken up with my sisters to protect our youth. This protest is led by Sister Patterson. She teaches our church Sunday school." Karen handed over the permit, and turned to smile at the reporter. "Thank you so kindly for coming out and making our cause known. It truly is a blessing to have the local news see this as newsworthy."

"Well, Karen, everything looks in order. As you know, stay out of the streets and private property. You are clear on what is public land?" Tate shot her a look that said what he couldn't actually say at the moment.

"Yes sir, Mr. Tate. Would you care to join our demonstration? It would be lovely to have the support of our local law enforcement officers," Karen said, in a sickly-sweet voice.

"Mam, while I can respect you for having your views, as long as I wear this badge, I cannot stand with you," Tate replied. "But I will say this, with or without my badge: I would never get behind anyone or thing that spoke hate out of one side of their mouth and turned around and preached about love and acceptance on the other."

"Miss, what are your group's desired outcomes?" the reporter jumped in.

"We want the school board to have a meeting with the parents again, the biological families of our students, and address our concerns." Karen smiled at the camera.

"So, you are now publicly announcing that you don't want the opposite side to have a say, because on October the 5th you had a meeting that got crashed by a same-sex couple, and your meeting ended with a result you are not happy with?" Tate rebuffed.

"I thought you didn't get involved, officer?" the reporter questioned.

"I typically won't, but this lady used her husband to push for a private public meeting. Basically, she let everyone know except the family she was going after, and it did not work out so well last time now did it, Karen? So you try again by drawing a more public audience, and now you are openly declaring war on same-sex couples. You want them to lose rights at school. What's next, hospitals? Do you need them to go around with a logo on them so the banks and restaurants can refuse service? Is that the hill you're going to stand on? Is that what the town I love will become?" Tate looked at her with horror in his eyes.

"Well, if they don't like good moral values, there are other towns, and if you don't want to stand with us, I'm sure the good people can elect a new Sheriff. Have a wonderfully blessed day."

"Wow, those are some good values you have. It's funny because my values tell me I need to treat other people the way I want to be treated." Tate walked away, shaking his head and texted Austin and Danny. "*Avoid the scout building. Karen is trying to start crap once again about same-sex couples.*" He waited, as he saw three little dots showing a response.

"*She wants a war; well I guess we have a few options.*" Austin was the first to respond.

"Danny, what does this lady have against us that much that she has to go after our children?" said Austin to his husband.

"Austin, she was this way when I dated you. Do you really think she would have changed after all these years?" Danny flipped over the pancakes before yelling for the kids. "BREAKFAST!"

The house shook and came to life as three hungry boys came charging down the hall into the kitchen, while Aurora took her time gracefully entering the room.

"Such pigs. Father, are all men like this when food is involved?"

"BURRP." Logan let loose a volley of belches.

"Cool, that was a good one. Wait watch this." Deven leaned to one side and a firecracker of a fart ripped out of him.

"Better check your shorts, kiddo. We can't send you home with skid marks." Austin laughed.

"Dad is used to it. We have belching and farting contests all the time. I guess that will change now that mom's back in our lives. Sir, can you tell me about my momma?" Deven asked as he picked up his glass of orange juice.

"Well, buddy, that neckless you wear is a special gift from your mother. NEVER take it off, okay?" Austin explained, when suddenly a rapid knock on the door made everyone jump.

Danny reached the door shirtless and in gray sweatpants. "Hello, come in. We just started breakfast."

"Honey, who is it?" before he could finish, Rebecca came running in to cover Deven in kisses.

"Were you a good boy for mommy and daddy? Did you behave and listen to mommy's friend?"

"Mommy?" Deven tested the word out as it was still strange for him to say.

"Austin, I see you've got the news on. That's why we came over so soon. I'm so sorry, I thought my mom would have given up on this after last night's events," Eric said, while tossing Deven's bed head into even more of a mess.

"Well, we have options. We can fight them on this. It would be a long, expensive court case, but then the town would raise taxes to cover the cost. We could also go back to home schooling the kids," Danny spoke out as he poured the adults coffee.

"She's not only targeting you as parents, but it's anyone and everyone LGBT. The English teacher Mr. Patterson, she just got him fired. If she doesn't have dirt on you, she has no problem making it up. Mother has done that for years." Eric rolled his eyes.

"Daddy, is Grammy being bad?" Deven asked while he looked at the paused image on the television.

"Yeah, sorry pal. Grammy is being very mean, and she is telling lies to make herself feel better," Eric said while squatting next to him and brushing his bed head down.

"Should we do something? Is there anything we can do to help?" Rebecca questioned.

Austin turned up the television again, and they all looked on in horror as several school staff members were being fired.

"Here at scout the people have spoken out about who they want teaching their children. With that in mind, any same-sex parents will now be limited, so only one of them is listed as the legal parent. They will need to list the other birth parent. To keep things fair, any student of a single-family home needs to have both parents listed as well," Dr. Johnson announced to the gathering crowd.

"Wait, that's not what I wanted. My Deven," Karen gasped.

"Well, you should be so proud, Karen. You got what you wanted. All these nice people are out of a job, and now even your own grandson cannot go to school here." Tate shook his head and picked up a phone call.

"Babe, yes, I know I need to play nice, but tell that to this devil of a woman. How do you know what I said? What wait, I'm still on camera! Oh, I need to go love. I will see you in a few." Tate turned several shades of red as he hastened away.

"This has nothing to do with my grandson," Karen called out to Sheriff Tate as he took off to his patrol car. The news crew cut off their cameras and wrapped things up, as the principal walked over to Karen.

"Well, Mrs. Matheson, the Sheriff is not completely wrong. You brought to light a wonderful position that both parents need to be listed on birth certificates, while highlighting the need for everyone to be out in the open. Deven has no mother listed on his paperwork, thus, as of tomorrow, he is no longer enrolled in our school. The good news is, the George-Blazek kids won't be allowed at school either. I say it's an overall win. If you can bring the correct documentation for Deven's birth certificate, we can get him back in school as soon as possible." Dr. Johnson turned and left Karen at a loss for words.

CHAPTER 25

HOME SCHOOL

"Austin, I'm truly sorry for all the trouble my mother has caused," Eric said while picking up Deven.

"Daddy, why is Grammy so mean?"

"Deven buddy, I don't know, but we will get to the bottom of all this drama. Did you like spending the night? I was a little worried since you guys fought at school." Eric shifted Deven in his arms.

"We're cool now, Dad. I was only mean cause Grandma said I had to be. But now that I spent the night, it's super fun. We played some games. It was great." Deven laughed while looking at both Logan and Ethan.

"Boys?" Danny questioned.

"What Dad, we played a game to see who could fart the longest and who could fart the loudest," Logan said, while picking up an apple.

"Logan, buddy, we had this talk. You can't play fart games. It's not polite," Danny chastised.

"Well, you can't tell us you played the fart dart game and

not tell us who won," Austin chimed in as he prepared breakfast.

"I DID!" Deven yelled out. "I won both in one fart!"

"Well, I have breakfast ready. Come join us." Austin plated the table.

"Now boys, remember, we don't have a lot of time together." Rebecca looked down at her watch.

"Rebecca, sit down. Your father and sister will be here in a few to have breakfast with us. They wanted time with Deven as well." Danny pulled up more chairs at the table.

"Danny, go get dressed please. While you're headed to our room, knock on Bou's door and wake the lovebirds," Austin said with a smile on his face.

"Austin, we were just so comfortable. Why are we up!" Bou pouted as he dragged his feet across the floor into the dining room where breakfast was set up for everyone.

"You know in this house we have breakfast together. If you want to go back to bed afterward, you can. In the meantime, pull up a chair, and I expect your soon-to-be wife will be out soon." Austin shot an Alpha look at his brother.

"She's on her way, but she might need a change of clothes," Bou said when he heard Lexi shriek.

"AUSTIN! I LOVE YOU!"

Lexi came strutting out in a pair of dark denim Capri pants and a Cashmere sweater with a pair of black pumps on. "Austin, it's just my size. This outfit is amazing!"

"Anything for my soon-to-be sister-in-law."

"Well, dig in, folks, before it gets cold." Danny directed the kids.

The phone rang and Danny went to answer as the broom closet opened to Tatian and her father walking in waving to Danny and taking their places at the table. Danny paced the living room and looked up at the television, then again at his mate and family in the other room. "I understand that this may be your position, but be ready. We want everything in writing. Form due cause down to every statement, rule etc. Damn right we have a lawyer. My father and I will represent not only my family, but every family you try to push out of a public school system." Danny hung up the phone and muttered cuss words under his breath.

"That's ten bucks in the swear jar, Danny," Austin called out.

"Oh, come on, I was not even near the kids!"

"House rules are house rules!" Aurora yelled out.

"You heard your little princess," Austin said, smiling while shaking the swear jar.

"Better keep that jar out, Austin, that was the school. Well, more like Dr. Johnson. He called to inform us in case we were not already aware of the news. Our children will not be going to scout public schools because of recent events."

"My mother." Eric shook his head.

"Well, he also informed me that it is not only our family affected by this new ruling. It will bar any student that does not have both parents listed on the birth certificate and enrollment papers from attending."

"That's just wrong!" Rebecca cried out. "That woman would do this to even our son? I know I am not listed on Deven's papers, but we can fix this. I won't let that evil woman mess with my son's education."

"Well, we will just home school the kids until they settle this, Danny." Austin didn't seem fazed about the situation.

"About that, any student who cannot attend in person, cannot and will not be eligible for home schooling through the scout public school system."

"Are you telling me we have to go back to Colorado?" Austin's voice caught a little, thinking of all the people he would have to say goodbye to because of Karen.

"We will get through this, Austin, but let's finish our meal and try to have a good day today." Danny sat down and loaded up his plate with French toast and fresh fruit.

A knock on the door caught everyone off guard. Bou got up to answer and was already being shoved aside by Karen.

"Where is he! Where is my little man? I Know you evil people have my grandbaby," Karen screamed as she pushed her way into the home.

"Karen, stop where you are! You are violating protection orders, and you are forcing your way into my home. Leave before I call law enforcement." Danny stood with his phone in hand.

"MOM!" Eric's voice boomed over everyone, causing even Karen to jump.

"Wait, what? You're here with Deven? Why?" Karen's face turned white.

"Because Mother, I chose my side of this war, and it's not with you. The people I let you keep me from were the very ones I needed to find Deven's mother. Yes, they helped find Rebecca. So I will stand with them." Eric crossed his arms and Deven wrapped his arms around his father's legs.

"Oh, you found her. That's good. We just need to get all the papers together and they will let Deven back into school!" Karen clapped her hands together.

"No, Deven will not go to school as long as you keep the George-Blazek kids out." Eric looked at Danny and Austin. "These guys are now my family, and I think I will move with Rebecca back home. Deven, what would you say about a little adventure?"

"As long as I get both you and mommy and can still have

sleepovers with my friends." Deven looked at Logan and Ethan.

"Dude, you can sleep over. Just don't eat whatever you had last night, king gas bag," Logan teased.

"Excuse you, don't speak to my grandson that way!" Karen chastised.

"Excuse me, Grams, but I think Mr. George-Blazek asked you to leave. I am with my friends and my parents. You are a bad, nasty lady and you need to leave." Deven pointed to the door.

Karen turned and glared at everyone, then she left with her head down. She walked out to her car and called Darla. "Darla, my grandson, son, and Deven's mother are all at Austin and Danny's house. I got kicked out. Eric is talking about taking my grandson out of state. Yes, I can meet you for brunch. Thank you, Darla."

Meanwhile, inside the house, the families gathered around to discuss the future they would work on together.

"So, this is my grandson's human grandmother?" O'Brien looked curtly at Eric.

"Sorry, we can't always pick our family."

"Blood does not make a person's family. It's how they are involved in your life. Eric, she can be your birth mother, but it looks like you have a family here." Bou smiled and raised his glass of orange juice.

"Cheers, here is to the family we choose and to making a better life for those we love." Eric raised his glass to Bou and his new family.

"Austin, we will take the kids to Colorado and register them there. In fact, call your bath daddy Kev up. He is an Alpha of the Celtic Rhino Pack. The pack moved here from Ireland about a hundred years ago." Danny looked up at his mate.

"I see. We will teach our kids in a werewolf school until we get this figured out. I will reach out to Kev later today. Besides, I need to put in a new order, since the kids got into my bath bomb collection." Austin shot the boys a look.

"So, this school. Is it only for werewolves, or could my son go as well? I mean, if you're okay with that, Rebecca?" Eric took her hand and placed a kiss.

"If Alpha Kevin will let him attend, I have no issue, but he will have to take up some lessons at home to learn about his Fae power." Rebecca looked at her father.

"It is settled. I accept you two as fated mates. I just want that woman to have nothing to do with my grandson if she is going to act that way. Tatian, my dear, I need to leave and plan for your children to return home, and for young Deven to have his tutor." King O'Brien stood up and walked to the portal.

"Grandpa, wait!" Deven ran up to his grandpa and gave him a big hug.

King O'Brien smiled, as his grandson wrapped around his leg. "Thank you so much, Deven. You have made this old man happy again."

"That settles it. I will have Kevin's school contact this school and get the student records transferred along with Deven's. We will get this sorted out. I'm glad that this week is teachers in service and holiday break, so the kids won't be missing many lessons."

"Breakfast has been fun, Austin, but if we're going to do this, I need to get some things settled and see if we need to get a rental property in Kev's pack territory. Bou, how do you feel about staying here and taking care of our house while we are away dealing with all these school issues?" Austin asked his brother.

"Lexi, how do you feel about being here for a while? I won't make any choices without talking it over with you." Bou looked lovingly at his mate.

"Bou, I am part of this family now, so yes, we can stay here and care for their home while we plan our own one. I just need to figure out some clothes." Lexi bit her lip.

"Lexi, we're going shopping." Austin pulled out his charge card and Danny just shuddered.

"While you all go out shopping, I guess I can start looking at rentals. Austin, care to open a portal to Celtic Rhino Pack? I will even get a couple of his bundle boxes." Danny walked up, kissed Austin, and briskly went to the master bath to get ready for the day. "Kids, get ready. We are going to see family today and getting out of town for a while."

"Daddy, I know mommy just got back in our lives, but I finally made real friends." Deven's lip quivered.

"Well, my little man, we need to go so they can get their day started, and maybe we can meet up later. Hey Austin, how much would it cost us to live near you all in Colorado? I'm sure the pack doesn't want a human on its territory." Eric looked down at the ground.

"Kev loves everyone. As long as the people in his territory respect everyone else, he has no issues. I will have Danny find a few listings and see what we can do for your family." Austin ushered the children to their rooms to get ready for their trip.

"Kids, go shower, and hands off my steamers. Get ready and be in the living room in fifteen minutes. Eric, here is my cell phone number. Call us later and we can chat. Deven, little man, you are welcome to spend the night anytime where we are staying."

Tatian stood up. "Well, I will take my leave, Austin. It seems like we all have a bit of a full plate. I need to go home and get ready for my kids to come home, and you all need to find a new home for your kids."

"Tatian, I'm sorry. Tell my folks we will be up to see them soon. Kev's territory is not that far from the clan's territory."

"I will Austin. Rebecca, I am so proud of you. You have your family, and once I get home I will have mine again finally." Tatian slipped through the portal to the garden of Mt. Evens Clan.

CHAPTER 26
GOOD ENOUGH

Austin picked up the phone, and paced the living room that was now cluttered with kids toys and clothes. Looking at the phone one last time, he called up Kev to negotiate housing. "Alpha," Austin started off with his usual chipper voice.

"Alpha? Buddy, don't call me that. It's Kev or bath daddy. You're a friend. No need to be so formal," Kev said while walking across the parking lot to his condo.

"Only being formal because I have a formal request." Austin quietly bit his lip, nervously twisting it between his teeth.

"Oh, a hum. Let me get my serious face on," Kev snickered, enjoying that he couldn't help but tease Austin.

"Kev..." Austin allowed himself to relax and fall into the conversation with nothing more than one last deep breath.

"Austin, what can I do for you?" Kev's voice was warm and soothing.

"Remember when I told you about that bitch Karen and how I was not looking forward to dealing with her again?"

"Do I need to send some help?" The change in tone could have cut the tension like a knife.

"Not exactly the help we're looking for right now, although the thought has crossed my mind. I need to teach the kids how to better manage anger and problematic people."

"Austin, what is it? You can tell me; we are friends, and I told you I am always here for you?"

"My clan seeks safe harbor." Austin finally let it slip out with a defeated breath.

"What are they kicking you out of Genesis Moon territory? I'll come crack heads open, I swear. I have no problem doing that. I don't care if your new Alpha has my name."

"No, it's not the pack. It's the townsfolk. They are passing anti LGBTQ laws and rules at the school. We can't list both Danny and I as the parent of our kids. I can't enroll them unless they have a birth mother and birth father listed on the birth certificates. We can't even home school them. The same rules even outlawed us doing that."

"Ah, and you don't want clan issues with your parents' side, so you seek my pack? The answer is yes, Austin. I will set you guys up with a pack house on the resort ridge to give you all some privacy, but still under our protection."

"Thanks Kev." Austin took in a deep breath and let it out slowly.

"There is more, isn't there Austin?" Kev's voice remained flat and void of emotion.

"I have one tiny wincey favor more, Alpha." Austin bit his lip, looking up at Rebecca and Eric.

"Austin spit it out." Kev drummed his thumbs on his steering wheel.

"Yes, Kev."

"Austin loves you, pal, but it's never small when you call it small. Last time I ended up having a sleepover at my house where your three little ankle biters used fifteen bath bombs in the hot tub!" Kev laughed, remembering the night Logan had dumped all fifteen in and cannon balled them into the middle of all the suds.

"Right yeah, I know. Karen has a son who wants to come with my family."

"What! You want me to allow a human to stay in werewolf territory?"

"Well, it would be him, his Fae mate, and their son."

"Wait, hold up. You're telling me hell hag Karen has a son who got himself a Fae wife, has a halfling son, and that he'd rather hang out with werewolves? How on God's green earth did he get a Fae to fall for him?"

"Eros rose bush on Mt. Evens had something to do with it, but anyway, he is getting brought up to speed and his son falls under Chimera protection, because he is half human, half Fae. It's not safe for him yet among the Fae, and it's no longer safe with the vampires near our territory."

"Malcolm and his blood suckers still hanging out? I would have thought we'd have pulled them back to their little strip of land, Daddy."

"Not quite. Elena has helped to keep the peace, but as you know, every family has their share of troublemakers. I can't risk one of them finding a defenseless Fae child."

"I have no issue with helping your newly found friends, but if his mother shows up on my territory, I won't give her any special treatment. Trespassers are Trespassers," Kev said through gritted teeth.

"That's fine and very agreeable by everyone." Austin looked around to make sure no one objected.

"Send me current information on everything and everyone: photos, dates of birth etc. I will have my mother contact and get transcripts, and if they try to pull any crap, I will have my dad get involved, since he stepped down as acting Alpha he took over the school with Mom."

"Oh, that will prove fun for the boys. I know they have your dad wrapped around their little paws." Austin started laughing, knowing Alpha Dean loved the kids and teased Kev about when he would have a pup of his own.

"Think that's funny? Well, I will just have to make sure the boys get an extra surprise each. Oh, and I can't forget about the little princess." Kev had a dark laughter break out.

"Kev, remember? It's your pack house. If they flood it with bath bombs, do you think your mom will hold us accountable?"

"Shut up and get your family up here and away from those redneck idiots. Regardless, I will set you up real nice."

"Kev, you have a business to run." Austin gave off his dad's voice.

"I know, and you and your other half both have businesses as well. While you're here, I might need to woo some of your major clients. Unless you want to bring your companies here..." Kev attempted to use his most suggestive voice.

"We can discuss that over dinner in a couple of days. I have to get the kids ready, and I need to get the house in order. Thanks once again, Kev. I will get all that you requested sent over in a few hours." Austin hung up the phone as the kids came running out fully dressed. "Perfect timing, with two minutes to spare."

"Yes, I told you Logan, if we used Dad's master shower with the two heads and sissy used the hall shower, we all could get done faster."

"BOYS." Austin's voice went up.

"Daddy, no shower steamers were harmed this time. I can assure you," Logan said, while raising his hands up in defense.

"Okay, well, we're going up to the school to see Ms. States."

The children all jumped for joy in unison. "We love Ms. States."

"Well, Ms. States is going to let us into the classroom so we can clean out your cabinets," Austin explained as he got eye level with the kids, adjusting their clothing so they didn't look like they'd dressed themselves.

"Daddy? Why are we going to school to take our stuff out? Do we have to leave because of Deven's grumpy old grandma?" Aurora asked, tapping her foot on the ground while crossing her arms.

"Well, it is a little more complicated than that, and it's more of a grownup issue. But once daddy gets home and we take care of a few things, we can settle all of this and try to explain what's going on."

Austin stood up and gathered his thoughts. "Bou, you and Lexi hang out here for now. I will be back with the kids in I hope less than an hour, but I know Ms. States will want to have some goodbye time with the kids."

"Sure bro, but are you not going to call Mom and Dad and let them know what's going on? After all, you're moving back up near them but not back onto the territory. Don't you think you might hurt Mom's feelings?"

"Bou, that is a conversation us adults will have later when the kids are all busy."

"Wait, we are moving again!" Aurora huffed and stomped across the room, making it shake until pictures fell off the walls.

"Damn it, Bou!" Austin glared at his brother, as he stood there listening to his little girl have a meltdown.

"Sorry, bro." Bou nervously smiled as he saw his future before him.

"Kids, out to the car now, we don't have time for fits. Keep it up and I will send you to Grandma Amy to clean the chicken coops." Austin raised his eyebrow at his little girl and a sudden chill filled the air as the two power houses, father vs daughter collided.

Aurora stomped off to the car, slamming the door behind her and leaving the boys to look at each other, before they shook their heads and tiptoed to the car to await their father.

"Bou, you owe me a month's worth of babysitting for the melt down you just started. This is just the tip of the iceberg. We are in for a world of screaming and crying and Goddess only knows what else."

"Austin, buddy, I'm so sorry. I will so do whatever you want." Bou started picking up the room, trying to change the subject.

"It's bad enough, Bou, that I am struggling to keep the clan and packs from fighting. As the Chimera, I am supposed to help these people, and all they have been doing is fighting. Now I have the issue of people attacking my family to deal with. I feel like I'm running away and it makes me feel like even more of a failure. Not only as the Chimera but as a father." Austin pinched his nose and took a deep breath.

"Austin, just chill out. We will all get through this together. Just one day at a time. But I will tell you this: if you wait any longer, I'm sure our little princess will eat your car."

"Crap, I can't have her destroying the car. I swear last time she tore up two tires before we got her to stop. Bou, I'll catch you later." Austin tore off out of the house and tripped over the tanks and dump trucks on the porch.

He was about to scold the children for leaving the toys out yet again, but at that point all he could do was let a tear run down his face as he walked up to the car. Looking at the children, he unlocked the car and helped each of them get in and buckle up.

"Look what you did now, sis, you made daddy cry." Logan took his hand and wiped the tear off of Austin's cheek.

"Now, now, we're going to have a good day. No picking on your sister. Let's go see our friend, Ms. States."

As Austin drove his children to school to collect their things, he talked to his wolf, Trey, "*Trey, are we doing the right thing here? I am the Chimera. I'm supposed to defend and protect my children, and here I am, running from our problems.*"

"*Sometimes it's better to step back and find a better way. These people are not our problem. We need to keep our pups safe, Austin.*" Trey receded to the back of Austin's mind as he finished the drive to the school.

Austin pulled into the school parking lot to see Ms. States at the door being berated by Mr. Johnson. Austin walked up to the two with the children in tow. Ms. States welcomed the group with a warm hello and a smile.

"Hello kiddos, I'm happy I could help you all gather your things." Ms. States shot daggers at Mr. Johnson.

"I Don't know why you feel the need to bring your children here Mr. Blazek." Mr. Johnson blocked the doorway.

"Mr. Johnson, move aside before I move you myself. I am no longer playing nice dad. I'm here to collect my children's things and give them a chance to say goodbye. If you and the school want to be pricks, fine, but know that I won't be playing nice anymore. Speaking of not playing nice anymore." Austin pulled out his palm pad and typed in a few things, when suddenly Mr. Johnson's phone went off at the same time as Ms. States'.

"Sorry Ms. States, it's all or none." Austin put his palm pad back in his pocket.

"What is this, Mr. Blazek?" Mr. Johnson looked at his phone that now had a locked logo across it and wouldn't open.

"Ms. States, please take the kids in to collect their things while I educate Mr. Johnson on the fact NRG and my husband's company bought and paid for all staff phones. Since our companies might pull out of this town, we are gathering our resources. So that ends all useless phones and services. That said, we should back your school security system up. You no longer will have the unlimited cloud server."

"You cannot just shut our system down!"

"We didn't shut it down. We just separated you from the cloud server. If you want that kind of service, the school will now need to pay for it. Now step aside, I'm going to my kids' classroom to clear their things." Austin pushed Mr. Johnson aside and walked to his children's classroom.

CHAPTER 27

KAREN STIRS THE POT

K aren blinked and stared off into the void. "This is not what I wanted for my Deven. We will just see about this. You can't just cast my grandson out!" Karen screamed out to Mr. Johnson, who continued walking away.

"So it's true, Mother!" Eric said through a clenched jaw, while holding onto Rebecca and carrying Deven in his arms.

"Eric, wait. Who is this tart on your arm?" Karen tugged at the arm that was wrapped around Rebecca.

"This, Mother, is the only time I will introduce you to her, not that you need to know her after today. Rebecca, meet Deven's grandmother. Karen, meet the mother of your grandson." Eric pulled free and headed to the doors.

"STOP!" Karen screamed.

Eric paused briefly. "What is it, Mother? We are pressed for time. I came to get Deven's records and collect his things, because they don't welcome him and his friends in this school."

"About that, if you have proof this tart is who she says she is, we can have her name put on Deven's birth certificate and he can stay!" Karen smiled weakly.

"This is the only time you get to see her and Deven. We're leaving tonight." Eric turned back to the school doors and walked away.

Karen watched as her son and grandson faded into the surroundings. Then, just as she was about to crumble to the ground, Darla walked up and caught her. "Karen, let's go. We can regroup and see about getting you custody of Deven. Just give me some time."

Meanwhile, in the office, Eric wasn't having the luck he thought he would have with Pam. "Pam, what do you mean it doesn't entitle us to collect my son's school records? You are kicking him out because of his birth certificate. I want the records. I am moving my son to a different school." Eric slammed his fist down on the counter.

"Eric, calm down. It is policy. Even if Austin walked in, he wouldn't be able to get his sons' file." Pam placed her hands on her hips.

"You mean he won't be allowed to get his own kids' records? He has three." Eric leaned over the counter.

"No. According to our records he has two, while Danny is the father of only one." Pam looked over the papers on her desk.

"Oh, so you have all of our records on hand already?" said Eric, reaching over for his son's folder, but Pam slapped his hand and pulled the file back.

"Eric, you need to leave." Pam was dismissing Eric when Austin walked in with the kids. "Austin, what are you doing? I told you I won't release any records for you. I don't care who your father-in-law is, or whatever it is you want to call Danny."

"No, but you can send the records for my children and

Eric's son to this school. Here is their email address, fax, and phone number. At least this school will educate our kids." Austin handed her a notarized copy of the school's paperwork.

Pam looked it over, and her brows furrowed. "You're taking the kids to Colorado? Eric is taking his son to Colorado? You know, all he has to do is get the paperwork showing who Deven's mother is." Pam pursed her lips. "By the way, miss, who are you? Why are you at our school? You are not a parent of a student. You need to leave. This is a private matter in determining who is Deven's mother."

"Oh, that would be me. Not that it is honestly any of your stuck-up snobbish business. We're still pulling our son from your school." Rebecca stepped forward.

"Well, now that we know who his mother is, Pam, we can rescind the dismissal for Deven." Mr. Johnson stepped out of his office.

"NOPE. We're taking our son, Mr. Johnson, and there's nothing you can do to stop us. So where do I need to sign for authorization?" Eric picked up a pen and narrowed his eyes at Pam.

"Fine, but he won't be welcomed back if this doesn't work out. I guess if you're going to side with them, you're not a fit for our town either. I'm sure your mother will be highly disappointed." Pam tossed the papers at Eric and walked away from the desk with files in hand.

"All right buddy, let's go pick up your stuff from Ms. States' class." Eric took Deven by the hand as he approached the door.

Austin held out a bag.

"What is this, Austin?" asked Eric.

"Ms. States had to leave, and she asked me to give you Deven's things. There is something special from her in the bag. She is not happy about losing so many of her students."

"All right buddy, it's time to go." Eric pushed Deven toward the door.

"Daddy, can Deven come play?" Logan pleaded with Austin.

"Buddy, we need to pack so we can go see Grandma and Grandpa Blazek before we visit bath daddy." Austin smiled down at his children.

"He's not bath daddy, he's Uncle Kev," Aurora giggled.

The group walked out of the school to find Darla and Karen standing guard at the exit. "Shi—" Eric said, but caught himself as he looked at Deven.

"Deven, come give your Grammy a hug." Karen squatted down, opening her arms in an over-the-top display of affection.

"NO! Grammy is bad!" Deven defiantly pointed his finger at his grandmother, shaking it.

"Eric, I will see you later. I need to get the kids home. Rebecca, I'm so happy to see you step up to Pam. That tickled me pink. All right kids, head to the car." Austin directed his children to the car.

"Mr. George, really, I must insist that the kids stay. I have some serious questions my office wants answered," Darla explained.

"Darla, you can call my father-in-law. He is our family lawyer." Austin took the kids and pushed past the two bitter women like they were not even there.

"Mr. George, you will regret this," Darla called out, pulling out her phone. "Karen, do you feel you were assaulted just now? I know I feel that way." Darla smiled wickedly.

"Darla, don't even try that shit," Eric snapped.

"Daddy said a bad word. That's five dollars to the no, no jar.

"Deven, get over her right now! Grammy is not letting your

father take you from me. You need to come stay with me. Get over here." Karen launched herself toward Deven.

"NEVER. Grammy, I hate you. You are a bully." Deven bolted past Karen and Darla, who was too preoccupied with her telephone call to realize that the dark blur that passed her was Deven.

"Deven!" Eric went to go after him, when Darla finally came to her senses and tried to corner him but it was too late.

"See, you're unfit. You can't even control a small child. This will go in my report. I don't think the judge will let you keep Deven after all of your recent behavior." Darla started feverishly taking notes.

"Who is this white trash?" Darla pointed to Rebecca.

"Are all you people in this town stupid or just rude?" Rebecca quipped out.

"Who the hell are you?" Darla now directed her question to Rebecca with more anger and hatred.

"I am none of your concern now. Out of my way, I need to get my boy." Rebecca attempted to push past the two.

"Well, that's a shocker. You're not listed as a parent, so you need to get off school property. You will force me to call the Sheriff." Darla pulled out her phone again.

"No need." Rebecca grabbed her own phone and hit send. "Tate, this old bat, who I can only assume is best friends with Karen, showed up at the school. Yes, we came to get Deven's things and his records, but they won't release them. They scared Deven off, and this bitch won't let me go find my son." As Rebecca was talking to Tate, Darla walked up to her.

"Who do you think you are, calling me a bitch?" Darla went to strike her, but Eric grabbed her arm and held it tight.

"Try to assault my son's mother, and my future wife and I will press charges on you so fast the state will see stars."

"Keep your bitch on a tighter leash and have her mind her tongue," Darla said, her left eye twitching uncontrollably.

"You little tart, who the hell do you think you are talking to my friend that way? Get off that damn phone and out of my son's life. I want my grandson." Karen's face was turning tomato red.

"Karen, you damn well know by now who the hell I am. I might have been away for many things—"

Rebecca was laying into Karen when the school doors swung open and Dr. Johnson walked out with a box, pushing it toward Karen. "Karen, I feel these records should be enough to help you start your endeavor. Why is the Sheriff pulling up to the school now?"

"This troublemaker called on me because I was asking about my grandson. The nerve she has. She isn't even a parent and here she is interfering with things."

"Records? What is this?" Rebecca walked over and used her long arms to snatch up a yearbook that was littered with sticky notes flagging former students or the stores that allowed LGBTQ staff to work there. "Oh, so now you are targeting."

"You keep out of this," Mr. Johnson growled out.

"What do we have here, folks?" Tate said, walking up to the group of adults who were at each others' throats.

"Tate, my son ran off and this lady won't let me go find him." Eric pointed at Darla. Suddenly Eric's phone blared some song from a television show. "Hey Austin, sorry I'm still stuck here at the school and Deven—"

"Yeah, I know. Deven is here having a snack, and the kids are going to settle down and watch a cartoon. Eric can come by anytime to pick him up. There's no rush," Austin said, and disconnected the call as Karen's voice screeched, "What! Tate, you get your ass over there and bring me my grandson!"

"Eric, Rebecca, you all are free to go. Darla, Judge Anderson wants you to swing by the courthouse. Karen, I don't have the time or energy dealing with you. Oh, and Mr. Johnson, you know it is still a hate crime to discriminate on the LGBTQ community? If you are planning anything, I advise you not to.

"Mr. Tate, please get off school grounds. Your services are no longer needed, nor are they wanted here."

　　　　　　　　　　　⟫

L ater that night, Karen walked into Rick's to see dancers on the stage in skimpy clothes and drag queens in the lounge. While no one was looking, she pulled a small jar out of her bag, opened it, and gently sprinkled mouse droppings as she walked around the club. She bumped into one of the drag queens.

"Well, as I live and breathe, it's Karen. What can we do for you here at Rick's?" Jason said with a Hollywood smile.

"Can you kindly show me where the bathroom is?" Karen said with a sweet smile.

"Down the hall and to the left." Jason turned and pulled out his phone, texting his brother Jacob.

"Guess who just wondered into my bar?"

"Who?"

"Karen."

"Shut up! No way is that bitch lost cause she knows nothing in that club would touch her with a ten-foot pole."

Jason was about to respond, when a badge was stuck in his face. Jason read the words "HEALTH INSPECTOR."

"Well, the polite thing to do is to say hello, my name is, and I work for, not shoving a badge in a guy's face." Jason pushed the badge down to see the dark eyes of a very short, angry woman.

"Sir, this club is officially closed by order of the health

inspector. We did a surprise visit, and you have mouse drop-pings throughout the club. I have seen dead bugs and some not so dead ones around the bar and by the ice machine. You also have half-naked men dancing around, and I am not too sure that follows the health code. Here is your ticket. This establish-ment is officially closed."

"You have to be kidding me?"

"Sir, I don't kid. Ladies! Gentlemen! This club is officially closed. You all need to exit the building in an orderly fashion. Put your drinks down now and get out."

Karen pulled her phone out and took a picture of Jason and the look of being utterly crushed on his face. Then she sent it out to her group with a tag line of "Another one bites the dust."

CHAPTER 28

FIREHOUSE

K aren walked out of Rick's filled with pride, knowing that one place was shut down and there were more to go. She quickly texted, "*They all are on their way out.*" Outside there were several town's people taking pictures of the club being closed down, while some of the patrons gathered together.

"What's all this?" one patron shouted covering his face.

"We are finding you all out. There is nowhere to hide. We don't want your kind in our town!" a bitter man spit out with a bucktooth smile dancing across his face.

"So what, you're going to harass us? You know you can't do that." A sassy twink flipped his wrist and pointed at the hillbilly.

"You would be surprised what we can and can't do legally. Smile." He pulled out his phone and took a few more pictures.

As the crowd filled the side walk someone yelled out, "Now that is what you would call a sidewalk sale."

Karen turned to see a seven-foot-tall drag queen eyeing the

crowd on the sidewalk like a child eyeing Christmas presents under the Christmas tree.

"What does a sidewalk sale have to do with these freaks?" Karen's shrill voice rang out.

"Well, those freaks and I are the same, sugar." She smiled smugly.

"Shit! You're one of those drag queens," Karen stammered out.

Jason came out, hung the health inspector's sign, and locked the doors to his bar. "Karen! You cunt, I knew you were behind this."

"Watch how you talk to a real woman freak," A man from Karen's crowd yelled at him.

"Fuck you and the small dick in your pants." Jason shoved past the growing crowd of onlookers, quickly got into his car, and locked the door. As his eyes welled up with tears, he pulled out his phone and called the only person he could at a time like this: his brother Jacob.

"Jacob," Jason sobbed into the phone as his face became soaked in tears.

"Yo dude, are you crying? Really, like an ugly girl crying? You're a man. What the hell have you done now? Did one of your dancers shoot you down again?" Jacob's deep, gruff voice mocked.

"It's not a guy. God, do you have to be such a dick? Just because I want something more than a thirty-minute fuck." Jason took a deep, haggard breath, taking a moment to collect his thoughts before continuing.

"Hey, bro, I know it has to be something big, but I need to let you go. It looks like a lady here is calling for help." Jacob sounded irritated to the point he gritted his teeth.

"Okay, call me when you can. It's important."
Jacob hung up the phone and walked out of the firehouse.

No sooner had Jason set his phone down and a baseball bat came flying through his windshield. Then it pulled out to be launched again and again. He turned the key to start his car as they launched a brick through his rear window.

"What the fuck!" Jason bellowed as he threw the car into gear and took off. As he was pulling out, another object smashed his driver side window. "Fuck this." Jason hit the street and floored it, as all along the block people were yelling hate speech and tossing piss-filled bottles, eggs, and flour at his car. Bricks were denting his 1985 Chevrolet Camaro all over the place.

Jason's wolf stirred in his head, piping up for the first time in months. "*Go back! Let us tear them limb from limb.*" Fire Vox's voice was deep and filled with hate.

"*We can't do that. We have codes. There are rules we follow. We have a responsibility to keep our kind out of the spotlight. You know how hard it was to contain the supernatural war only a few years ago.*"

"*Do you think I care?*" Fire Vox growled out.
"*Austin would be mad at us, so would Trey!*" Jason snapped back.

"*Damn human, even though they are not our mate, we care too much about what they think... I'll get you for that dirty trick.*" With one last low growl, Fire Vox moved to the back of Jason's mind.

While Jason debated calling his brother back, he called Sheriff Tate instead. "Tate?"

"What is it, Jason? I am kind of busy. I am getting calls all across town of violence and disturbances." Tate clicked a few buttons on his patrol car's laptop.

"Yeah, I am one of the victims, and I didn't feel safe calling in, because, well, one of your deputies was there when I was attacked, after Karen got my club closed down." Jason looked at his car, seeing the damage he knew he would have to cover himself.

"Okay, shit man, are you all right? Do you need medical care? Wait, did you just say one of my deputies was present when you were assaulted?"

"Yes sir, Berry was there when my car got smashed. He just put his light on me and smirked as they launched bricks at my car."

"Do you need medical?"

"Really, Tate?" Jason snorted out.

"Sorry, bad habit." Tate let out a deep chuckle.

"I'm glad you are aware of us. Austin was right trusting you." Jason bit his bottom lip.

"Austin had no choice. Umm, my girlfriend is a vampire hybrid. My sweet mate is a vamp, and I couldn't be happier. Well, I would be if I could actually have the night off like I planned, but no, someone got the hornet nest stirred up."

"Rub it in. Not all of us have found our mates. You know that sucks, man. You're a human and found your mate, and here I am, a gay werewolf who was kicked out from my pack by the former Alpha. I fell for a guy I can't have, and Selene still torments me with no mate. Now I get beaten up by the town I grew up with for being gay. All because of Karen and her oh so holy crusade."

"Sorry, Jason, I have to go. I'm getting a dispatch to the firehouse." Tate quickly hung up the phone, triggering alarms in Jason's head.

Jason took the next turn and headed to the fire house entrance, trying desperately to link his brother or his wolf, Stargazer. Getting no response, his pulse quickened as fear crept up in his chest. Jason's worst fears were met as he pulled in to see Jacob with a crowd standing over him. Tate was already on the scene, fighting the growing crowd back to get to the victim who was still getting pummeled.

"You filthy, dirty, sinful heap of trash. This entire time you served in the fire department and you were queer. How many times did you try sleeping with the men here? You freaks all need to burn in the fires of hell." Another punch to Jacob's already bleeding and broken face. It was then that Jason saw the small flow of crimson on the ground around his brother.

"WHAT THE FUCK IS WRONG WITH YOU MOTHER FUCK-ERS!" Fire Vox and Jason bellowed in unison, catching the crowd off guard by the power of his voice.

Tate pushed through the crowd to see the look of utter shock and horror as Deputy Berry looked up with a fist covered in blood.

"AHH Sheriff Tate. Ah Jason, Jacob is alive. I must have got here just before you. I don't know who did this, but once he is secured, I will head up the investigation." Berry quickly attempted to wipe the blood off his work gloves.

"Berry, stand up and turn around. I am placing you under arrest and relieving you of your duties." Tate quickly unarmed Berry and took his keys, while placing handcuffs firmly on his wrists until he winced in pain. Jason ran to scoop up his brother.

"Jason, it looks bad. I think it's best to take Jacob." Tate paused, looking at the mob that was still swarmed around them.

"Sheriff, what happened?" The chief of the fire department yelled as he jumped out of his barely parked car. "Jacob!" Tanner looked over the crowd. "You people make me sick with your bullshit. You all better get out of here before I take my turn of vigilante justice. I have a fire hose that I am dying to turn on someone. Now get out of here and don't you dare follow them!" Tanner walked over and pulled the fire hose off the nearby truck.

"*Home*," was the only word Stargazer spoke to Fire Vox through mind link, and Jason knew what home was—not his condo across town.

"We need to go to Gen—" Jason stopped for a moment.

"Yes, I will escort you to Genesis Moon Estates. It's not far, and I will have Austin contact the guard." Tate pulled out his phone, texting Austin. "*Need permission to cross. Coming in hot. Injured party of three.*" Tate helped load Jacob into his cruiser after seeing the damage to Jason's car. "No way are we taking him in that. It's not safe to drive that far. Tanner, do me a favor and keep Berry here nice a wrapped up till I get back. By the way, don't get him wet. I need all that blood as proof of his crime."

"That's the son of a bitch that beat up my friend? No problem." An evil grin danced across Tanner's face.

"Tanner, no violence. I need the charges to stick."

"Fine," said Tanner, his face showing Tate all he needed to know. Berry would be unharmed, but not very comfortable until his return.

As they finished loading up Jacob, Tate got the text he was waiting for. "*All clear. Cherries and blueberries are fine, just no siren, that shit hurts our ears. BTW I will meet you there.*"

"Sheriff, that is a misuse of town resources," Karen said smugly as she arrived on the scene. She crossed her arms as a wicked smile pulled up at the corner of her mouth.

"Would you rather I stop this?"

"Yes."

"Oh, then I shall place each and every one of you under arrest for violence and hate crimes, because those charges are coming and you are at the top of my list, Karen." Tate's eyes narrowed.

"I am untouchable. You have no proof I did anything. Freedom of speech, dear sir. Remember, you are to uphold the law and constitution." Karen's thin finger poked Tate in the chest.

"Freedom of speech does no cover speech that pushes for violence and riots, and you just assaulted me while I was actively carrying out my duties. Karen." Tate snatched her hand and spun her around with more force than he thought he had to place her in cuffs. He cuffed her to the end of the firetruck. "Now Karen, you will stay here until I can retrieve you. Tanner, no one can take her but me."

"Ten four big boss." Tanner just started laughing as Karen struggled to free herself.

Jason picked up a few of the items that had spilled out of Jacob's jacket, as he carried him to the car to have and old man grit his teeth and speak with a clenched jaw, "Just keep walking queer."

Jacob let out a muffled groan as he stirred in the back of the cop car. "Sorry bro, I can't just leave you here. We need to go home, and it's going to be a bumpy ride. We're not riding in style. Some asshole shattered all the glass on my car. Tate is taking us home. Austin got us clearance." Jacob tried to move, but only hot searing pain ran through his body, and Jason could feel the twin bond for the first time in years. His eyes welled up with tears, while he tried to draw out all his twin's pain, as Tate flew down the road back to Genesis Moon.

"Not safe here," Jacob's voice came out as a barely audible whisper.

"I agree, but maybe now that Joe is gone, they will let us back into the pack." Jason brushed bloody strands of hair off of Jacob's face. The healing process had started, but he needed to be seen by healers.

"Not allowed on pack grounds?" Tate asked over his shoulder.

"That's up to Alpha Kev. Hopefully he will grant us passage and safe harbor," Jason sighed. "We have one person I could call and try to smooth things over with Kev."

"Your precious untouchable Austin," Jacob spat out, coughing up blood. "I still don't understand why you didn't mark him. You could have had Austin and I could have had Danny, but no, my brother is Mr. Perfect." Jacob coughed up blood as he grasped his side.

"Jacob, shut the hell up." He pulled out his phone and called Austin.

"Hello?" Austin hastily answered the phone while packing things and getting ready to jump to the pack boarder to get Tate and the two he was bringing into Genesis Moon.

"Austin, this is..." Jason took a breath and held it, praying to Selene it wouldn't trigger any raw or painful memories. "I know, I promised after what happened between us all that I would keep my distance. Austin, it's—"

Austin cut Jason off with his firm and assertive voice. "I Know Jason. I have caller ID."

"I kind of figured you would. I know we don't deserve the help, but we are in danger. Karen..." Jason cried, reliving his nightmare.

"That bitch is after you two now?"

"My club got shut down. Shortly after she came to visit, the health inspector showed up. I got roughed up a little. My car was totaled. I went to see Jacob, but they got to him first. He is in terrible shape. Thank you for letting us cross over into Genesis Moon territory. Is Dr. Stone still the pack doctor? Because Jacob is looking bad."

"Quit crying to your loverboy, but tell him thanks from me." Jacob continued to cough.

"Jacob, you're still coughing up blood. That should have stopped by now. Doctor Stone needs to see you right away."

"Guys, are you near the border yet?"

"Yeah, in like five minutes."

"Good, I will see you soon." With that, Austin linked Danny. *"Loves, I am off to the pack. We have drama. Your mom is coming over to watch all the kids while Eric packs up his house. Kev has everything set for us. I love you."*

"Love you more," Danny said back.

CHAPTER 29
THE GUARD

The night air hung thick as Frank restlessly patrolled the pack gates. "I can't believe it. Kevin has been the new Alpha for six years now, and I'm still on guard duty," Frank muttered to the additional guard member he was stuck on patrol with that chilly night.

"Dude, I get you have been on guard since the Stone Age. If you were going to be named Beta, he would have done it by now. So do us all a favor and shut the hell up. We have a job to do, so suck it up." Zaiden's voice was laced with anger at hearing a senior member of the guard acting like a child.

"Hey, you're the rookie. Just shut up and watch the road to town. I need to go take a piss, or do I need to ask your permission to do that too? Maybe you need to hold it for me to make sure I know how to piss since you seem to know how everything works around here." Frank stormed off angrily to the nearby mulberry bush.

"Hey, you might need to pull that up really quick, we have cherries and blueberries coming up the road right now." Zaiden's voice had a little catch in it, because when you are part of a werewolf pack this close to town, it's never a good thing to have the cops show up.

"Shit." Frank came running back from the bush with the front of his pants covered in piss.

"Dude, no need to piss on yourself unless you are into that shit." Zaiden laughed as the Sheriff pulled in.

"What the hell are you here for?" Frank spat out.

"I was told I could gain access," Tate explained.

"I don't think so. Without a warrant there's no entry. This is private land." Frank took a rag from the guard desk and wiped the piss off his pants.

"Need I remind you, boy, I am an officer of the law."

"Need I remind you?" Frank mimicked and mocked, curling his lip up in disdain.

"Excuse me?" Tate looked menacingly toward the guards.

"That doesn't explain those two," Frank said, pointing to the twins in the back of the squad car.

A whirl of white and golden light appeared next to Sheriff Tate's car, and Austin stepped out, clearing his throat and eyeing Frank.

"Austin, what the fuck man? you can't just do that in front of a human. You're risking exposing all of us." Frank tossed the rag to the floor and slammed his fist into the desk.

"Excuse yourself, dumb ass. He is not only human, you idiot, he is our ally. His bride to be is the vampire princess that keeps Malcolm at bay. Besides that, he has known of our kind for some time. And as far as these two go, they are here under my protection," Austin growled out, causing Zaiden to bow his head and bear his neck in submission.

"Zaiden, you pussy. Why are you—" Frank began saying, when he was interrupted by a commanding voice.

"Because he knows Austin is an Alpha by birth, and you would do well to listen to him. He could easily challenge you and take you down, Frank. He is not the skinny little nobody you used to pick on. Need I remind you it's because of him we all survived Alpha Joe?" It was the voice of Alpha Kevin of the Genesis Moon Pack.

"Chimera or not, he's still a nobody to me, and not even a member of this pack. I don't give a shit." Frank stormed off to the gates to ensure they were locked, so Tate couldn't enter.

"I, interim Alpha Kevin of the Genesis Moon Pack of Nebraska order you to stand down, Frank." Kevin's amber eyes glowed.

"Oh, I'm so scared the interim Alpha gave an order but can't pick a Beta in what, six years now?" Frank picked up his bag and started walking off into the woods. "If you're so big and bad, you can take my shift, I'm going home."

"You worthless bitch." Kevin moved to go after him, but Austin reached out to stop him.

"Kevin, we need to see Dr. Stone right away. We had some gay bashing happen in town and the town's folk tore up Jacob." Austin's smooth voice calmed Kevin, and he looked in the back seat.

"Shit, whoever these bastards are, they are not playing. Yeah, take them into the good doctor. I have a question for you, Austin, why not transport directly to the sick house?" Kevin opened the gates so Tate could drive into pack territory. "Sherriff, take this road down to the oak, turn left, and go six blocks. I have already linked to the doctor. His staff will be waiting. Austin, if you have a second, I need to talk to you."

"Tate, you're fine. I will catch up in just a few." With that, Tate took off down the path outlined by the Alpha, Kevin.

"Kevin, thank you for your help. I am so glad you and the pack have been more open to the LGBTQA members." Austin wiped a tear from his face.

"I hear things are getting more hate filled in town. My

heart hurts, but we cannot open our grounds to everyone. We still need to protect the paranormal community. I know what Jacob did to you. I'm glad to see you are allowing him to get medical treatment, but what would you like us to do as a pack?" Kevin looked at his feet and drew circles in the dirt.

"I still think Jacob is a worthless pile of dog shit, but do I think he needs to be punished more? That was yet to be decided, but for now the ass whipping he received was hard enough. The town turned against not only him but his brother. Jason's car is totaled, and I don't know how to tell them yet, but their apartments both caught fire before I left. The fire chief was looking around for the arsonists."

"Shit, they really aren't playing down in town. How is the Chimera clan holding up?" Kevin looked up with soft concern in his eyes.

"We're moving again. We can't stay. I won't risk my kids. If this was a supernatural problem, it would be one thing, but they can't even attend school; they were kicked out simply because there is no mother on their birth certificates. For now, we're in town, but not for long. I'm also taking Eric away with us," Austin said smiling.

"Wait, Eric, as in Eric Matheson?" Kevin's look of shock was all Austin needed to let loose the deep laughter he had been holding in.

"As shocking as it seems, he actually turned out to be one of the good ones. Eric's son Deven, is half Fae. Rebecca, who is from my father's clan lands, is his mother. Thus, Deven is under my protection as a hybrid, as per Selene and the other gods. Speaking of them, I have a feeling one of them is behind Karen, and that's where she has been getting all her power. I'm only trying to figure out why someone is starting shit. It's been almost a decade since I released them back into our world. Some of them never learn. Locked up for six hundred years and

P.A. POWER

still they act worse than Logan and Ethan when they want the same toy." Austin let out a deep sigh.

"Well, if there's anything we can do to help here at Genesis Moon?" Kevin asked, leaning back on the guard shack.

"He can help." Austin pointed over to Zaiden, who was walking back up to the guard shack after doing his rounds. Zaiden came up to them, grabbed a bottle of water, and took a deep drink, setting the bottle down and wiping the slick layer of sweat from his brow.

"This green horn?" Kevin chuckled, wiggling his eyebrows at Austin. "He's still green behind the ears. Reminds me a lot of you, Austin, before you got Trey."

Zaiden looked over at the two men, as their faces turned bright red.

"Umm, what can I do for you, Alpha George-Blazek?" Zaiden rubbed his lean muscular arms while his fingers shimmered in the gentle glow of the moon.

"So, do I tell him or are you going to?"

"Zaiden, are you part of the Alphabet?" Kevin asked smiling, "because, as you know, we fully support that here in Genesis Moon."

"NO!" Zaiden made to run back into the woods to get away from the two Alphas.

"Zaiden, if you are, it's fine." Kevin tried to reassure his additional guard that he was safe to be who he was born to be.

"Zaiden belongs under my protection. He is born from white witch and werewolf blood."

"He gets his wolf here in like two weeks, right Zaiden? Wait, you mean a white witch like Candy? Are you sure about that, Austin? I know you can tell a hybrid only by looking at them with all your damn gifts, but really, we have a werewolf with witch power? How is that going to work?"

"Yes sirs, no one was supposed to know. I was sworn to

secrecy. I was adopted. My father made me promise not to tell anyone. Do I have to leave now? My mother was a white witch who died in the battle six years ago. My father died from a broken heart when I was twelve. I have no one to guide me with my powers. I'm barely learning how to be a werewolf." Zaiden sat on the ground with his head hung low and cried a steady stream of tears.

"No, that's not true. Candy will help you with your powers. Here is her card. You call her any time you need anything. In fact, I will have a spare room at my house that Bou and his mate are staying at in town. I know Claira and Marshall adopted you, but it's time you awaken your magic side. In Genesis Moon, we don't hide our gifts. Sorry Alpha Kevin if I overstepped." Austin smile cheekily at Kevin, seeing full well on his own that he was happy Zaiden's missing puzzle pieces would fall together at last.

"Well, guys, Sarah is waiting for me. She wants her, umm, peppermint stick." Kevin let out a sheepish grin as he stepped behind the shed and tossed off his clothes, allowing the pale moonlight to dance across his body, as fur rippled down him. Letting out a single howl, he took off for the pack house at a dead run.

Zaiden looked over at Austin in bewilderment, and Austin pulled him into a hug. "Welcome to my family, bud. One thing you will learn once you meet your mate, is that if she is a wolf and goes into heat, you better beat feet home, because a were-wolf in heat is not only endless sex, but if she goes into heat without her mate, every single male will try to mate her. This might be her first heat, so I know Kevin is going to be trying to put a pup in her. He has been trying to do that since the night he could claim her." Austin shook his head as Zaiden's eyes grew in size.

"Oh, please tell me someone told you about the birds and

the bees and other fun stuff?" Austin turned to watch the changing of the guard come on.

"Someone said the prodigal son came home. You can't be here without seeing Katie and Samantha. They are still living in the pack house, even though she wants to take up the new condo where Danny used to stay."

"Oh, I got to go Zaiden, I need to see my little sis." Austin reached out his hand and tossed out a light orb making a portal to the pack house back door.

As he walked through, he turned to Zaiden. "Be seeing you soon Zaiden." With that, Austin faded away as the portal closed on the guard shack.

"Zaiden, why would Austin be telling you he'd be seeing you soon? He has a mate, and you turn eighteen soon, so you are far too old for his daughter." Mathew teased his best friend.

"Dude, here is a report. Some of us don't have our wolves to support us as we run the perimeter." Zaiden tossed the clipboard with a report on it to Mathew.

"Wait, where is the old bitty who likes to whine?"

"Who are you calling old bitty? Just because I'm an old son don't mean I can't tan that ass of yours," Hank growled out.

"Hank, sir. No, not you, sir. Frank was not at his post again at shift change," Mathew stammered out, forgetting Hank was supposed to do random audits.

"I will inform Beta Jeff. Not another word. Once you get a rank higher than Omega, we can talk. Question me and I will make you clean the toilets in all the pack parks with a wolf's tongue holding the toilet brush. Do I make myself clear?"

CHAPTER 30

PACKHOUSE

T ate's arrival at the pack house brought the place to life with all the rumors buzzing around. As Austin stepped out of the portal to the familiar back door, he couldn't help but smile. Looking at the steps, he noticed they were no longer worn and broken down anymore. He walked up to touch the cold iron handle, when a voice from the past startled him from behind.

"Aren't we a little too old to be sneaking in the back door like some juvenile delinquent?" Katie's voice was light, showing no judgement. Katie stepped out of the shadows, casting a motherly gaze upon Austin, taking in the man he had become. "Well, you seem no worse for wear," Katie smiled while making eye contact with Austin. She could tell, even in the pale moonlight, six years had passed and Austin looked as if only a day had gone by since the epic battle.

"Luna?" Austin was taken aback by Katie's surprising appearance. He stepped back, taking in her hair with a dusting of silver around the temples. The dress she wore was not a designer name, but still pleasing to the eye.

"Nope, wrong title Mr. Serious, I gave that up. It is no longer my responsibility. I get to just relax now and worry about Sammy." Katie nervously fidgeted with the wrinkles in the fabric of her dress.

"Speaking of the little angel, where is she?" Austin cast his gaze around to see if she was hiding around the back door of the pack house. Realizing that it was just the two of them, his expression fell. "Where is she? I was hoping to see her. I know it's unexpected and unannounced, but the last time I saw peanut was a week after she was born."

"She is up in her room. I have told Kevin to let me move into the new condos down on Bolder Avenue, where Danny's condo used to sit. Sadly, this Alpha won't hear of it. You know for someone who at a wave of your hand can teleport anywhere, you never could come back here. I know you have brought the kids to see Doug's family. Lucky for me, when you have them stay with Doug, he is kind enough to bring them over here for supper. I would say I raised you to have better manners, but the both of us know that's not true. If I could start all over though, I would teach you that."

"You sound like Kevin. Oh, you want better manners? Let me get the door for you." Austin opened the back door expecting the old creaking noise, but it was gone. He stepped aside to allow Katie in and followed behind her.

"You always were the gentlemen. I am so proud of you. Where are those babies by the way Mr.?" Katie shifted her gaze, giving him a smile with a side eye.

"The kids are home. This was not initially a social call. We had some violence in town, and we needed the pack doctor to look at Jacob." Austin's voice shifted as he said Jacob's name.

"Jacob? What happened to him? Is he trying to steal someone else's man again? Oh, I know it is probably a sore subject. Sorry, that's a dirty joke. I'm sorry, Austin." Katie pulled Austin into a warm embrace.

"Ha ha, Mom, my man is safe. I bit him. He is mine. Trey and I don't share. But if he was a threat, I would just teleport his ass to Florida to the swamps." Austin smiled, remembering the poor bastard that pissed off Selene.

"Oh, yes, the lovely swamps in Florida. I wonder how that jack ass is holding up. Trying to take my boys, and Phoebe away. Thank the Goddess you were there." Katie started to tear up.

"Brian?" He started telling Katie the news he thought she should already know but pulled out his phone and bit his lip as he texted Brian.

"I know Austin, Brian is a powerful man and very strong minded, but ever since he lost Ted he is not as strong and would be no match, not only for that Alpha, but his pack members that came with him." Katie pulled a tissue from her dress pocket and dabbed at the tears forming in her eyes.

"Mom," Austin said in a sweet but firm tone while texting Brian even more feverishly. "*BRIAN! You never told mom. You understand she is going to lose her shit on you when she finds you have been holding back on this information.*"

Brian got Austin's angry text and quickly responded. "*Dude, what the fuck are you talking about?*"

"*You never told mom you got Ted back! She is almost in tears over here.*"

"*Yeah, So. Why does that matter right now? I have my wolf, Kevin is the Alpha. Things will not change. I am getting wedding plans made with Phoebe. Ted is happy with our new station in life. So just chill. Why is she even at your place right now?*"

"*I am at Genesis Moon. Because of what the town has done, I need to move. They beat Jacob half to death, and he had to be seen by the pack doctors.*"

"*Wait, hold up, you're at Genesis moon? What is this bullshit?*"

You're moving like the fuck you are. I am in my kitchen. Open me a portal like now!"

"Hey mom guess who's coming for a visit," With a twist of his wrist Austin opened the broom closet door to show Brian standing with a less than pleasant look upon his face.

Brian eyed Austin head to toe, and without looking at his mother he said, "Hi mom, please excuse my rude and unexpected visit. I need to kick someone's ass for threating to move out of state once again."

"Now boys, no violence. You know how Kevin is about things like that. Brian, it's so good to see you. I know Sammy will be happy to see the two of you." Katie quickly mind linked her daughter.

"Sammy, come to the kitchen, please. I have something to show you."

"Yes, momma," Sammy replied in the link as she skipped down the hall, heading to the stairs to the kitchen. Soon, a bright-eyed blond girl came dancing down the stairs to see her mother and the two men locked in a staring contest. "Brian, Austin!"

"Mother, you don't play fair," Brian said through gritted teeth.

"Well, I am your mother. No one ever said I played fair. Besides, I can't have you hurting Austin just because he is leaving town once again." Katie looked over at Sammy as she locked eyes with her mother and nodded her head. "So, Brian, do you have anything to say?" Katie walked over, pulled Austin's phone from his hand, and started reading the text messages between the boys.

"You know when you were growing up you two would never do this." She waved the phone like a carrot in front of the guys. "After the war, you became thick like thieves. Now I know you're not biological or legally adopted brothers; it's like

Brian's bond with Kevin. Before I read this, Sammy told on you. Sammy came back to me with a gift from Selene. She can see a person's wolf, even out of wolf form. Brian, I will ask once more..." Katie's Luna aura radiated off her body.

"For not being Luna, you sure pack a punch with that." Austin pulled his phone out of Katie's hands. "Now you cannot blame me for his choice. It was up to him and Ted to decide to tell you on their terms. Now, how is my little peanut?" Austin reached down and pulled up behind Sammy.

"Oh, Trey is pretty. You smell like; mommy what was that spice we used on the pies?" Sammy put her nose to Austin's shoulder.

"Nutmeg and cinnamon?" Katie looked at her little girl, puzzled.

"YES! Austin smells like nutmeg and cinnamon!" Sammy squealed.

"No, Sammy, my scent is vanilla and baked goods, but I know someone who smells like nutmeg and cinnamon. He is my little cinnamon roll, Logan." Austin cast a glance to Katie, letting her know he needed to talk with her later in private.

"I already know what you're about to say, Austin, and don't you dare, my little girl is only six!"

"Logan is the same age. Well, you were there when he hatched. She was born soon after. But let's not put the cart before the horse. Maybe we can have a play date and see how they react. It might be as simple as him reminding her of the pies you just made today. We have twelve years to figure dynamics out."

"Fine, we can table this conversation, but speaking of pie, how about we all sit down and I will get us some pie and coffee? We can talk about how you two boys broke this lady's poor little heart hiding such good news from me." Katie placed her hand over her heart, mocking them as if she was dying of a broken heart.

"Mom, you're no longer in drama class, enough of the theatrics. Ted was settling in and I was getting used to having my wolf. My mate is still getting used to having her wolf man back. Since that is already out of the bag, I guess Phoebe can meet up with you, and the pair of you can plan our wedding ceremonies. Keep in mind Sammy here will have to be both flower girls."

"YES!" Sammy exclaimed, squealing at the prospect of shopping.

"Why do I have a feeling I am going to seriously regret this?" Brian placed his face in his palms, while Katie slid over a large piece of pie with a cup of coffee.

"She takes after her momma. We love shopping and spending money. Especially if it's not our money. Lucky for you sir, the family coffers are full of funds set aside for your wedding day—if the day would ever come that is." Katie rolled her eyes as she sipped her coffee.

A kitchen Omega walked in. "Lady Katie, are the rumors true we have a human here and he brought the twins back from town?"

"Yes, it is true," Austin spoke up calmly.

"Excuse you? Who are you when I asked Lady Katie?" The young Omega scuffed at Austin.

"Watch how you talk to him, child. I helped raise him until he could reunite with his family." Katie's former Luna aura radiated off her body once more.

"My apologies Lady Katie. Sir."
"As Austin stated, yes, Sheriff Tate is on pack grounds. The Alpha already knows and approved this happening. Any Omega should know nothing should happen on pack grounds without the Alpha knowing. Kevin may seem sweet, but he is

still our Alpha, and he has a temper. Those werewolves that are here seeing doctor Stone are from our pack. Someone did not officially make them rogue. My late husband did not approve of their life; thus he kicked them off pack lands but kept them on a leash to do his bidding." Katie rolled her eyes, reliving the text messages she read on Joe's devices after the war.

"Oh."

"This one that I told you was raised by me, he is also Selene's favorite." Laughing, Katie turned to Austin. "Austin, I was just teasing."

Austin's phone rang and he felt pin pricks of danger riding up the nape of his neck. Picking up the phone, he said in an urgent voice, "Hello!"

"Austin, come home NOW!" Panic rose in the caller's voice.

"Why?! Is everything all right? I am catching up with Brian, Sammy, Katie, oh and making sure the twins get treated by doctor Stone."

"I think that can wait. It's Karen. She, she just—" The phone went dead as whoever ripped it from Bou's hand smashed it.

When home is no longer home, I took your safe place from you. Austin's heart dropped from his chest and dark thoughts raced through his head. "*Trey, what's going on? I feel danger, but we are safe. Bou just called and now his phone is dead. Do we rush back? Do I just teleport?*"

"*What if? What if? Our pups are in danger, Austin, and they are in the human world. We cannot just go popping up. When in a jam, use their own power play to our advantage.*" Trey's voice reverberated in his head.

Austin closed his eyes and concentrated on Bou calling out to him, but the mind link was too far.

"*Trey, we're too far away to mind link. If I can't get Bou, I know we can't reach our pups.*"

"*Silly human, you have the Sheriff, have him give you the express ride. LIKE NOW!*" Trey's voice was anything but calm at this point. Austin pulled out his phone and texted Tate, "*911 on my way. I need you to lights and siren me to my house. I think my kids are in danger, and I can't use magic. I'll be at the border.*"

"*On my way.*"

Just like that, Austin turned to his family enjoying pie and coffee. "I'm sorry. I need to go. Something is not right."

"Oh, be careful. Brian sit down and let Austin deal with this parenting problem. When you and Phoebe have your own pups," Katie mused over her coffee while running her hands through Sammy's golden hair.

"Mom, really?" Brian glared at his mother before taking a drink of coffee and shoveling another bite of pie in his mouth.

Austin closed his eyes and concentrated on the pack border, until a portal opened before him and he walked out into the crisp night air.

CHAPTER 31
BROKEN

"Austin, again with the portals in front of the human," Jerry teased jokingly, pointing his thumb at the waiting Sheriff's car.

"Jerry not now. I need to get home and I can't use magic, so Tate is giving me a ride home."

"Should I send pack members to provide backup?" Jerry straightened out, ready to let his wolf out for a run to town.

"Jerry, we have to stay low key, but I appreciate the offer." Austin got into the car with Tate, and they took off down the road, lights and siren all the way to Austin's house.

"So, mind telling me more about what the '911, get me home so quick is all about?' Do you think Danny, or the kids are in danger? I would call a deputy to go to your house, but as you know, I don't know who we can trust right now." Tate turned down Austin's street, and Austin jumped out before he could even come to a complete stop. He was out of the car and running up to the house, only to see the front door kicked in, broken glass from the windows, and the one word, Austin hated the most: fag.

"Austin, do not, I repeat, do not wolf out," Tate said, coming up with his gun drawn looking for the intruder.

"Tate, my kids are gone! Deven is gone. Bou and Lexi are missing! Bou's phone is in pieces over there." Austin sniffed the air, frantically trying to pick up a scent and coming up with nothing. "Whoever it is that did this was human. I can tell it was not another werewolf or anything."

Tate pulled out his walkie talkie, "Tate to dispatch."

"Dispatch, what can we do for you, Sheriff Tate?" the chipper dispatcher's voice danced in the air.

"I need an A.P.B. put out for three male minors, one female minor, a male adult, and one female adult. They have been taken from the George-Blazek home."

"Oh my God, please tell my Doug's grandkids were not taken!" Her voice was now shrill and on edge.

"Sadly, yes, and so was their step uncle and his fiancé. I will send over the current pictures. I also need to find Eric. His boy was having a sleepover here, and he's gone as well. They have broken into the house, and it's clear there was a struggle."

"I will send the officers I know you can trust. Tell Austin I am an ally."

"I will, thank you." Tate walked into the kitchen to find Austin shaking while holding a note.

"Austin, give me the note. It's evidence. We will find your kids." Tate put on a glove and gently took the note. He turned it over to read:

Freaks and queers, you all need to go. No man shall corrupt the minds of these children. They have been taken from you and given to a wonderful Christian family. We will rename them with more appropriate names, and we will teach them you were sinners and will burn in hell. Leave now and never come back. You will never see these children again. Get in our way and you will go away on our terms. No one will come looking for your bodies.

"Oh God, Austin, we will find them." Tate was interrupted by three squad cars pulling up as Danny walked through the closet door in a rage.

"WHERE ARE OUR KIDS!" Danny roared as the three officers came in with guns drawn.

"Sir, put your hands in the air and back up," one officer yelled out a command.

"This is my house!" Danny turned to have his face meet the end of a gun barrel.

"Alice, guys, stand down. That is one of the homeowners and parents of the kidnapped kids. It was a kidnapping. We have the note; but no ransom. It looks like your kids were taken just now. Fuck, what kind of note is this?" Tate put the note in a baggie. "Alice, I trust you to get this to the lab and run prints on it. You're a mother yourself. You know their pain." Tate pointed to the two men.

"On it, boss."

"Boys, do a sweep. If anything shows up, let me know."

"Tate, I am going to show you and only you this." Tate motioned for his officers to do a check as Danny pulled a brick out of the wall and pushed a release button for a hidden door to open.

"Holy mother of technology, you have all this in your house? Well, this will make finding the ones to blame fairly easy." Tate looked over a wall of monitors that covered the outside of the house, and all the common areas of the inside.

"Here is my business card. Send all these files over. Make sure they are backed up and saved. I trust very few town's people right now." Tate looked at the screen. "Son of a bitch."

"What?" Austin screamed as he pushed Tate out of the way.

"Mother fucking bitch! Darla is in on it." Austin bolted for the door as his phone rang.

"Kev, I don't have time for this right now. I have trouble with the kids."

"Well, it's nice you think this is Kev, but it's actually Rob. I was calling to let you know that the school is refusing to submit to our inquiry on the four kids' records."

"Oh, shit, sorry Rob. We have some drama going on. This town crossed the line, and it is taking everything I have not to break the rule about exposing ourselves to the humans."

"Anything our pack can help with, you know no one knows us, so it might be easier... I know Kev would love to pay a visit," Rob chuckled.

"These damn humans have kidnapped my kids," Austin growled.

"What!" Kev roared in the background. "Austin open a portal for us. In ten minutes, my warriors and I will be there."

"Kev, you don't have to. We don't want to be a problem." Austin looked at Danny, whose eyes were black like onyx.

"Austin, I am an Alpha. You asked to stay with us in our lands. Thus, by werewolf law, I am your acting Alpha. Austin, open the portal," Kev demanded through the phone.

"Our packs will burn this town to the ground to get our kids back, Austin." Danny closed his eyes, taking in a deep breath to calm Adonis from coming to the surface.

Austin closed his eyes, took a deep breath, and opened the basement door, opening a portal to Kev's pack house in Colorado. He looked around and nodded to Tate, who ushered the rest of the officers out of the house in time for Kev and the Celtic Rhino Pack to arrive.

With lightning speed, Alpha Kev was the first one through the portal and up the basement stairs. "Where do we want to start the hunt, Austin?" Kev growled.

"This video shows the social worker, Darla, was here, and I can see the kids in the back of her car. But no way could a little woman like her take out a full-grown werewolf, a hot-blooded siren, and a half-blood Fae child along with our three children," Danny snickered. "Sorry, two of the three will have full Chimera powers while Logan is a full-blood werewolf."

"Wait, you already know what the children will be? That is amazing, but why is Logan only werewolf?" Rob asked as he scrolled through Danny's security films.

"We knew before they hatched, but that is okay." Austin looked around his home, now filled with a growing number of Celtic Rhino Pack members, when a knock on the door made him jump.

Running to the door, Austin flung it open to see someone running away, and a note stuck to his door.

Danny pushed Austin to the side and took off after the guy who ran to his beat-up car. Ripping the car's door off the car, Danny reached in and pulled out a shaking teenage boy. "Who the fuck are you, and what do you know!? You posted a note on my door. You're coming in with me." Danny dragged the kid in crying.

"Let me go. I am only dropping off a message. I have nothing to do with whatever you are so mad about. Man, let me go!"

Kev walked out and grabbed the kid's face to make him look up and see his onyx eyes. "So, if you're just the messenger, who gave you the job to deliver news like this?"

"I was just approached by a lady who said she saw this note on your door earlier and the wind must have caught it. She asked if I could go put it back, because she was late getting the kids off to Grandma's house."

"What did she look like?" Kev got the pungent odor of

urine, and he looked down to see the teenager had pissed his pants.

"I don't know. It was dark, and she was in some kind of red sedan. She had three boys and one girl. They all appeared to be the same age, but it was obvious they were not all related. Please, can you let me go?"

"If I set you down, you will come inside and tell us everything. Those kids were not hers. She kidnapped them, and the note she had you deliver is not a traditional ransom note. It's more like 'screw you, I got your kids. Now leave town before you regret it even more. '"

"Wait, she kidnapped those kids? Oh my God, I don't want to be charged with accessory to kidnapping. I wouldn't make it in prison."

Kev sat the kid on the ground, and he didn't run. He calmly walked to the house and walked in past Austin, waiting to be directed where to go, seeing a house full of powerful men he did not know.

"All right, sit here. Don't worry, they won't hurt you. I want as many details as you can give us. Time is of the utmost importance. Three of them are my children and one was a friend visiting." Austin sat across from the scared teenager.

"Where is Deven!?" came the distraught voice of a panic-stricken father.

"Eric, sit down," Danny commanded.

"NO! I thought my son would be safe here. Where is he!"

"One guess, Kev, this is Eric. Eric, this is my friend Kev, and Rob, his right-hand man. Those guys over there are the personal guard for the town we're moving to. They are here to help us get back what your mother and Darla took. The only thing is, they did something with Bou and Lexi."

"How?" Eric looked at the teenager, and his eyes narrowed. "Andy? Andy Johnstone?"

"Yes, sir."

"How the fuck are you involved in all this?"

"They tricked me into delivering that note. I am so sorry, I thought that was Deven. The lady said she was on her way to Grandma's house."

"I swear if my mother is behind this, not even the devil will help her!" Eric stormed out of the house.

Kev looked at three of his guards. "Follow him and give him any help he needs within reason. He and his son are under our protection."

In unison they all nodded. "Yes, Alpha."

Austin sat there looking at the letter, reading it repeatedly, and each time his eyes welled up with tears. Danny pulled him off the sofa and into his arms where he let himself go into uncontrollable sobs.

"Austin, it will be okay. We will get our kids back. I need you to stay here and do not be afraid to use your powers! I am off to hunt down those who harmed my family."

"NO! You're not leaving me home alone. I am coming out to play, and it's time to use my powers. I will take to the air. I will link you to what I see. They will regret coming after our family." Austin walked out to the back-yard, looked around, shifted into his dragon, and took to the sky.

"So is his dragon always the size of a hawk?" Rob asked, looking perplexed at the size of the dragon high in the air.

"Nope, he can control his size, and I would say it's for the best, because if someone saw an enormous dragon in the air, this town would shut down in panic mode." Danny saw Austin disappear and linked him. "*Austin, my love. I love you. We will get our kids back.*"

"*Danny, I am broken. The Chimera is me. I am supposed to be so powerful, yet our own kids have been taken and by humans no less. I see Darla's car, but no sign of her or the kids. It's parked behind the old movie theater."*

"We're on our way. We have Eric and three of the pack guards from Celtic Rhino on their way to Karen's house."

"I doubt she would be stupid enough to take our kids there, but she might have Deven. I am getting a calling to the lake south of town. Someone is drawing me to the water. I will patrol along the way."

"Follow your heart, baby, but if it gets dangerous, send me a sign. I will not allow myself to lose the kids and you on the same night. I won't lose you again, after what happened to you six years ago."

"Six years ago, I was drugged and beaten up. I am now at my full power. May the gods have mercy on the one who took my babies."

Kev and Rob pulled Danny from his mind link to his mate by clearing their throats. Meanwhile, Tate looked around the room and viewed the security files. "Danny, I noticed whoever was here knew where the cameras were, because they blocked them out, and knocked them down. They even used infrared lights to blind the cameras. What they failed to realize though, was that the town uses your security system. Any chance, as it is your system, you have a back door hack?"

"As a lawyer, I should say no officer, I do not have access. But as a father..." Danny raised an eyebrow.

"I'll tell you what: if I walk outside to clear my head and I come back and I magically have access to the video in question, I won't be able to prove anything. All I care about is getting the kids back, because if it endangered your children, my child will be too."

"I can't argue with that."

"Wait, this human knows all about us and you seem to be so relaxed about it?" Rob eyed Tate and sized him up.

"Truth be told, Rob, he has been blessed, so he is not quite all human. His mate is Princess Elena." Danny smiled, looking at Tate.

"Wait, the vampire princess from across the river?" Rob looked at Tate in awe. "Besides the fact she is a human hybrid, way to go man. But does her daddy know his little girl is brewing one up in the oven and you're not married?" Rob eyed Tate's naked hand.

"We will be married soon. But that will wait. I want to bring the George-Blazek kids home first." Tate stretched, grabbed his hat, and smiled as he walked out the door.

CHAPTER 32
LAKESIDE VISIT

Austin glided over the town, keeping his eyes peeled, but he couldn't find any sign of his children. He passed over parks and school grounds, but they were nowhere to be seen. The night air was crisp and clear. If he had not shrunk so small, the town's folks would be scared of him. His heart felt heavy, as Trey was howling in his head, crying for his pups. "*Trey, you're right. We need to be alert. They will know we are hunting for them, and maybe somehow, they will hear us. They have to hear us. We need our pups to be safe. I swear we are leaving this place. I can't stand Karen. The evil cow has something to do with the disappearance of our kids. I still can't figure out how she managed it.*"

"*So, I can take over vocals?*" Trey howled with delight and readied himself.

"*Yes, howl to your heart's content.*" Austin allowed Trey to come to the surface as he glided through the air to the lake. Trey let out a long howl that echoed across the town and they waited on the airwaves for any response.

"*Well, we can only wait to see if we hear a response from*

the children." Austin used his wolf and dragon hearing combined, only to pick up nothing in response to his calls.

"I don't hear our pups, but I can hear the guard's response. They have cleared the south end of the town and are moving north. They are worried about the dairy farm."

"They don't have to worry about that. I will have princess Elena deal with them. They know if my kids show up on their land and I am not there... well, the sun will be the least of their worries."

Suddenly, down by the lake there came a calming blue light that called him to land just nearby. As Austin approached, the familiar glow of the light from Selene stepped out as he landed. Austin quickly took his human form and greeted the Goddess like an old friend.

"Selene, it is lovely to see you, but this is the worst timing for a visit." Austin stopped in his tracks as two figures stepped out of the water. "Amphitrite, Poseidon." Austin did a bow to the two ancient gods.

"Child, no need to bow. You saved us, remember? We should pay our respects to you, isn't that right, Poseidon?" Amphitrite nudged her husband, who rolled his eyes.

"I see you are still wearing my trident, young man. I am to assume your mate has the other one still." The firm voice of Poseidon showed he was not completely happy his wife gave away not one, but two, of his prized tridents.

"Poseidon, if you don't knock it off I will put you back in that prison world myself! If it was not for this man and his husband, we would still be separated, and they would imprison me under the sea. So show him some respect." Amphitrite smacked Poseidon on his broad, muscular chest. "I swear you act like those were your only two tridents. Keep it up, and I will have Hermes run an errand for me and take all six hundred and eighty-three of your tridents and leave them with your brother."

"Yes, dear. Austin, I'm sorry if I came across like that. It's because I'm not used to sharing my toys."

"Poseidon, Amphitrite, we don't have time for this right now. Austin, have you noticed anything strange going on lately?" Selene asked as she sat on a tree stump.

"Besides my children being kidnapped, and I was hunting for them when I was assuming you beckoned me to the lake?" Austin looked up at Selene with a less than pleased look on his face.

"Now, here here. I know you are upset, so I will let that look slide, but I am not beyond slapping Treyvana back into her box. We came here to warn you. As you know, the war we won gave the old gods their freedom, but not all the gods and pantheons were good for mankind. One of those is Eris."

"Eris? Who the fuck is that, and why should I care?"

"Why should you care? That foul hag is the goddess of strife and troublemaking. She is a downright thorn in all of us gods' sides. You, my dear boy, are her newest fixation."

"Do you know where my kids are?"

"No, even now that we are in the mortal world and away from that prison, we are still limited. I swear, whoever filled your heads with this sawdust notion that we are all omnipotent, all knowing, and all powerful... We may be gods and goddesses, but..." Poseidon patted Amphitrite on her thigh. "We still have our limits. Much Like Apollo and the nectar of the gods, it has its limits as we do. Surely you have tested your limits, young Chimera?"

"What do you mean by my limits? I am not a god. My limits are very clear. I am a Chimera, but I will age and die like anyone else. I have not even tried to fully power up after I destroyed Joe and that devil creature."

"Sugar pie, you remember the gifts I gave you and that hottie of yours that smells like hot chocolate. You know, chocolate with hints of vanilla? I believe his name was Daddy? No. No. Danny." Amphitrite blushed a deep shade of red.

"Son, be happy you have a husband, not a wife. After six hundred years of us being locked away from each other and she calls one of her heroes a daddy."

"Well, he is a daddy. The father to our three children that are still missing right now. If he is lucky, I might just call him daddy when he plays his cards right. So no, I am far from upset on the slip of tongue, but I must insist on letting me find my children." Austin felt a tingle on the back of his neck.

"You feel that, don't you, Austin?" Selene said, as she stood up and strolled to his side, placing an arm around him in a motherly embrace. She took Austin close to herself and whispered into his ear. "Follow your heart. Listen with all the gifts that have been bestowed upon you."

"What is that? I feel the world around me crying out as if it is in pain, pulled in so many directions." Austin closed his eyes and let his other gifts take over. I can smell orange creamsicle, cinnamon rolls, and citrus and mint. I also smell a faint smell of lilac and roses." Austin's eyes flashed open. "I can smell the kids! Why can I smell the kids? I swear if any of you..."

"Oh, piss you, old shits, you just had to involve yourselves in my bit of fun. I have stirred the pot, now to watch him steam up, boil over, and prove my point. No mortal should have that much power just given over to them," came a voice from the tree line.

"Eris, I presume. Come out and face me, you hag." Trey's voice came to the surface, letting his intentions be known. "I am the Chimera wolf and you, I presume, have taken what is mine, and I want it back. You took my pups; my wolf wants his pups back. It's the worst crime you could do. An Alpha who marries an Alpha and has pups makes powerful pups."

"Selene, keep that mutt on a leash. Poseidon, do you think it wise for someone so ill-tempered to be gifted with that trident?"

"Don't you understand that pups were, are, and always will be off limits? Since you're not denying involvement, it is safe to assume you are behind the shit from Darla and Katie."

"What does it matter, potatoes to potatoes? Either way, both end up smashed and no longer what they once were."

"You would think that for the princess of chaos, you would have some balls—oh wait, wrong gender—the guts to step into the light. I would hate to label your gender without seeing you or asking you. So are your proper pronouns bitch and cunt, or what?" Austin goaded this mysterious god.

"AUSTIN GEORGE-BLAZEK evil goddess or not, please mind your manners!" Selene chastised.

"Eris, what have you done to my children? If one hair on their heads is harmed that six hundred-year imprisonment will be nothing compared to a father's wrath!" Austin rotated his head and popped all of his joints.

"Oh, I am so scared the little baby god is making demands. Do you feel oh so powerful now that you realized that you and that dog of a man have immortality?"

"What?" Austin was surprised as he attempted to mind link other pack members.

"Oh, no, none of that. I can't have you summoning an army to attack me when I was only doing what needed to be done.

"Did they not tell you that a tattoo that calls forth a god can only wield the powerful weapon of a god? Dear boy, in having you fulfill their prophecy, they made you and your mate into gods. Your children were conceived before those tridents were in your arms." Eris smirked while crossing her arms and stepping into the light.

With the speed and gifts of the elements, Austin was upon Eris, pinning her to the ground with another trident in hand.

"Fool! Attack me and I'll destroy that trident from your mark, so you will once again be powerless."

"Foolish goddess, I summoned *my* trident, made and forged by my own hand. Now, where are my children?" Austin demanded as he pointed the tips of the iron laced trident to the base of her skull.

"So, you're not as stupid as I once thought. Your time is running out, though. Your human law system seems to be quick to action in matters of children." With that, Eris chuckled, then cackled and faded into a dark mist that dissipated as she vanished.

"Austin, you have your answers. Now, go." Selene displaced a pack of wolves to hunt Eris. "We will deal with her. She admitted to crimes against you the CHIMERA. We have strict laws with our children and what is permitted. She rolled over and gave you information on where to search. Be swift, but remember, they are only humans under the control of a sick goddess."

"Selene, Amphitrite, Poseidon. I make no promises. No one messes with my babies!"

Austin took a deep breath, then linked Danny. "*Courthouse.*"

Danny quickly responded, "*Meet you there.*"

"Well, I need to go, and I will use all my powers from now on. I guess I have that right as a minor god. Thanks for telling me about it."

"It is not just you, Austin. Danny is in the same boat. Eventually you two will have to make yourselves look older, or one day everyone around you will look old and you will still look eighteen."

"So that's why I keep getting carded. What of our children?"

"I will gift them with eternal lives longer than the normal werewolf or hybrid. They two will need to learn to move and change who they are and age without aging. We will help where we can. Even as gods and goddess's, free or not, we still have rules." Selene kissed Austin on his cheek and faded away, as Amphitrite and Poseidon both turned into water and blended into the lake.

Austin shook his head and flicked his wrist to open a portal to the rear of the courthouse when his wolf piped up, "*You know Danny will not be a fan of you using magic to transport us to a town like this. I am just warning you. I don't plan on getting Adonis mad at me.*"

"*Trey, this is for our pups. All rules are out of the window now.*" Stepping through the portal into the dark alley, Austin proceeded with caution.

CHAPTER 33
MIDNIGHT COURT

Once in the alley, Austin quickly readied himself by calling Doug. "Doug, why are the lights on in the courthouse?"

"It seems they are having an emergency T.P.R. for someone's children."

"YEAH, MINE!" Austin growled out as he ripped the courthouse door open.

"Who the hell are you? You can't be in our courthouse. This is a closed matter." One of the courthouse guards aimed a gun at Austin.

"Aww, the little courthouse bitch thinks I fear a gun. You have my children, and you have kidnapped them. I take what is mine!" Austin bellowed out, as Darla came out of one court room, moving the children from one room to another, while Karen walked out with Deven crying in her arms.

"Grammy, why are you doing this to me and Daddy? We just found Momma and you're doing this. Why?" Deven was struggling to free himself, but he appeared weaker than normal.

"DEVEN!" Austin yelled out.

"Austin? What are you doing here? Guards, get him. Lock him up. He is the father of those children that were are endangered." Karen pointed at Austin.

Danny and Kev, with Rob and the pack guards, came rushing in, pinning all the guards down, as Austin walked up to take Deven, but he could sense something was wrong. "I gave him a shot. He is sedated, but he should be safe."

"I don't have to give him up to anyone. I got emergency custody because my son left him in your unsupervised care. Well, that's what we told the judge." Karen half laughed at the idea.

Danny walked up and forced Deven out of her arms, as he grabbed on to Danny for dear life.

"Get me daddy please," cried Deven.

"Daddy is right here bubby." Eric stormed into the court house, taking Deven from Danny's arms.

"Mother, you are dead to me. Once Doug fixes what you have done, you will never see me or my son again. To me, you and father are dead to us. I hope you are happy."

"DADDY!" Aurora cried out as Darla struggled to pull the kids one by one from a side office into a courtroom. Darla looked up to see both Danny and Austin rushing down the hall.

"I don't understand how the hell you're still standing, little girl. I gave you enough medication to sedate. You should have passed out a long time ago. I don't know what is going on and why this is not working on you three little shits, but it will all soon be over, and your parents won't be able to stop it. Once we put you in protective custody and end parental rights, you will all be given good Christian full names, and all traces of the past will be lost. There's no reason such heathens should be allowed to have children."

"Aurora sing for daddy!" Austin yelled, running down the hall.

"Okay daddy." Aurora cleared her throat.

"Here we are, once again, dealing with this evil woman.
Seems like just
days ago, she pushed into our lives.
Ignoring our cries,
She tells us no more goodbyes
Darla needs
to go away
Ripping us from home today
She forces us into tears
Taunting our fears
Once you forget
No one will know
What powers we hold
Now we demand release."

With that, Aurora shoved Darla off of her and ran to the room where her brothers were still locked up. Once inside, she untied her brothers from the chairs Darla had confined them to.

"You can't do this. This is a house of law. We will have you in court." Darla stood up and ran her hand over the cut she found on her leg. "You know, I think you assaulted me, Danny. Why make a child pay for the parents?" An evil grin spread across Darla's face as Karen rushed up to her hysterically.

"Eric is here, and because of them, he has Deven."

"That's okay, we have the judge on our side. Let's get into the courtroom. That will be the only thing that matters." Darla urged Karen to go into the courtroom so they could seal it and not have anyone interrupt the proceedings.

"Danny, Austin, Eric, I know you don't want to do this, but we now have no legal choice. Because of Karen and Darla, we have to have you and the kids in front of the judge. Failure to do so will make you look bad and give them the power to take the kids," Doug said, out of breath as he fixed his tie.

"Fine, very well," Austin mumbled as he tried the door. "That bitch locked or blocked the door."

"STEP ASIDE!" came the firm voice of Adonis as he shoved hard on the door, knocking the two women over who were blocking the door with their bodies.

"You brute, did you have to knock us over with such violence?"

"Ask me a stupid question Karen, you will get yourself a stupid answer. Do you really want me to answer that?"

"Good, I got here before they could do anything. Doug here has the security footage, not only from the George-Blazek home and the hidden cameras they all didn't know about, but also the ones on top of the streetlights for a three-block radius, showing them taking four kids, and two adults by piping some kind of sedative into the house. They all never stood a chance," chimed in Tate who had arrived with Doug.

"You will have a hard time proving that one Tate. I won't call you Sheriff, because after tonight we will have you removed from office. You know we cannot have someone who is, well, let's just say, living in sin, be the one to enforce our good Christian town laws." Karen smirked and rolled her eyes.

The judge entered the chambers, and Karen and Darla both over acted injuries as they went to their side of the courtroom. "Are you ladies, okay? Did I miss something here?" The female judge motioned around the room.

"Oh, we can settle that later, your honor. we need to settle the matter of the children first. They are the priority. We can press our assault charges later," said Darla.

"Your honor." Doug motioned for the three fathers and four children to take a seat on the bench behind his podium.

"Doug, I was not expecting you here. We, in fact, do not need you here for this. Please see your way out."

"I think not, your honor, as these men and their children are my clients, and you and those two seem hell bent on terminating parental rights without a fair shake, you better believe I won't leave. Try to force me, and I will take this to every chain of command in the country, and you will lose your robe over this. Do I make myself clear, your honor? You and I both know this entire thing is a sham. Danny, do your thing."

"With pleasure dad." Danny pulled his father's tablet out of his bag and logged into the court house cameras, then he uploaded to a private server all the footage from when they entered the courthouse until that moment. "Done."

"Wait, what did you just do?" The judge sat up, looking puzzled, knowing it was never wise to pick a fight with the Blazek family.

"Oh, we just secured footage of everything in case someone tries anything funny."

"Fine Doug, you can stay. Darla is your first witness." The judge motioned to Darla.

"Your honor, let's call Deven to the stand. Oh, wait we can't. He seems like he is asleep, or like someone drugged him with something."

"Not true, your honor." Austin placed a hand on Deven and hummed, and he woke up and was fully angry at his grandmother.

"Grammy you're a bitch and so is she," he yelled, pointing to Darla.

"Hey now, young man, you know we don't call adults that," Eric's firm voice rang out.

"Sorry daddy but Grammy is a B. She stuck me two times in my arm with something, and I don't know how we got here. Grammy is evil. She wanted to take me away from you forever."

"Your honor, that is..." Karen started to sway and look intoxicated.

"Young man, do you stand by what you just said? If they drugged you, why are you so awake?"

"HE fixed me. He knows how to return to the sender," Deven said, before he realized his mistake.

"See, your honor, filling these children's heads with such devious lies." Darla stood up and helped Karen to her seat.

"Fine, next witness."

"Your honor I want to call Aurora George-Blazek to the stand."

"Very well, come up here child, and mind your tone."

"Yes, your honor." Aurora happily skipped up to the stand.

"I don't know how she is standing. I gave her enough tranquilizer to put her to sleep. I should pass all of them out," Karen said through gritted teeth, but loud enough that everyone in the chambers heard her, even though they ignored her. Doug only took notes and motioned for the guys to remain quiet.

"Aurora, what grade are you in?" Karen asked from her seat.

"Umm Karen, I am in kindergarten with your grandson."

"So, Aurora, would you agree that most children in your class have one mommy and one daddy?"

"Yeah, but some have just one mommy and no daddy. Like Deven had just his daddy and no mommy. But he is lucky cause his momma is pretty and has found his daddy and him again."

"Okay sweety, please just answer the questions. No extra talking."

"Fine."

"Aurora, what would you say to someone who says your dad and his friend are not a good fit for you?"

"My dad and daddy are just fine, Karen. Our family is just as good as anyone else."

"Again Aurora, keep to the question."

"Fine," Aurora pouted.

"Since you seem unable to follow basic instructions, do you know your ABCs? I highly doubt you can, and it would not be your fault," Karen said smirking.

"Yes, I know my ABCs. A. B. C.D. E, F you Karen cause you're a B," Aurora sang.

"AURORA ROSE GEORGE-BLAZEK, you stop right now!" Danny said, standing and giving his daughter one simple look.

Aurora put her head down. "Sorry daddy but she started it. I know two wrongs don't make a right, but still... Some strange men broke into our house, and Uncle Bou and Aunt Lexi passed out. Lexi was making dinner, and suddenly she was on the kitchen floor, and some guy was looking at her with a funny look in his eye. He tied her up and dragged her off. Then some guy came and tied all of us kids up. I acted like I was asleep, and I heard him say Karen paid a pretty penny to have us all taken, but not a single hair on Deven's head could be harmed."

"Young lady, stop right now. You can only answer questions when they are asked of you. I will toss anything else you say out." Darla stood up and crossed her arms.

"Doug, do you have anything to add?" the judge begrudgingly asked.

"Yes, I do. Sweetheart, tell the courts what you remember from tonight's events."

"Objection, your honor."

"Over ruled. Let's see what the child knows."

"Do I have to say it all over again, your honor? Or can I pick up where I left off?"

"I will permit you to continue, honey, but keep to the facts. Do not sugarcoat things."

"Well, once we all got to the courthouse, Darla injected all of us with something, and it made us sleepy. We woke up tied up in room 133. Karen came in and took Deven out, and that's when Darla came to drag me in here. She was complaining someone should drug me enough that I would be asleep."

"Your honor I object. There is no proof."

"Your honor if you please." Doug held up his tablet.

"Sure, why not Doug? The entire night has been a shit show anyway." the Judge tossed her hands in the air.

Doug linked his tablet to the projector and played the video of them dragging the kids into the courthouse and injecting them with a mysterious solution. Aurora had stated that the enhanced audio would play exactly as she had said.

"Doug, I have heard and seen enough. Karen, Darla, did you think because we belong to the same church and country club that I would side with you? You must be kidding me. Look at all this evidence we have. Karen, I advise you to get a lawyer, because you are going to need one. I already fired Darla as caseworker, and she still attacked this family. You are on video injecting these kids with what I assume are sedatives. You are under arrest. Bailiff, place Darla and Karen into custody. Karen, you better hope that husband of yours can bail you out. I could not care less that you're the mayor's wife."

"Your honor?" Austin stood up, holding Ethan's hand and Logans.

"Yes, Mr. George-Blazek?"

"Can you force them to tell us where my step brother and soon to be sister-in-law are? If not, our private security detail will go over every square inch of this town, and I am sure you don't want the public eye of the nation on top of this town."

"Austin, are you threatening a judge?"

"No, your honor I am giving you all the information to form a judgment."

"Karen, where did you put the two adults?"

"Hell, if I know Seth took a liking to the lady and Rodger took the guy somewhere, they were to release them at five o'clock in the morning."

"Sherriff Tate, hunt down Seth if he has done anything to that young lady. We need to use whatever force to bring my brother into custody. Lord knows that son of a bitch is a perv."

"Your honor," Darla protested.

"This case is dismissed and so are all pending charges to the George-Blazek family. If you even try, the two of you even attempted to contact that family, I will toss you both in jail and toss the key into the river." With that, the judge banged her gavel down, dismissing everyone.

"Austin, we will meet you at your place and then we can go to mine to collect the rest of our things. The West Side moving company you set us up with were champions," Eric said with a wink as he picked up his son and walked out, never looking back at his mother.

"Dad, thank you. As you know, this town is not safe for us anymore. I would prefer if you and sis took mom back to Genesis Moon. But that is your choice. Bou is to keep our house up for us. But we are leaving tomorrow afternoon destination Celtic Rhino territory," Danny said, picking up his little princess.

"All right boys, let us get princess here home to bed. We have a lot to pack and get done before we say goodbye to this place." Austin led the two boys out of the courtroom and headed to the vans Kev and Rob had waiting for them.

CHAPTER 34
TRIDENT'S GLOW

"Bath daddy!" the three children squealed in delight, running up to Kev and giving him a large group embrace, while Rob stood there holding the door with his mouth agape.

"Umm Alpha Kev you smell like eucalyptus, just like my favorite bath bomb," Aurora squealed.

"Umm, hello I'm here too you know," Rob mumbled under his breath, but Aurora heard him all too well.

"Beta Rob, no one can forget you and your cinnamon and clove smell. You should make that into a bath steamer if it wouldn't get you into any trouble," Aurora said smiling walking up to Beta Rob. You are Alpha Kev's right hand and we know if it was not for your pack coming to save us, our dads would have had a harder time of it. Thank you for rescuing us." Aurora hugged Robs leg, leaving him speechless.

"I-I."

"You asked for the attention, Rob. Let's get these pups home, so they can rest and finish packing to come stay with us. I don't want to stay a minute longer than we have to in this town. Anywhere that isn't inclusive and filled with love, isn't a place I want anyone from my pack to be in, always living in fear like that." Kev picked up Ethan, who instantly nestled himself in his arms.

"Well, well, looks like our Alpha has a natural talent. Ethan can't, or won't fall asleep in anyone's arms like that other than Austin's." Danny looked on at how at peace his little boy was in Alpha Kev's arms.

"Oh, no, no, no. Don't get any ideas. My Luna and I are not ready for kids. We may or may not even have a pup. We will know when the time is right. For the time being, your pups can fill any void, right Rob?" Kev looked over his shoulder as he fastened the now sleeping Aurora into her car booster seat.

"Safety first, little one." With that, Rob kissed his fingers, then placed them on her sleeping forehead.

"Austin, Danny, I don't know how you managed, but you two raised some special pups." Rob looked one more time at the sleeping pups, closed the door to the van as quietly as he could, walked back over to the second over-sized van, and got in with the rest of the pack warriors.

"Austin, not that I'm looking, but why is your arm glowing under your sleeve?" Kev asked, nodding his head to Austin's forearm.

"Crap, we need to get to my house and be on alert. Danger is near," Austin muttered while drawing his sleeve up, showing the glowing trident.

"I never knew a tattoo could glow. Especially when danger is near. Did you have some white witch spell the ink before you were tattooed?"

"No, it's a tattoo, but it's also a real trident, like the Chimera. It comes with my job. Danny has one as well." Austin looked up to see his neighborhood coming into view, and Eris was standing in the middle of the road. "What does this bitch want now? I thought I made it clear at the lake that I won't tolerate people fucking with my family. Its one problematic son of a bitch after another."

"Daddy has a potty mouth. That is money into the bad word jar!" Logan said as his eyes flickered. Between his one blue and one green, both were turning crimson red and black.

"For him not being a full-blooded Chimera like his siblings, those eyes told a different story. He was young to shift, but his wolf seemed to be at the surface." Kev took a deep breath and looked again at the child.

"They have a sizeable chunk of their powers already, but they haven't shifted yet. It's just a matter of time. I know that sometime soon, probably once we're in your territory, they will fully shift. For now, I get to step out and deal with this goddess."

"Good luck with that. I don't know how my men can be of help going up against a goddess." Kev looked at Eris and back at Austin, only to watch Austin dissolve into mist and appear on the road near her. "Man, does he know how to leave and entrance?"

"Yeah, yeah, so he can do a few party tricks—" Rob stopped mid-sentence as he witnessed Austin pulling the trident from his arm and shifting part way to be as tall, if not taller than the goddess of chaos, with blue pearl wings coming from his back. "What on Earth?!"

"Oh, that wicked lady is in for it. Daddy is going into his mega form. No one wants to see Daddy hit that level. We better hold on to your car seat, sissy," Ethan giggled, wiggling his nose as his eyes turned silver.

"Oh, Ethan, your eyes are silver," Aurora exclaimed.

"Yours are turning." Ethan pointed to his sister.

"Kids, there will be no transforming in the van. Your dad

told me to get you in the house." Kev looked back and gave the kids all a stern look of an Alpha's command.

"Yes Alpha," they all called out, but they turned to each other and talked in an unrecognizable language.

"Twin speak, sir. The two are twins and they taught it to Logan. Not to mention they have the gift to mind link and a lot more," Danny said, while looking down at his glowing tattoo. He linked Austin. "*My trident is glowing as well. Do I need to come out and play?*"

"*No, get our kids to safety.*"

"*I am one thought away. No need to play super wolf out here.*" Danny chuckled and closed the link.

"All right my little minions, into the house and finish packing what you think you must have once we settle in at Alpha Kev's pack in Colorado."

"Yes Daddy. Will Dad be okay?" Aurora asked, looking perplexed at the standoff in the road.

"It's okay, sweetheart. The magic is concealing them and the humans can't see them. Now, get to packing or you will go without. Scoot." Danny playfully swatted at the children to get into the house.

"I see you still hold dear that trident, poor fool. You don't even have the power to wield it, let alone know how to use it properly." Eris' voice crossed the street in a wicked hiss.

"Eris, what's it like being the goddess of bitches?" Austin mused, goading the goddess to make a move.

"Think you're cleaver? I know the rules of engagement. I can't directly attack you or your family because you were the one prophesied to liberate us. To be honest, not all of us wanted to be liberated, because now I am forced back into my old role. Anyway, I will get the pleasure of making them suffer." Eris gestured to the humans and werewolves around her. "But since we no longer have time restraints, those who know how to reach out to us older gods and goddesses, also know how to put limitations on us. I dislike being controlled by a simple human. Witch or not."

"Aww." Austin took his index finger and thumb and rubbed them together.

"What is this? " Eris copied the gesture.

"I am playing the world's smallest violin for you. Can't you hear it? No. Then I guess I really couldn't care less that your actions are being stopped, and it's pissing you off. But once you fuck with my family, then we're on. I can play ball just as much as the old gods. Trust me, Poseidon and I have an under-standing. Hell, he even taught Danny and I how to maximize or power."

"You have no power. You're human, with a relic of an old worthless god."

"Mind your mouth before he fixes that for you."

"I don't fear him or any of the other pathetic pantheons. I will raise this town to the ground with strife. Karen and Darla were already against you, so I started on your family. Raising kids none the less. Over the years, I have sowed the seeds of hatred for your kind. Now I get to enjoy the fruits of my labor, as they hunt you all down and either beat you to within an inch of your life, or chase you out of town. Once that is done, well, they can have a little peace as I feed on the hate."

"So that's your gimmick. You do this to feed off of the hate and strife to gain power."

"Cleaver little human." Eris mocked Austin as if talking to a baby.

"Human? You know better. I am the Chimera." Trey's eyes flashed as his head morphed into the head of a wolf and the trident glowed.

"Oh, so what now, is the dog coming out to play? Is he up

to date on his shots? I would hate to have him put down being a mutt and all."

"Watch who you call a mutt, tramp," Trey growled out.

"Tramp?" Eris stumbled over the word.

"Oh wait, my mistake. No one would touch you, even with the devil's dick."

"You shut your mouth. How dare you speak of my jelly-bean?" Eris' eyes glowed with anger, as she summoned dark skeletons from underground. Attack him, my minions!" Eris screeched.

Austin hummed and the sound vibrated out around them and bounced off the houses. The skeletons started to stumble and dance around as if they were drunk before bumping into each other.

"What are you going to sing them to death? Minions, I said attack him, or better yet, attack the house." Eris flicked her wrist, opening a rift allowing more skeletons out of the underworld.

"Are you working with the underworld now? I know you bring strife and troublemaking, but to control the bodies of the dead?" Austin and Trey asked in unison.

"Worry not about who or what I can control," Eris hissed out as she grazed her hand over a ring with a skull that had ruby eyes. "Get those worthless brats and drag them to the keep!"

"Daddy!" Aurora squealed, as a skeleton chased her out of the house.

"Baby girl, you have permission." Trey's eyes glowed an eerie electric blue.

Aurora stopped dead in her tracks as Danny came running out of the house. "NO Aurora! Daddy is coming!"

"It's okay daddy, I love you." Aurora took up a fighter's stance as her eyes glazed over, turning purple.

The skeleton warrior stopped a moment and sized up the little humanoid victim before he started slowly stalking up to her again. Danny rushed out to save his daughter when the skeleton screamed and more warriors crawled out from the ground surrounding Danny. Alpha Kev and Beta Rob and their warriors rushed to the door.

"I need six of you to stay with the children. We need to fight them off and help Danny get Aurora back. Austin, Danny, any way to stop the masses?"

Austin broke eye contact for a second to see Aurora charging up to the skeleton, then he looked back to see Eris reaching into her gown and pulling out a metallic spider. Once it hit the ground, it shattered into a million little spiders all crawling toward the house. Eris cackled as the color faded from Danny's face when he saw Logan being dragged from the house.

"NOW Aurora!" Austin yelled.

Aurora sprang from the ground and flipped into the air. Then she morphed into a half-wolf and half-dragon creature, and she threw one hand into the air, catching the moonlight. Then, making a fist, she swung her hand at the skeletons that were dragging Logan, and at the same moment she released the light she had trapped, and it went flying out like silver spears, crashing into the skeletons and turning them into dust.

"Thanks sis, can I play too?" Logan asked with an impish look on his face.

"Do your worst, just don't burn any homes down Logan!" Danny yelled as he cracked the skull of a nearby skeleton warrior.

Logan took a knee, placing his hands on the ground, and he hummed louder and louder. Eris turned to face Austin once again. "So, she has powers already at a young age. All well and good, but she will burn out soon enough. Little ones have no endurance. Oh, little boy seems to take after you and likes to hum. What is he going to sing me to death? My minions will get both of your brats."

"You understand you drew first blood? Eris, your punishment is coming." Austin pointed to his little singer as hot air came out of the rift. Hands made of earth and steam reached out, scooping the spiders into the hot abyss. The ground started to gently open up soft spots around each of the skeletons, and they seeped into the underworld once more.

"This is not possible! It's not fair! Strike me, you fool! Use your powers on me!" Eris screamed at Austin, then turned her attention to the kids. "I dare you to try that on me, you little mutts!"

"Logan don't," Aurora said, walking up to her brother. That's what she wants. If we attack, she can use more of her powers. She is an old ugly god that no one loves and she is just bitter." Aurora turned to face Eris. "Bitter party of one, your table is being served." Aurora smirked at Eris and waved.

"Foolish girl." Eris raised her arm up to strike Aurora, when a blinding light flashed before everyone, freezing time.

CHAPTER 35
OH, GODDESS

"Not my baby, you bitch." Selene appeared in a blinding blue light. Stepping out of the light, she back handed Eris, sending her rolling across the street. Then she brushed her gown down and shook her head, before walking over to Aurora, squatting down to eye level, and smiling. "How is daddy's little princess? I saw how powerful you have become. You are so strong, Aurora. I'm so proud of you. Can you help me out with a little favor?"

"Anything for Auntie Selene." Aurora perked up.

"Do you think you can get your brothers and go through the portal in your closet to Grandma and Grandpa Blazek while us adults take care of this problem?" Selene smiled sweetly at Logan and Ethan, who were now standing at Aurora's side.

"You heard Auntie Selene boys off to GGs. Now march!" Aurora spun around and pushed her brothers into the house.

"Selene, how dare you get involved? This does not concern you!" hissed Eris, picking herself up off the ground.

Danny kissed the kids as they passed, and headed to Aurora's closet door. "Listen to GG, you hear me?"

290

"Yes, Papa," Aurora said, rolling her eyes.

"Young lady, do not sass me." Danny's voice had an edge that let Aurora know quickly to change her tune.

"Sorry Daddy, we will be good." Aurora stepped into the house with her brothers and was soon out of sight. Danny paused and took in a deep breath, allowing Adonis to take over. The sound of bones cracking and shifting echoed down the block.

"Oh, look Selene, one of your little mutts is coming out to play kid games," Eris mused as she tried to open another rift and was stopped.

Austin was tapping the butt of the trident on the ground, eyeing her next move. "Selene, thank you for stepping in since she attempted to attack my pups. Do I now have permission since she drew blood first?" Austin's eyes narrowed to almost slits as he glared at Eris.

"I did not draw the blood of your mutt child."

"No, you just attempted to send your underlings after her until she kicked their asses back to the underworld." Austin didn't hide the pleasure he felt witnessing his daughter's powers.

"Eris, you do not need to be here. Why are you stirring the pot? If you'd rather be imprisoned, that can be arranged. The fact the other gods have allowed you to carry on as long as you have leaves me shocked. I only stepped up once you attempted to hurt a child. You know we banned striking down children, let alone children of the gods, long ago." Selene stood to her full height, with Austin to her right and Adonis to her left.

"So you would step on the neck of a sister goddess to lower yourself to their standards? Forget the fact they are men for a moment. But they were once human. They have no celestial blood in their veins. Selene, you are such a waste of a goddess."

Eris looked around and all of her destruction was slowly evaporating.

"What is the matter, Eris? All that hate, all that discord and destruction is slowly going away? Have you not heard of me this entire time? Did you think I was tapping my trident for nothing? While I was tapping in a rhythmic pattern, I was also doing a siren song of return to sender. All the damage you have inflicted on this land has returned to you. Well, where ever you lay that wicked little head of yours." Austin's eyes flashed electric blue as a surge of power rolled off his body.

"Y-you can't do that. You are nowhere near that powerful." Eris staggered to gather her strength.

"I would advise you to go before you do the wrong thing that allows me to use the full scope of my power." Trey's voice overpowered Austin. "You came onto our territory. You threatened to harm my family. Sending your minions to attack my children. Eris, you are lucky I don't run you through with this trident right here and now. Once I settle my family, I will talk to the council about your actions. Everything you did tonight risked exposing the mortals to the immortal world. It was hard enough covering up the war six years ago. If you loved your little prison world so much, then go back to that pocket dimension and leave this reality alone."

"Big words from a little wolf," Eris scoffed.

"Little?" Austin shook his head. "You understand that as the Chimera I control my size. I am part werewolf, dragon, and triton. I have the blessing of the elementals. That is why my powers are where and what they are. Attempt to harm my family, or anyone who falls under Chimera protection, and I will bring wrath on you like no other." Austin snapped his fingers and a portal opened behind Eris. Placing his palm out in front of him, he blew across the street, causing Eris to stumble into the portal.

Before Eris could figure out where she was sent, she heard her father's voice. "Eris, what do you think you are doing? The Chimera is protected. He is a minor god, but a god all the same. Him and his partner helped save us all. This behavior reflects on me and I will not have it. Do not attack them ever again." Zeus's voice boomed out across his chamber.

"How did he send me here!" Eris screamed, while throwing a full-fledged adult tantrum.

"If you will act like a child, you will be treated like a child." Zeus snapped his fingers, sending Eris off in a black mist, leaving her wailing voice behind.

Meanwhile, back on the mortal plane, Austin turned to Selene. "Why does she have such hatred for my family?" He took a deep breath and let it out, slowly deflating to his normal human size. "Adonis, the danger has passed. It's time to bring it down a notch."

"No, we have visitors coming." Adonis sniffed the air.

"Adonis, my child, he is right, the oncoming car is full of humans. When they see me, they will see just a beautiful woman. They can either see you as a dog, or as Danny."

"Fine." Danny shifted back to his human form. "Well, being a partial god has its perks. I don't have to worry about shifting naked anymore."

"I don't see that as a perk, Danny. I enjoy seeing those golden bronze buns."

"You can see them later, once all this drama is over and we're out of this damn town," Danny growled through a clenched jaw, as a van with blacked-out windows drove down the street and stopped short of Austin and Danny. Someone from inside the van opened the door and shoved Bou out with such force, that you could hear the bones in his arm crunch as he hit the street. The man inside attempted to have one last try at caressing and touching Lexi. "Such a waste. We could have had some fun, but the boss won't seem to let me. You know, I could show you a lot in a matter of minutes."

"Touch me, you slime ball, and you will sing soprano for the rest of your god damn life." Lexi struggled against her bindings.

"Now, now, such a feisty little kitty. Let's see if daddy can make you purr and not hiss." The man ran his rough, callused hands up Lexi's exposed thigh, creeping higher and higher.

"You pig! Get your hands off of me." Lexi struggled further back in the van to get away from her assailant.

"See, you know you want this." the strange man undid his belt and reached to unbutton his pants, when he was suddenly yanked backward out of the van and hit the concrete with a deafening thud.

"Lexi, it's me. It's okay. I'm going to touch you now and take off your bindings."

"Bou?" Lexi's voice quivered in anticipation of her mate's touch, but also of the freedom that was upon her.

"Yes, my love. Did that fucker hurt you? I don't know how they sedated me, but they really knocked it out of me. I'm so sorry I failed to save you. Austin will have my hide if we don't get out of here and save his kids."

"That won't be necessary Bou, the kids are home safe with GG Blazek," Austin said, walking up and grabbing the unconscious lump of a human from the ground and tossing him in, once Bou and Lexi were free of the van.

Danny walked up to the driver side window to see a deputy trying to engage the van to drive, but he was only managing to spin his wheels.

"What the fuck man? You got that dumb ass and his whore?" Before he could finish his words, Danny's fist went flying, contacting his jaw, and breaking it in multiple places.

"That is my brother and soon-to-be sister-in-law. I have

you on video and audio admitting to your crime. So, say goodbye to ever working for law enforcement, because even if this sick, sadistic town won't do anything, trust me we will take it at the state level. If we don't get satisfaction on that level, I will take it one step higher."

"Goddamnmootherfufer," the driver mumbled through his broken jaw and the ensuing excruciating pain. As he slammed his foot on the gas, the van took off faster than he intended and he had to jerk the wheel not to crash into the line of cars on the side of the road.

"Austin, were you holding the bumper so he couldn't leave?" Danny asked, walking up to his mate and pulling him into a long kiss.

"What? Little old me? I thought by now these clowns would realize this family is not the one to mess with. We are over the top physically fit. There is an outdoor training station for us. We have security that rivals the FBI building down town. But hey, if they want to be the village idiots, let them. Because when you mess with my family, the gloves come off."

"Speaking of family, Tate, you better go check on that deputy, not to mention your bride. Malcolm has already started shit. Now this with the townspeople. The last thing we need is someone messing with the little spud." Danny looked at a very red-faced Sheriff Tate.

"If any of them hurt my little moonflower, I will need you to be my lawyer." Tate rested his hand on his gun while taking his other hand to pull out his phone. "Hey honey, I'm just calling to be sure you are okay. There has been a lot of drama as of late, and I want to be sure you and my little spud are doing okay."

"Little spud? What do you think I am, a farmer's field or something? I know I live on the dairy farm for now, but really Tate?"

"Aww, come on moonflower, my name is Tate. People call me Tater tot. So naturally my child is my little spud." Tate's voice became chipper and overly bubbly.

"Eww no, we will wait until he or she is born before we make any nicknames up. Do I make myself clear?" Elena's voice was firm, and Tate knew not to question her further.

"Yes, moonflower. I love you, and I am coming to get you. You should come back to my condo. I know you're in a den of vampires, but I would honestly feel better falling asleep tonight with you in my arms after today's events."

"I heard all about it, and I agree. I have already packed my bag and will wait for you. Drive safe. I don't trust these people, nor do I trust Malcolm's people. If daddy were to find out I am with child and not married, he would flip. But if he found out I am with child and was attacked by one of our own, they would wipe this coven out of existence."

"Well, let's not let anything happen. I will be at the dairy farm in ten minutes." Tate hung up the phone and walked over to his car. "Austin, keep me in the loop."

CHAPTER 36
CELTIC RHINO

hile the Chimera clan gathered together once more back home, safe and sound, two blacked out vans rolled up and the Celtic Rhino Pack piled out.

"Okay, boys, patrol the yard until we leave. No one is allowed on the property without Austin or Danny's permission." Kev yelled out his commands before entering the house.

"Kev, I am so thankful for the pack's help in getting our kids back. I don't know what I would have done if I had lost my boys and my little princess." Austin went over to the hall closet to get more luggage for the kids to use. "Logan, honey, come get your suitcase."

"Thank you, daddy. Alpha Kev, you came back." Logan dropped his bag and ran to hug Kev.

"It was nothing, squirt. You're pack members now, so it is my job to be there for all of you. Speaking of that, Austin, can I use that portal and head home? I need to surprise my girlfriend with something." Kev let a gentle grin dance on his lips.

"You know, Kev, one of these days, you will have to share

her with the pack. We will need to know the Luna," Austin said while opening the pantry door to show the Alpha's kitchen on the other side.

"Man, this is crazy. You got that gift from the gods." Kev let out a gentle whistle. "She is not the official Luna yet Austin, but if that day comes, you will all know."

"Yeah, we have a few gifts, but like the saying goes, sometimes it's better not to know, then life can be a surprise. Take your time, Kev. The pack respects your choice. Well, here is your stop, my friend, be seeing you real soon." Austin stepped aside so Kev could walk into the portal to the pack house kitchen.

Rob entered Austin's house as Kev crossed over. "Great, I get to babysit the warriors." Rob rolled his eyes and took a seat as the portal back home closed.

"He said he had a thing to work on back home, sorry Beta." Austin picked up a stuffed teddy bear as Ethan let out a blood-curdling cry, breaking the otherwise quietness of the house.

"Well, I can see as the room empties it's only going to get louder." Austin dusted the dirt and lint off of a teddy bear as Ethan came running down the hall. "Ethan." Austin's voice came out smooth as glass as the red eyed crying boy came running down the hall to the safety of his father's arms.

Austin held out the teddy bear gently, making him dance in the air.

"Freddy Teddy!" Ethan's voice jumped an octave once he saw his missing bear.

"Squirt, how old are you?" Rob asked from the couch, eyeing the child questionably.

"I will be seven this spring," Ethan responded, without looking up as he snuggled with his best friend.

"So, you will be seven and you still have a cuddle buddy?"

Rob let out a half chuckle mixed with a sound of disappointment.

"Why not? You still have a cuddle buddy." Ethan looked up and defiantly stared Rob in his eyes in a showdown, emulating the power of an Alpha in training. Then he walked up and tapped Rob's wedding band with a quick little finger. He snapped his fingers and walked back to his room.

Robs jaw dropped. "What?"

"Ethan." Austin gave his son a father's 'mind your manners' look while holding back his smile of pride.

"What Dad? Uncle Rob should know better. I am your son. What is that Grams B always says? Don't ask a smart butt question if you can't handle a smart butt answer." Ethan placed his hands on his hips, cocking his head to the side.

"That's definitely not how my mother would say it." Austin put his own hand on his hip and cocked his head, mocking his son lovingly.

"Dad, Grandma cusses. I can't." Ethan spun on his heals, springing to his room to finish packing, now that he had his cuddle buddy back.

"Well, Austin, Sandy will be so happy to teach your kiddos." Rob pulled out his phone, taking notes at Ethan and his bear along with his sassy attitude.

"What is that supposed to mean?"

"Nothing. All that sass, I expect it from little Aurora, heck the way you two dote on her, I'm surprised she didn't get the master bedroom." Rob shook his head, still entering detailed notes into his phone. Then his phone pinged, notifying him of an incoming message.

"What now, Rob? We don't have time for any more drama, and I don't have the patience for any more bullshit. I want to get my family out of this town."

"Austin, has anyone ever told you that you are wrapped tighter than a drum?"

Austin looked across at an almost empty living room to meet the gaze of Beta Rob. "Rob, sorry. It's just I feel overwhelmed with all this drama. First, back home in my parents' territory, the three factions, merfolk, werewolves, and dragons, were fighting with each other over the stupidest crap."

"Typical family drama." Rob leaned against the wall next to the fireplace, inspecting his nails. Then he picked up his phone once again, and looked to see if he had any more messages.

"I used to feel safe here. Now our kids have been threatened, then taken to the courts during the night. I swear, if I could, I would send Karen to the bottom of the Black Sea." Austin slammed his fist onto the back of the couch, causing it to break.

"Alpha Kev will not be replacing that couch, just to let you know. Would you cause discord for the Black Sea to ease your own pain? Granted, Karen is a pain in the ass. But would you put that problem in the Black Sea?" Rob raised his eyebrow while holding back a snicker.

"Let me through. This is my house." Danny's voice could be heard in the front yard, getting louder as he was arguing with the guard.

"Sir, we have orders no one in or out per Alpha, Kev."

"Let my husband in, Charlie." Austin stood at the front door with his arms crossed, staring down at the Omega guard, questioning Danny.

"You know, Austin, you might be friends with my Alpha, but the attitude you have..."

"Oh, you think this is an attitude? I'm about to have an MBF." Assassin's eyes flashed with lightning, and a strong Alpha aura rolled off of him as he stared down the Omega who dared to question him.

"What the fuck is an MBF?" Charlie scoffed, as he looked Austin up and down.

Danny let off a stifled laugh as he rushed past the guard who grabbed his wrist at the last moment, pulling him back behind the line of defense.

"It's called a major bitch fit. Unless you want your ass handed to you, you better let go," Danny growled out through a clenched jaw.

"Who are you to talk to me like that? I can definitely see who the bitch in this relationship is and who seems to be neutered." Charlie let out a snicker as he looked at his friends.

"Can you now, Charlie?" Rob said as he stepped out from behind the door. "You do realize, Danny is a pure blood true Alpha. He comes from the Blue Sapphire Pack of Arizona. Austin here is a freaking Chimera."

"Chima who?"

"Chimera dude, are you that stupid and not knowing what happened six years ago? Regardless, Austin is for my pureblood Alpha father and mother. Only difference is he is a tribe red. He has a siren." both Danny and Austin briefly cut Rob off.

"Triton." they say in unison.

"Sorry, triton, dragon and werewolf, who is not only blessed by the elementals, but by the gods and goddesses. So are you really going to stand there and act like an ass?" Rob stepped to the edge of the porch.

"Beta." Charlie's eyes grew to the size of saucers, and his voice stammered as he pointed to where a blue shimmering lady was sitting on top of the roof.

"Selene." Austin smiled, recognizing his old friend.

"Selene?" Rob spun around and bowed to the Moon Goddess.

"Come now, Beta, please keep your pups in line. I would

hate to turn a blind eye to Austin or Danny." Selene smirked and snapped her fingers, disappearing in a beam of moonlight.

Charlie instantly let go. His eyes darting around the yard. "Alphas? Magical powers? Blessed by gods and goddess? Shit, they are on a first name basis with the Moon Goddess. What did our office sentence set for Beta? I demand answers."

"Charlie, last I knew you are an Omega, and we are Alphas. Your Alpha is our friend and your Beta here is also our friend. Question us like that again, and we will see who is really in charge here."

"Austin, do not use your powers on him." Danny slapped Austin gently across his chest.

"We need to finish getting this house in order. I don't feel Bou and Lexi will want to stay here after what happened tonight. I don't trust any of my family to this town."

"Austin, if Bou and Lexi want to, they can join your family in our pack until we get things figured out. I may not be the Alpha, but I am the Beta. Charlie, you will pay for your disobedience when we get home. Speaking of home, Austin, when do you think we will be ready to go?"

"Depends how we're departing." Austin's voice was no longer smooth like glass, but frigid, with a hard edge.

"Don't worry, Charlie here will run back without using his wolf. Anyone who feels the same way can join him." Rob pulled out his phone and texted Kev. "Yep, it's an official Alpha order now. Start going, Charlie. It's a long run back to the pack. Don't forget you have duties in forty-eight hours." Beta Rob's booming voice gave Charlie no other option but to run. "The rest of you pack up in the vans and head home. Austin mind if we take the quick way home? I know you have been transporting stuff to the pack."

"That won't be an issue. I am just waiting for, well speak of the devil, Eric, Rebecca, and Deven."

"So, um, how are we to get all this to Colorado?" Eric pointed to the pickup truck overloaded with boxes.

"The wife used magic to pack, didn't she?" Austin laughed, knowing Fae magic all too well. Rebecca blushed as she and Deven went inside to check on the other children.

"It's that obvious? I have never seen a woman, not only wipe out all my, umm, corn, but also cry over all the things she missed out on. Austin, I have one quick question, since you know more about Fae folk, how quickly can you tell if... well you know?"

"Oh, you're asking if you should get a three bed instead of your two-bed condo? I would suggest getting, if not now, maybe in a year or two, a sizeable piece of land and building your own house, because Rebecca definitely wants an extensive family."

"That works for me, because with a large family comes lots and lots of practice." Eric wiggled his eyebrows and darted into the house.

"Beta, I need one of your men to drive that beast to Colorado." Austin tossed Beta Rob the keys and walked inside.

"Who will I choose, hum? Well, Eddie, you can drive this wonderful truck all the way back to the pack. I know you won't dare pick up Charlie, because if you do, I'm sure Austin will tell me. Trust me, you do not want to be on the receiving end of Austin or Danny's wrath."

"I understand Beta, besides, I know what he did for not just his pack but for all of us shifters. He has all my respect." Eddie bowed, taking the keys and running to the truck.

"Well, you all got your orders now get." Rob turned away, looking for another glimpse of Selene. "Man, wait till I tell the Alpha I got to meet Selene tonight."

"Are my little impromptu visits that well-loved? It is so nice knowing my children are getting along." Selene's voice danced around Rob.

"That we are Mother Moon Goddess. It is always a pleasure to be in your presence." Rob walked into the house and gently closed the door behind him.

CHAPTER 37
REVENGE

E ris paced the room her father sent her to as punishment. "So, this is what return to sender looks like. My room took on the destruction." She attempted to use magic to correct the damage, but getting nowhere, she screamed, "WHAT THE FUCK!"

Looking around her chambers, she saw her witch's looking glass. "Let's see what those worms are up to now." With a wave of her hand, the water rippled as images of Austin and Danny came into play. "Are you kidding me? How can it be? Those filthy animals have so much protection. Selene is always putting her two cents in where it doesn't belong." Eris slapped the water's surface, distorting the image. Once the surface settled down, Darla and Karen came into focus. "Those two worthless worms! I have plans for you yet." Eris leaned into the water, her lips just above the surface, as she mumbled something to the ladies.

"Karen, I cannot believe you almost go us caught."

"Darla, what the hell are you talking about? It was you that got too greedy. I got my Deven. Well, I had my Deven and now, because of you, he is missing." Karen tried once again to call her son, Eric.

Darla looked at her phone, then at Karen, a grin running across her face. "Well, Karen, my eyes on the force say they saw your son and grandson running off to the old dairy farm."

"Why on earth would he go to that godforsaken place?" Karen frowned at Darla but turned to go to her car.

"Where are you going, Karen? Do you honestly expect Austin to just let Eric go after all this? If he truly did something to Eric's mind like you suggested over coffee, I wouldn't go up against him alone."

"Then jump in. We're going to find my son, and prove they've taken him to that run-down farm. Wait a minute, that Malcolm character and his creepy family moved on that farm, and I'm not impressed with what they did with the place. I swear something is not right with that group."

"Sources say they are drug dealers, and the cops just can't catch them." Darla put her phone in her bag, but not before looking at the blank screen. Once again Darla forgot to charge it and now it was dead.

"Oh, good idea. I'll shut my phone off as well, so they can't track us. Darla, I knew I kept you as my friend all these years for a reason."

"Besides, so you could be a power-hungry bitch and forget all about me on your way up, you mean?" Darla shot a dirty look at Karen.

"Darla, really now, it is not my fault they caught you. Hell, I will talk to Judge Pennington to get your charges dropped. But let's go prove how unfit my son is with my grandson."

Eris smiled as she watched her plan of revenge play out before her. Looking up, she rolled her eyes in disgust at the destruction of her room.

"Honestly Eris, I don't understand why you have to be so hateful. You understand Austin fulfilled a six hundred-year-old prophecy that saved us all? Had he failed, that creature would have put an end to all of us old world gods and goddesses." Zeus's words filled the room before he did. He looked around shaking his head. "It took a lot of dark magic to do this to the human world, and he simply deflected it back only onto your room. I have to hand it to the kid after only being a minor god for six years. He has control of his powers. I am grateful that he showed restraint. He had every right to come at you full power. I really can't believe you went after his children."

"I was only doing what I thought was right. They don't deserve our powers. Nor do I feel like I should have to respect him. His life is but a blip in our existence." Eris picked up a broken vase and slammed it into the wall, shattering it even more.

"Sometimes, when you can't change your views, you need to change perspective and direction, Eris." Zeus cleared his throat, eyeing his daughter.

"I don't need to do that. Just because you're my father, doesn't give you the right to imprison me in this room."

"You better take the time and realign your thoughts. I am your father and the supreme father of most gods." Zeus conjured up a chair to sit on since most of the furniture in Eris' room lay in ruins. "You are—"

"I am what, Father!"

"You know what you are, daughter. I am so disappointed with you. Please leave the Chimera clan alone. I will not protect you when you cross that line. If you don't believe me when I tell you that Austin can and will crush you if you cross him. He has many of your siblings on his side. I can't make any promises, but I will try talking to him about not seeking revenge." Zeus snapped his fingers and in a lightning bolt, he was gone.

"Pompous old fart." Eris walked over to her looking glass and waved her hand across it, bringing in the image of Karen and Darla arriving. "Oh, perfect timing. Let's see what can happen now." Eris gently tapped the water like an insect pulls on the strings of a spider's web. "Wake up. You have visitors. Well, if you want to be so gracious as to call them visitors. I think it's more like a walking buffet."

Malcolm's eyes flashed open in his nest deep underground in the dairy farm house. "Wake up, my warriors. I believe we have a meal walking into our home. Keep them alive. Fresh meals do not just simply walk in that often."

"Yum, a warm meal. We will welcome them with open fangs, boss. In fact, I think we have two perfect spots for them in the barn."

"Darla, what was that?" Karen used her flashlight to light up the growing shadows.

"Karen, I don't know. This family gives me the creeps. No one ever sees them that much. The one girl out here runs with the Sheriff. She seems to be the only somewhat normal one." Darla pulled out her phone.

"Are you expecting a call or a text? You keep pulling that damn thing out, Darla? You are worse than my Eric. He could never keep it in his pants."

"Well, that's obvious. How do you think you got a grandson? Hell, I bet you have more than just the one. But because, as you said, he can't keep it in his pants, you just don't know where all of them are located."

"That is not what I was saying, and Darla, you can be a real spicy bitch. With a mouth like that, I am surprised you're not some street walking whore."

"Whore? Excuse me, but if I remember correctly, in high school you were the one always hiking up the long skirts your daddy made you wear. Turning those long skirts into barely allowed miniskirts just to get the boys' attention. I remember all those days you changed your clothes in the bathroom before first period. You act like some holy Christian when in fact you are the wolf in sheep's clothing." Darla shoved her phone in her purse while uttering curse words at Karen.

"You know if you took that dick out of your mouth, oh wait last time you had dick was when you let the quarterback of the football team screw you under the bleachers the night before the big game."

"I never—"

"Well hello ladies, welcome to our home, but wait, we don't remember inviting you," came the silky-smooth voice of one of the vampire guards.

"We came for my grandson. I know he is hiding here with his father," Karen said while blushing at the robust physique of the man before her.

"Forget her. She is old, married, and has grandchildren. I am younger, and my breasts are more perky and firm." Darla puffed out her chest, trying desperately to show off her rack.

"Yeah, if you like a cup with no experience." Karen elbowed Darla in her ribs, causing her to step back. "Hello, my name is Karen." Karen presented her hand to the guard without thinking about it.

"Hello Karen, why don't you come with me, while Darla here goes with my brother, Ivan?"

"Well, if his name is Ivan, what's your name?"

"Ben, well, more like Benjamin," Ben said, kissing the top of Karen's hand.

"Oh, I love Benjamin so much more than just Ben." Karen blushed as Ben's eyes glowed purple.

"What's with the eyes?" Darla questioned, as Ivan walked up with glowing purple eyes as well.

"Follow us ladies," Ben and Ivan said in unison, taking the ladies by the hand and leading them into the cellar by the barn.

"Jericho, we have two new trespassers to add to the bank. Malcolm said to tell you not to drain them dry. We really need to keep our living blood bags around longer. I hate that imitation blood, and we may not hunt the town's people. The only time we get fresh blood is when they foolishly trespass. Theodor, take these keys and dispose of the car. Here, take their purses with these damn cell phones. We almost got caught last time because someone forgot to dispose of the phones." Ben looked at Theodor with a distant gaze.

"Well, bring them down to the cleaning station. I will have Elly strip them, scrub them clean of all perfumes, and put them in the correct gowns." Jericho motioned for Elly to come and take the ladies, who were still under the spell of Ben's eyes.

"I am very grateful that you glimmered them. When a donor comes to us in fear, it makes the blood bitter."

"Yeah. Yeah. What is the point in putting them in different gowns, doc?" Ben questioned Jericho.

"Look around you, dear boy! Some of us have gained taste. These gowns are like labels on a wine bottle. You don't stock your red wine with the white. So why put an AB-blood that has a wonderful full bouquet of flavor next to that?" Jericho pointed over to the old homeless man that wandered in last winter. "That trash heap is B- and tastes as bad as he smelled when he first walked in. Malcolm insisted we keep him alive. I give his blood to the lowest members of this coven. But his darling," Jericho ran his fingers along Darla's neck, "will be put in the private top ranking. We will enjoy this tasty little treat."

"What about the one that goes by Karen? Where does she rank on your perfect little scale?" Ben hissed.

"Aww, did Karen compliment you and make you fang out? Wipe the drool off your face. If you were not an immortal, you could pass for her son, not a lover. She is tasty, has a full body, but kind of a smoky after taste. She will be high reserves, so sorry dear boy, you won't be tasting her blood soon." Jericho laughed while turning away.

"I did my job. I brought in the food from outside," Ben hissed.

"Yes, and such a good little spider you were. But the masters are at play now. We control what you get and don't get. Be happy I don't feed you them bums blood." Jericho waved Ben and Ivan off.

"I will complain to the high council. The first guard is me. I should have a say in my food," Ben hissed out as he headed to find Malcolm and address his desire to be allowed Karen's blood.

Eris stood up, excited to see all the strife playing out without her having to be there to stir the pot. "Oh, those simpleton humans are falling for all my tricks. Even that worthless bag of bones. All it took was whispering in his ear for a few days, talking about how caring the new family on the dairy farm was for poor souls. The job they would give him. I just didn't tell him the job it would be. Honestly, he should be thankful he is alive after all. Obviously, I must not be breaking any rules, because their own god has not stepped in to stop any of this." With a wave of her hand, the witch's glass went dark once more.

CHAPTER 38
BL⚸D OATH

T ate sped down the road toward the dairy farm with his lights and sirens blazing, muttering under his breath, "I Need to marry this woman before she shows off my little spud."

Over the radio, he heard the mindless chatter going on about the unique events that transpired in the town. "Officers called to the block of Santa Fe Road and Lewis. Caller states a strange dog is in the road chasing after its own shadow. Animal control on route."

"We have a code 376. The mayor states he has not seen his wife all night. If anyone sees her, please direct her to call her husband. I am sick of him calling dispatch every thirty minutes."

"Zoey, she was last seen at the fire house causing trouble over an hour ago and I am going to be out for the rest of the night. I have family matters to deal with."

"Ten four Sheriff Tate. I didn't realize you had family in town. Maybe you could bring your parents around. I would love to meet them." Zoey giggled as she talked through the radio.

"Zoey, I have a girlfriend, soon to be my wife. If my parents come to town, it will be to greet my wife."

"You know what, Tate, you can be a real party pooper. Since you are clocking out for the night, turn off your siren and lights. I would hate to have people accuse you of misuse of power."

"I got it, Zoey." Tate clicked off the siren, finishing his drive in silence.

He pulled up to the main house and left his lights on, stepping up to the door. Before he could even knock, Elena opened the door, shoving a bag at him, and giving him a warning shot. "Honey, what's wrong? I can't even get to the door, and you're already shoving your bags on me."

"My father knows something, and he is coming," Elena hissed. "Here, take this. I will grab my purse."

Tate took his soon-to-be bride's purse and pulled his phone out to a call from Austin. "Tate, congratulations on the new spud. Sorry, I couldn't help but overhear your news. I know you are not planning on living in that small, one-bedroom apartment, and because they attacked my family in this home, Bou and Lexi don't want to stay here now. Would you like to live in our home rent free? Only catch is you have to maintain the property. With that said, we can have a workaround to the vampire rules."

"That would be amazing. I am sorry you have to leave. Yes, Elena and I would be honored to take over your place. I think it would be the icing on the cake for Karen to see me and my pregnant moon pie living in the house. She caused so much drama over the place."

"I know, her head would be spinning. Well, I have already sent the family ahead. Pack warriors from Colorado are driving

Eric's truck. You don't have anything incriminating in your apartment do you Tate?" Austin chuckled as he stood in the living room spinning his trident around playfully.

"Umm, no. I would say don't go looking for things you don't want to find." Tate's face turned red thinking about the state of his bedroom. Let alone the dirty clothes he would take Elena home to. "Well now, you have me thinking Elena is going to kill me once she gets to my place. She is going to want to clean all night. Shit."

"My house is not dirty, thank you very much Tate." Austin cleared his throat and concentrated on the task at hand.

"Austin, your house is amazing, and we can move in starting later this week. Right now, everything needs to get cleaned, sorted, and packed. I know I have a mountain of dirty clothes and I'm sure Elena has a few pairs of panties that I may or may not have stolen from her in my bedroom."

"Umm yeah, let me just clear the vomit from my throat. Okay, we're clear. The key to your new place will be on the bottom side of the swing on the porch. You can redecorate or move things around. Your apartment is now fully settled. Your dirty clothes, yeah, those are cleaned. I never want to move a straight man again. You all can be dirty. I thought my kids were bad. Tate, you will not have this happen again. Keep things clean. You will have a maid come once a month. She is a Siren that lost her pod, and she doesn't want to return to the sea. I paid her, but she will take tips." Austin chuckled.

"Wait, you already moved me? Wait, you just magically moved me?" Tate's voice had a hitch and a gentle quiver.

"Tate, I had Candy's help, but she animated. I teleported, and she sent everything through a cleaning spell, so I cleansed all the negative energy. Like I said, you will have your share of things to put up. I am leaving one of the extra cribs for you. Tell Elena I say congrats and enjoy. I am getting linked to get up to

Colorado. My kids are driving Danny nuts." Austin quickly hung up the phone, and walked through his portal to the Celtic Rhino Clan, leaving Tate bewildered on the front porch of Elena's ranch style home.

"Baby, we have an issue." Elena came out with her head down.

"Well, one of our issues just got solved, thanks to Austin and Danny. We get to live in their house since Karen chased them out of town for now."

"Well, that's just nice of him. Now we have to pack and move your apartment to that six-bedroom house." Elena rolled her eyes, thinking of all the work.

Tate walked up, taking her gently in his arms, looking down for the soon to be baby bump. Running his hand gently across her belly, he said, "No honey, Candy and Austin moved for us. He left us a crib and we can decorate how we like."

"That will work if Austin did the decorating. We won't need to move anything, but it might be all for naught. We have a bigger problem than that right now. Apparently, we have two people that trespassed onto the farm. Now I cannot confirm who it is, but I can tell you it was someone from town."

"Well, until someone officially listed them as missing, I am not looking. I will say I am officially off the clock. Right now, all I care about it getting you out of here and to safety. You know I can't have anyone hurt you or our little peanut."

"That is what I need to warn you about. Tate, daddy knows!"

"Well, hello my midnight child. Who is this human, and why do you smell like him?" Lord Allen's voice was harsh, with a frosty edge.

"Father, I want you to meet my destined mate, Tate. I don't care if you don't approve. We already have the blessing from up high." Elena pulled Tate close.

"Yes, the Strigoi overlord already told me he blessed this blasphemous union. I am not pleased, but I see he has a white witch in his circle." Lord Allen pointed to Tate's ring.

"Well, I am not turned, but I have it if it comes to that. With this ring I will have the same gifts as my soon-to-be wife. It is an honor to meet you," greeted Tate, holding out his hand swiftly.

"You will learn to speak only when spoken to, human." The quick hands of one of Lord Allen's guards greeted Tate before he knew what was happening.

"Oh, Father, I see you brought your pet. What's this one's name?" Elena smiled while cutting eyes at the guard.

"You know all too well I care not to learn their trivial names." Lord Allen stepped around Tate to greet his daughter face on.

"Well, Father, you might need to select yourself an additional guard if he ever puts his hands on my mate."

"Threaten me, will you? You worthless mix blood bitch—" before the unknown guard could finish his words, Tate had blurred over, picked him up, and body slammed him to the ground, trapping him by his neck and squeezing tight. Tate's eyes turned black as night and fangs showed through.

"Test me, touch my mate—my soon to be wife, the mother of my unborn child—and you will not live to taste blood again." Tate pulled himself together and stepped back, taking a deep breath. His eyes returned to normal and his teeth retracted.

"Wait, what is this nonsense?" Lord Allen looked at his guard on the ground, then to his daughter, and lastly to the man he had assumed was only human.

Before Elena could even say anything, Tate realized his fatal mistake: he had let the pregnancy be known before its time. Elena gave him a dirty look, then looked at her father without faltering. Standing tall and proud, she said, "Yes, Father, I am with child. Yes, it belongs to my mate. And no, there is nothing you can dare do about it without violating several accords. Absalom blessed us. My advice, Father, is to be proud my mate stood up to the guard with no knowledge of how to fight vampire style. He is a good man. I have my station here and will not leave my lover."

"That's very well and all my child, but I will deal with this disappointment soon enough. I have gotten concerning reports about your brother holding humans once again as living blood bags. If this thing you call a mate is, in fact, the Sheriff, we might have a case for him." Lord Allen went to knock on the door when a whiter than usual Malcolm opened it.

"Father, Elena." He greeted them both as if touching them would cause his skin to burn from his body. Looking at Sheriff Tate, he said, "Human, what do you want? Just because you know of our kind, and I foolishly let you entertain the thought of being with my sister before, my leniency is over. I should kill you where you stand."

"Child, is your family always this stupid, or do they not understand a direct coven law that I have put out to all covens? I, Absalom, declared you two bonded, married, and mated in my eyes. I will not force the mark, because it would take young Tate's humanity away. You three better knock it off before I take your undead life from all of you!" Absalom bellowed from the top branch of the silver maple tree right off the porch.

Absalom was upon them all in a blink of an eye and took Elena's hand, placing a kiss on it. "Young Austin, I see, has given you all his home. Only those he gives permission can be on his property. I helped him put up the barrier spells to keep out anyone you do not desire to let into your home. That includes anyone a vampire may have compelled." Absalom gave Malcolm a dirty look.

"So they are leaving here together?" Malcolm looked baffled until he saw Elena resting her hands on her tiny baby bump.

"He got you knocked up? I should have known. Well, you're his problem now. I want you completely out of his house. Father said you should never have come here, and he was right." Malcolm turned up his lip in disgust.

"This is one of many I plan on having with this woman." Tate looked down at Elena, kissing her passionately.

"Tate, can we go home now?" Elena leaned into him, watching the men in her life cringe away.

"Not so fast. First, I want him to walk the grounds with us, and we can discuss the custom of the blood oath. If he is going to be a part of this family, he must take part in all of our customs. Failure to do so is an executable offence." Malcolm looked smugly at Sheriff Tate.

"I will walk with you, but I will say now already, unless someone has filed a missing person's report, I have no power to do anything if you have living blood bags."

"Wait, you know of those? Elena, are you telling family secrets?" Malcolm's voice matched his eyes, both filled with fire and anger.

"Can we get this over with, so I can take my wife home and enjoy my night?" Tate looked at his watch, then once again at Malcolm.

"What are you in a hurry for? Won't Austin and Danny help you move? Like making sure you check the place for fleas?" Malcolm let out a stifled laugh.

"That's enough of that. Yes, once we've done their walk and talk, we can get you and Elena home. But now that her coven knows she is expecting, regardless of their opinions, they must risk life and limb to protect her and the coven young." Absalom snapped his fingers, bringing them all to the sub-basement, where the guards were fighting to keep Ben from muscling in on the high-profile blood donors.

"It's not right. I brought her. She should be my reward for all my hard work with the coven." Ben was now thrashing on the ground.

"Who did he bring in, thinking he should have feeding rights over Jericho?"

"Specimen 8706." Jericho looked down at his roster.

"Son of a Bitch." Tate's voice echoed in the basement.

"Son, you know this woman?" Absalom questioned with a smirk on his face.

All eyes in the coven fell upon him as his pulse quickened. "Sadly, yes, and she will be missed. That's the mayor's wife. She would have arrived here with..." Tate looked down the line to see Darla hooked up to a machine draining her blood one bag at a time.

"Don't worry Sheriff, we take one bag at a time and they are none the wiser. We inject them with an enzyme to make them produce blood at a faster rate. We can harvest a bag a month," Jericho said, smiling at the full bag before him.

"Now how about we talk about this blood oath? Since you will be part of this family, you need to take a blood oath to promise your life to protect the family. Obviously, you can't bite and drink the blood, so we will supply you with a small sample."

"He cannot do the blood oath until after the baby is born." Elena slapped Malcolm in the back of the head. "Tate, let's go home for now. You are off duty."

"I am off work, so I can clearly say I know nothing. I'm leaving now. If you want to keep Karen and Darla for a month it's up to you. It will be a hot mess for them to figure out, so I would suggest you make sure there is no way to track them here." Tate looked Lord Allen square in the eyes. Then, turning to Malcolm, he said, "Since this is your clan inherited from your father, I don't want any harm to come to my Elena's family. I will protect my wife. She is my priority, but you are important to her, too, so I leave you with this warning: Karen is not a prize. Elena, my love, let's head to our house and make it a home. Austin and Danny will visit once things settle down. His new Alpha for the Celtic Rhino Pack seems nice." Tate kissed Elena on her head and led her to his patrol car, leaving Malcolm fuming in the barn.

Join your favorite characters from the chimera series in book three. This will be a story to sink your teeth into Forbidden Human Love.

ABOUT THE AUTHOR

ABOUT THE AUTHOR Hello, my fellow readers! I'm so happy you could join me for book two The Chimera Clan. I strive to create an exciting world where you can lose yourself in not only the story but each of the characters. I truly enjoy storytelling. As you can, tell I can have a flair for the dramatic side of things. I work in healthcare currently as my primary occupation, but I enjoy writing at night. It is a rare sight to be seen that I don't have one of my many notebooks near me. Being married with three fur kids keeps me active, but I make sure I have time to write out more adventures for the chimera family.